Blind

Killer Instincts

Sidney Bristol

Inked Press

Thank you, Shawn, for never complaining too loudly about my crime shows.

Hope is being able to see that there is light despite all of the darkness.

–DESMOND TUTU

1.

EMMA RATION was a women who didn't spook easily, which was a good thing since dark spirits haunted her. She toyed with the discarded wrapper from her straw and glanced toward the door. The latest serial killer creepadoodle wanting to interview her was late.

She sucked down some of her sweet tea and glanced at the Dr Pepper clock on the wall. Fifteen minutes late. If this guy wasn't here in the next ten, she was gone. The evening crowd was trickling in, and business was picking up. The last thing she wanted right now was to be the sad, depressed person eating alone. She knew enough of the servers that they might ask her where Derrick was, and then she'd have to explain why she'd left his sorry ass.

The door swung open again and she glanced toward it, her gaze sticking like glue to the nearly six foot hottie that entered—all by himself. He had one of those strong, square jaws with a nice five o' clock shadow, dark hair, and the bluest eyes. She chewed her straw as he searched the patrons.

So what if she'd broken up with her jackass of an ex a few days ago—a rebound was a good thing, wasn't it?

The hottie paused by the hostess stand and pulled out his cell phone. The hostess, a girl named Rachel, stood bent over the podium, no doubt giving him an excellent view of her ample boobage. Emma had been like Rachel once. She'd bussed tables and waitressed in high school for cash, under the table. Even met a few boyfriends in the process. If she was lucky, this guy could be her boyfriend for the night.

Her cell phone rang, startling her out of her drool-fest. She groaned at the name Jacob Payton flashing on the screen. Looked like her serial killer intellectual dinner date at least had enough courtesy to tell her he wasn't showing up.

"Hello?" she said.

"Hi, Emma?"

The hottie at the door had his back to her now, and damn what a view it was.

"Yeah, you're late."

The hottie glanced around. His cell phone pressed to his ear.

"Yeah, I know. Sorry about that. Are you here?"

Oh fuck me...

The hottie was the creepadoodle. Not that he looked anything like the guys who normally wanted to pick her brain about the TBK murderer. She did her best to weed out the real sickos who got off on murder fantasies, but the only people interested in a guy who killed a dozen people were a special lot.

Jacob Payton was not what she'd expected. From their phone chats, she'd anticipated a thinning, mid-forties man with a thousand yard stare. Oh how wrong she'd been.

Emma cleared her throat. "Yeah, I'm in the back corner, blonde, staring straight at you."

His gaze landed on her, and it was as if the restaurant faded away. For a few heartbeats, they were the only two things in existence. It was as if she could feel his heart beat, the caress of his eyes across her skin, and the flutter of his pulse.

The corners of his mouth lifted slightly. "I see you."

The noise of the restaurant crashed in around her, destroying the momentary spell. Her stomach was full of butterflies now. That was a smile that could do dangerous things to a girl if he ever truly unleashed it. She shifted in her seat, suddenly anxious.

She hung up and hastily smoothed her hair down. Her level of effort for this little meet-up was next to nil. Most of her stuff, including her make-up, was in boxes in her best friend's spare room, waiting for her to decide where she'd land next. At least her iRIDE tank top showed good cleavage. She picked at the lint clinging to the ribbed fabric, willing herself to appear a little more presentable.

"Emma?" Jacob came to a stop at the end of the booth.

"That's me." Her throat was horribly dry all of a sudden. She grabbed her tea and took a sip, giving him a slow once-over. Damn, he was fine, toned, and tan, plus no wedding band. If this weren't business he would so be a jackpot. "Have a seat?"

"Thanks." He quirked a brow at her, seemingly amused by her appraisal, and scooted into the booth to settle in across from her. "Sorry about the wait. There was some traffic and I took a wrong turn."

"Not from around here, I take it?"

"Oh, I am, I live closer to downtown."

Which was probably why they'd never crossed paths. She'd remember a man like him. Despite her inner vow to keep it professional, looking at him reminded her of the months without sex. She had needs.

"You are not what I expected." She propped her chin on her palm, curiosity piqued. It was way too soon to jump into another relationship. After the disaster with Derrick, she really needed to take time to prioritize her life. But a one-night stand? That might be the perfect thing to get her back on her feet.

"Yeah? What were you expecting?" He leaned toward her, one arm on the table.

"A professor, maybe. A stuffy intellectual type." She measured the width of his shoulders with her gaze. The man had to be a regular at the gym. Those forearms! She was willing to bet he had a great grip.

"I'm afraid I'm not that smart." He spread his hands while he studied her closely. She had a feeling he was much smarter than he appeared. "How do you do this? Do you want to eat first or get the *other* stuff out of the way?"

Right. He wasn't there to see her, not really. He was here about TBK. Cock-blocked by a killer.

She took a deep breath and shook off the lustful fog. It was time to put her business hat on. "Ground rules. You can't pull any of the documents out of the sleeves. You can take pictures of them if you like, but no flash. Also, you can't take pictures of me."

"People ask for pictures of you?" His brows drew down into a line. "I mean, you're beautiful, don't get me wrong, but I'm guessing that's not what people are taking pictures of you for?"

She chuckled. It was nice to be called pretty, even if he was covering his ass. "Yeah, I used to not think it was that big of a deal, then this kid took some pictures of me, started stalking me, and creating his own TBK letters with my pictures." She slashed her hand across her throat. "No more."

"Wow, that's crazy. I don't blame you. I promise, no pictures." He held his hands up. His gaze flicked from her face, down, and back again. Interesting.

"Awesome." She leaned forward, crossing her arms on the table. If boobs were what it took to distract him, she wasn't above using them. It was a little harmless flirting. "I will answer questions, but if I don't know something I will tell you. Um, I won't call my daddy and I won't tell people where he lives now. He wants nothing to do with this stuff, as you can imagine. He's actually gone completely off the grid and is impossible to get hold of, so don't waste your time. Any questions?"

Jacob chuckled, his gaze firmly on her face. Damn, resilient bastard. Was he onto her trick? "You've got this down to a process, don't you?" He mirrored her pose, his shirt straining across his wide shoulders. How she'd love to discuss anything else with him.

"I think it's helpful to be up front about this stuff, instead of misleading people."

"You consider this a service?"

"That's the best thing I can think of." She bit her lip. *You always stick your nose where it doesn't belong.* "What about you? What's your interest in TBK?"

He shrugged. "Curiosity."

Liar. If he was just curious he'd have asked a lot more questions. He was looking for something specific. It wasn't any of her business what that was, so long as he followed her rules. The TBK collection was to keep the memory of the victims alive, after all.

Jacob cleared his throat. "Ration. That's Cherokee, right?"

"Uh, Navajo actually. I think I'm like, one-tenth." She grabbed the ends of her blonde ponytail. "I bet I look real Navajo, don't I?"

"No, not really." He almost smiled, a slight upturn at the corners of his mouth. He struck her as the kind who didn't smile often. She was willing to bet that if he ever did, it was to be appreciated at length. Then and there it became her personal goal to make the man grin. "Navajo, huh?"

"Yeah. Family moved here in the sixties to start fresh." She spread her fingers. "Look how well that turned out."

The fresh start had turned into a massacre with only one living survivor. Her father. The rest was a bloody, sordid history that never got easier to live with.

"Damn." He shook his head. "Why do you do this? It seems like it would be hard on you."

Emma bit her lip. Jacob wasn't following the usual pattern of questions. His inquiries were personal, which she wouldn't normally allow. There was something different about him though.

She shrugged. "I didn't know my grandparents, so it's kind of a way to stay connected to them and my roots. There's so much history we lost with their death. I started out collecting information about the family, and then I stumbled onto the letters TBK sent them. Collecting the TBK stuff was really an accident. I was documenting their death, and I got curious. So I talked to another family. They really liked the account of my grandparent's lives and wanted me to do it for them. There was one catch, they didn't want to keep it. They told another family, that family contacted me, and it just turned into this—thing. Besides, someone has to keep a record of what happened or else people forget, and we should never forget the darker side of humanity. If we forget where the line is, what's too far, we lose our humanity."

He studied her, gaze slightly narrowed. It was intense, unnerving, and she liked it. He was a far cry from Derrick, that was for sure.

"What's your interest in this?" Jacob asked.

"Honestly?" She bit her lip. This was far more personal information than she usually shared and there was no good reason for telling any of this to him. Except she felt like it was important he know.

"Yeah."

Don't say it. Don't say it.

"TBK destroyed my daddy." She shrugged, trying to swallow down the hurt and years of anger. She'd worked through it, but there was no changing the pain TBK had caused her—and he was dead. "I thought if I got to know his parents, I might understand him better."

A year before she was born, Grandma and Grandpa Ration were murdered in a gruesome style in front of her daddy. He was seventeen, forced to watch their death, and the only survivor of the TBK attacks on the unsuspecting Oklahoma City residents. The serial killer earned his name due to what he did to the bodies. Torture. Blind. Kill. Over and over again.

Some people theorized that TBK knew he was about to be caught and wanted a living legacy, others thought his MO was evolving. Whatever the truth was, TBK was a sick fuck who'd branded her family with the spirit of evil. It was a mark Emma could feel on her soul.

Jacob reached across and brushed his fingers over her knuckles. She jerked her head up, unaware she'd dropped her gaze to the table. He squeezed her hand for a second, as if he understood. She mustered a little smile, uncomfortable with the sudden depth of emotion.

"Did it help?" He kept his hand over hers, her skin tingling where they touched.

"Not really. I mean, I get why he's messed up, but that's about it."

"I get it." He paused before continuing more slowly. "My father saw some things when I was a baby that changed him, too. Mom never talked about it until he passed away a few years ago, but it was clear in the way she talked about how things used to be that what he saw changed him. The version of him I grew up with was—haunted."

She nodded. Haunted was how she felt most of the time. How many times had she used that exact word to describe how her father looked? "Yeah, exactly."

A little of the tension eased out of her. Most people didn't understand, and not that she thought Jacob did, but at least he made her feel like not so much of a freak. Hot and sensitive, he was too good to be real.

One corner of his mouth curled up in a bit more of a smile, and he let her hand go. She missed the warmth immediately, but she was a big girl. That said, the way he was looking at her said one thing: *Interested.*

She didn't normally get involved with the people who came to talk TBK, but weren't rules made for breaking? Besides, Jacob was from the other side of the tracks. She'd never see him again.

"Why don't we go ahead and order something to eat?" Jacob grabbed one of the menus and flipped it open. "What's good here?"

"Everything." She was short of breath, and her skin still tingled. This was crazy. She could not seriously be entertaining the idea of a one-night stand with him. She needed the distraction of food to help ground her.

"That doesn't help me narrow it down."

"Depends on how hungry you are and how much meat you think you can handle." She pressed her lips together as soon as the words left her mouth.

Jacob glanced up at her, one brow quirked. "I don't know. How much meat can you handle?"

"Enough." She grinned, fanning her face and flipping to the last page of the menu. Was it hot in here, or was it just her?

"Is that you?"

"Uh..."

He leaned over and peered at the picture spread across the bottom of the page.

Oh. That.

Emma and the rest of her motocross team were lined up across the bottom of the last page, decked out in their riding gear, numbers plastered across their chests. Some of them wore medals, a few hoisted trophies, and there she was, right in the middle. The only girl in bright pink.

"What's this?" He stole her menu and held the picture up.

Why did she pick this restaurant? She could have picked any place, and she'd gone where she was most comfortable. Where she knew she wouldn't run into Derrick.

"You race bikes or something?" he asked.

"Or something." Inwardly she cringed. Not many guys thought a chick racing dirt bikes was sexy. It was dangerous and dirty.

"You've got three medals and two trophies. You must be good." He handed the menu back, his gaze a little warmer than before. If she'd thought he looked interested before, there was no denying it now.

"I'm very good at what I do. Know what you want?" She stared at the menu and wrestled internally with her libido. Sleeping with a client was bad for business.

"Yeah, I think so." He flipped his menu closed.

She felt his gaze on her and heat rolled over her body. By the end of the night, if she didn't spontaneously combust, she'd have to take a real cold shower.

"Would you show me what you do?" His voice was lower, inviting her to do wicked things, at least in her mind.

She fanned herself with the menu again and forced herself to meet his gaze. Just because he'd caught her by surprise tonight didn't mean he was going to get the best of her. "Oh, I don't know if you could handle that."

"I'm pretty capable." The way he tipped his head forward, the slow, lingering gazes— they were having more than a little impact on her body. Her nipples chafed against her bra, and her panties were becoming damp. Exactly how capable was he?

Emma waved the waitress down and they ordered. She ignored the pointed glances toward her male companion. She knew too many people who frequented this place. In hindsight, it might not have been the best place to meet, but she'd wanted to avoid her ex and knew he wouldn't come here for anything.

"So—"

"I—" She chuckled and gestured for him to speak. "You first."

He cleared his throat. "I hope I'm not being pushy here, but I understand that you have some letters TBK sent to your family before their—death?"

Cock-blocked again by a dead serial killer. She hated that bastard. It was probably for the best anyway.

"Don't be silly. That's why you contacted me in the first place. And you can call it a murder. I'm not sensitive about it." She shrugged and pulled a scrapbook out of a portable plastic filing box she'd brought with her. "TBK stands for, as you probably know, torture, blind, and kill. He gave himself that name, and we know that because he signed it on all his communications. TBK was known for sending letters to the police, newspaper, and even his victims. He liked people to be scared. Sort of a mind-fuck. Anyway, while a lot of the letters were sent to the police with details about his future victims, a couple of times he even told them how he was going to pose a body, and he did send some to his victims before the murders. My grandparents actually got several from him. The problem was that he messed up their address, so the letters bounced up and down the street before one of the neighbors walked them down to the house and left them in the mail slot after their death. They were actually boxed up when the house was cleaned out, and I didn't find them until a few years ago, which is why they were never in the official evidence at the trial."

"Really?" He held his hand out.

"I have to warn you, these are graphic." She held the book to her chest and watched his face carefully. She kept the letters separate from the books about her grandparents. Not everyone wanted to be exposed to them. TBK had a flare for the gruesome and there was no doubt he'd positioned the bodies to have the most impact.

His features tensed a little and he nodded. She handed the book over and let him flip it open. For several moments he stared at the first one, his brows drawing down and his lips squeezing together.

"Are these consistent with his other letters?" Jacob continued to pore over the first page, which was the least offensive of the collection.

"Yes. I had them compared to the documents in evidence downtown."

"And the cops didn't want these?"

She shrugged. "Why? TBK was dead. They didn't need them. The notarized certificate of authenticity is on the last page if you don't believe me."

Jacob flipped to the next page. "TBK."

"Yeah, he signed them all by hand, while the rest of the letter was a hodgepodge of words cut from magazines and stuff. I think he thought they could figure out who he was by his handwriting."

"But he still risked signing them?"

She shrugged. "Ego maybe? It doesn't make any sense to me, but neither does killing a bunch of people."

He quietly perused the last pages, only glancing at the notarized certificate before handing the book back to her after a few moments. "You have some other letters?"

He was persistent. He didn't even glance at her boobs now, and that was a shame. All business, no play.

"I do." She filed the scrapbook back in her box and retrieved a second thick book full of plastic sleeves and pages. She handed it over with a shrug. "I have letters from three-fourths of the murders."

"Really? How did you get to keep these?" He seemed horrified, but she couldn't wrap her head around why. What was it he was looking for? She tried her best to stay out of her clients' business. Maybe she should have asked Jacob a few more questions about why he was so interested in TBK.

"TBK was meticulous about how he picked his victims, but he wasn't so great about making sure the letters got to people who would open them. A lot of the families got the letters and hid them. Some of the letters were lost in the mail like my grandparents'. I really came into them by accident. Like the first family, they sort of threw them at me. They were ready to get rid of them, but didn't want to trash them."

"The cops didn't want these?"

"The families never turned them over. It seems like some of them pushed stuff under the rug to try to move on."

"That's hindering the investigation." His frown deepened.

"Maybe to you, but for them it was survival. These people were grieving and trying to put tragedy behind them. They did it however they could. It might not have been the right way, but it's what they did."

He wasn't like the others. Usually the people who sought her out spent forever poring over the words and the pictures. He seemed to be after something specific. He clearly wasn't going to outright ask her what he wanted to know, and for some reason she couldn't stop wondering why. She had enough issues without adding another, but she could never keep her nose in her own business. She wasn't about to judge them. She didn't need any more cracks in her glass house.

JACOB TRIED TO FOCUS ON THE FOOD. The barbecue was some of the best he'd had in ages, and he was pretty picky when it came to calling food good. But any time he'd begin to mull the flavors over, Emma would dip her finger in the sauce and lick it off, and he'd be back to staring at that mischievous smile, those dark, soulful eyes.

Emma Ration was not the woman he'd expected.

He'd read her file, knew enough of her life story that he'd expected to find some washed-up, hard-used woman working an angle. But she was different. Unlike her father, unlike Jacob, TBK hadn't left a mark on her he could see, and he knew the darkness of humanity. He saw it every day, working the streets of Oklahoma City. But despite his gut feeling about her, he still couldn't trust her. Could he? Did he dare lay it all out on the table and pick her brain for real? No, he didn't. People like her didn't trust cops. So he'd torture himself a little more by watching her eat a sandwich like it was the best erotic film he'd ever seen.

She was attractive in her realness. He couldn't think of another word to describe it. Emma was authentic to who she was, and maybe that person was a little redneck, a little rough around the edges, but she didn't seem like she was about to apologize for it.

He'd have liked to be interviewing her father, but the Ration family survivor was next to impossible to find, as was his wife, Emma's mother. There was also a baby momma and a younger son who was in the Navy before getting thrown in the federal prison. In a family of questionable people, Emma stuck out. There were two things in her file, a DUI and an altercation where no one had pressed charges. It sounded like some guy had tried to intimidate her, and she'd shown him how bad her bite could be.

Emma was the kind of woman he needed to stay far away from. And yet, he'd kept digging.

Thanks to social media, it was pretty easy to track down her current activities. She was a huge motocross racer, or whatever they were called. She had a website dedicated to metal sculptures she made out of reclaimed trash. And she had a job at a garage that appeared to specialize in recreational vehicles.

To top it all off, she was easy on the eyes. Her tank top stretched across ample breasts. It was a show of will he didn't just stare at them all night. Her left arm had a tattoo from shoulder to elbow of a dirt bike chick soaring through the air, done in pretty fine detail, against a backdrop of what he would call a race course. There were a few other tattoos, but he hadn't paid attention to them. Her smile kept snagging his attention. There hadn't been much to smile about these last few years, even less now. He was almost jealous of her easy ability to simply be happy. What was that like?

Emma glanced up and caught him staring at her again. One side of her mouth kicked up. He wanted to lick those lips.

"Do you have any other questions for me?" she asked between bites.

He was pretty much done with what he needed. He could pay now, get up, and leave, which was the safer option. But it had been so long since he'd sat and eaten a meal with another person. A hell of a lot longer since that person was female and beautiful.

"How'd you get started racing bikes?"

"Mm, that's personal." She waggled her finger at him.

He wanted to peel back the layers, find out who she really was. What her secret for not allowing TBK to get to her was. Maybe he could learn a thing or two from her.

"You didn't mind so much earlier. You don't share personal information until the second date?" Wait, what? His mouth was getting away from him. But he did want to see her again, even if it was the worst idea he'd ever had. As soon as she knew he was a cop, she'd run from him. Of that he was certain.

She sputtered, caught off guard.

"I mean, I figure since I'm buying you dinner and it's just the two of us—this is kind of a date." That was stretching the truth, but would it be so bad to see her again? He wasn't breaking any rules.

"But you forgot our third wheel." She nodded toward the box.

"It's a dead guy and paper. I refuse to think that he counts as much as I do. I mean, I'm alive and breathing—and paying for dinner." And she had been staring at him earlier as if she'd rather eat him than the chopped brisket sandwich she'd ordered.

"Yeah, not first date material, sorry." Her mouth curled up in that damn smile that made him want to pry her open, figure out what she was thinking. He was good at reading people, but right now he couldn't get anything from her.

He sighed and balled up his napkin. Fuck it. He wanted to see her again. "Damn, do I get to practice for this next date now?"

"Hm, maybe." She glanced up at the ceiling, as if she were thinking.

"For our real first date, what would you like to do?" She didn't strike him as the dinner and a movie kind of girl. Emma was a woman who did things.

"You assume I'd go out with you." She jabbed a fry at him.

He reached out and grabbed her wrist, holding it while he leaned across the table and took the morsel of food from her fingers with his mouth. She stared at him, her eyes growing wider the closer he got. His lips touched her fingers as he bit the fry off and she sucked in a breath. Oh yeah, she wanted him, she was just playing hard to get.

He leaned his elbow on the table and gentled his grasp on her wrist. Emma glanced around, her cheeks growing pink. Good. She was making him fucking crazy eating a damn sandwich. He'd rather lay her out and make a meal of her.

She seemed to pull herself together a bit and leveled a glare at him.

"You're so sure of yourself." She tugged against his hand, but he didn't release his grip on her.

"Not really, but when you see something you like, you don't let it get away." That sounded either smooth or creepy. He couldn't quite decide which, but romance wasn't exactly his strong suit.

She bit her lip and nodded toward the menu. "When I was a teenager, my brother Travis got a dirt bike. His momma wouldn't let him keep it, so I got it by default. I started racing in high school against the boys because there wasn't a division for girls, and I kind of kicked their asses."

God, that little southern twang when she spoke did something to him. And she had a mouth on her that would make his mother blush. Most women needed a toned down version of him. He had to watch what he said, keep a tight control on his anger, and never talk work. Emma wasn't like that. He felt more like himself than he had with another human being in ages.

His smile widened. "I'd like to see that sometime. You still race?"

"As often as I can. Fuck. I love it." She brushed the crumbs from her sandwich off her fingers. "Are you from the FBI or something?"

Jacob's eyes widened and he swallowed his bite of food hurriedly. Damn. She was more perceptive than he'd expected, too. She might be more than a tad bit country, but that didn't mean she was easily fooled. "No. Why would you say that?"

"I've been trying to figure you out since you sat down. You aren't like the intellectuals or the creepadoodles that usually want to see this shit. You're younger, hot, fairly normal, and I think if you wanted something you'd go for it."

"And that makes me FBI?"

"It doesn't make you the type I usually see. You're too old to be a student doing a research project. Journalists take lots of notes, ask hundreds of questions, and almost always focus on the negatives and sensationalize stuff. I don't see journalists anymore, it's too upsetting to the families, and I don't have that kind of time. I figure you have to be FBI or something like that. Are you?"

"No." He took a long drink from his glass.

His game was up. He wouldn't lie to her, but telling her the truth was likely to put an end to this dinner. Emma's dad was notorious for not speaking to cops. It was actually a blessing the man had gone into hiding. It meant there were no longer panicked calls to cops by reporters trying to get a story out of the infamous Ration family. Considering what had happened to Emma's brother, and even to her, Jacob didn't expect her to take the information well.

"You aren't going to tell me, are you?" She wiped her hands, and goodbye was written all over her face. If he didn't come clean, he could kiss the possibility of a second date goodbye.

He sat back in the booth, stretching one arm out over the cushion, studying her. What was he thinking? This was business, not hitting on a girl. He had to remember there was something else going on, something bigger than either of them.

"Did you enjoy your meat?" he asked.

She snorted. "It's good. You handle yours okay?"

"Yeah, it's pretty good."

"You're not going to answer me, are you?"

Jacob had to do it. Like it or not. He sucked in a deep breath and counted to ten, calming himself. "My dad was the detective in charge of the TBK case. He arrested Mitchell Black."

"No fucking way." Emma gaped at the man across from her. "Are you a cop?"

"Yeah. Detective, actually." He shrugged and glanced away. Studying the cases, he hadn't liked how her dad was handled, or how little the cops had done to mitigate the media coverage on the families. But he'd been a baby. And his father had changed with that case.

"And you let me sit here and talk shit at you that you already knew?" The fury radiating off her was enough to make a lesser man duck and take cover.

He hated the way she stared at him now, anger, hurt, confusion all there for him to see. Fuck. This was not what he wanted.

Jacob leaned forward, hands upturned. "Look, I wanted to see the letters. I didn't mean to piss you off. A lot of really shitty stuff went down on those last few TBK victims, and things should have been different."

"I think it's time for me to go." Emma grabbed her filing box and slid out of the booth. She kept her head down, not looking at him anymore. The flirtation and chemistry was gone.

"Emma, no." He dug out his wallet, dropping a generous amount on the table to cover the meal and tip, while she fled from him.

It appeared the distrust of cops was a family trait. He shouldn't take it personally, but Jacob's whole life was about making Oklahoma City a safer place. Sure, there were a lot of fucked up, dirty cops out there, but that wasn't him. Yeah, he had his issues—too much anger, short fuse, but he kept his cool on the job. He'd show her.

Jacob strode out of the restaurant, pausing long enough to tell the hostess his payment was on the table before jogging out into the parking lot. He glanced left, and then right, before catching sight of a blonde ponytail.

"Emma. Emma, wait!"

She glanced over her shoulder at him but didn't stop. That would be too easy. He'd bet money she was as stubborn as a mule.

Emma stalked between the cars. He didn't want to run her down, but like hell he was letting her leave yet. She had to understand. She might be in danger, too.

She reached a silver pickup truck sitting on the edge of the dirt lot and the lights flashed. She reached for the handle, and he closed the last foot of space between them, planting his hand on the door and shoving it closed.

He could smell the faint scent of oil and lemons on her this close. Her ponytail brushed his chest when she glanced over her shoulder at him, but her face was hidden in shadow. She was close, so close he could touch her. Would she let him?

Business. He needed to stop thinking with his cock. He was a better detective than this.

"Damn it, let me explain, okay?" he said.

She side-stepped away from him and backed toward the bed of the truck. "And why should I?"

He held up his hands. "Look, I know your dad doesn't like cops. I understand why. In his situation, I would be pissed off, too. But if I'd told you I was a detective, would you have let me within ten feet of you?"

She glared at him, the truth burning in her gaze. He hated that look.

"No."

He glanced away, his lips pressed into a line. There wasn't anything he could do to make her listen, hell, his lieutenant actively shut him down. Why should she be any different? Except, for an hour, he'd thought he'd found someone who really got him. Too bad she didn't like cops. After this, she probably wouldn't speak to him again. If she blocked his number, he wouldn't be surprised. If this was his one chance, he had to get through to her. Make sure she knew what was out there.

Jacob turned his face slowly toward her once more. She was still studying him, but glanced away hurriedly when his gaze met hers. He hated that she wouldn't even look at him now. "I got a letter two weeks ago, and another a couple days after that. I thought the first one was a load of shit, so I tossed it in the garbage. Then I got the second one. They were sent to my house, not the station." The images were still branded into his brain. He doubted they were stock images. Whoever those poor souls were, he hoped their death hadn't been on par with what the TBK victims had suffered.

She flinched, jaw dropping and brows drawing down, as if to say, *What did this have to do with her?*

He licked his lips. Lieutenant Miller had told him he was wrong, that this was someone screwing with him. But Jacob's gut told him differently. There were so many things fucked up with this situation that he didn't know where to begin, but Emma deserved to be warned. She needed to know. He shifted his weight from foot to foot, hands clenched at his side.

"They're copying TBK's style, but not the method."

She froze, her beautiful face a contorted mask of disbelief and fear. There were innumerable theories that Mitchell Black's sudden death in prison was a conspiracy. What if they'd never caught TBK?

"What does that mean?" she asked.

"I—I don't know. Originally, the first two victims weren't related to TBK until years later. Most of their possessions were destroyed. If there were any letters to kick off the murders, we don't know they exist. Am I right?"

"Yeah. I talked to the Strouds and the Lambs. They didn't know much, but I always thought they were hiding something." She hefted the filing box up so she carried it with both hands to her chest. "What are you saying? Do you think TBK is still out there?"

Jacob shook his head. "I don't know. My dad put him behind bars, and it fucks with my head to think he got the wrong man. I want to believe it's a copycat, but I can't risk that it's not. And it's not a fucking coincidence that he's sending me letters. That's why I looked you up."

"Why? You thought I sent them?"

"It was one of my initial assumptions, but I ruled that out before I ever spoke to you."

"Oh." She blinked. "Do you have the letters on you?"

She knew more about TBK than any other living person. Her eyes on the letters would be a great help in putting his mind at ease that this was a copycat.

He thumbed over his shoulder. "In my Jeep."

"Show them to me?"

"Yeah. Come on. Want me to carry that?" He gestured to the box.

"No thanks." She tossed a glare his way as they began walking.

One...two...three...

He kept counting until he got to ten, but he was grinding his teeth already. Why couldn't she understand he wasn't the enemy here?

"I don't want to cause you any trouble or anything. I know about your brother. I know about you."

She stopped, and he turned to face her. If looks could kill, he'd be ten kinds of dead right now.

"So what? Do you know about what my daddy did to me, too?"

He stared at her for a moment before nodding. He'd read the whole file, cover to cover. At first it was to figure out who she was, but her pictures and everything penned on those old pages had drawn him in. If he were really smart, he'd have sent his partner to meet with Emma, but he'd wanted to meet her himself.

"And that what? Makes me supposed to trust you because you can read a file? Detective Payton, we might share a dark and gruesome history, but that's it. You don't know me, I don't owe you anything—"

"I'm not saying you do."

"You think you understand me? You can flirt with the poor, pitiful daughter of the TBK survivor and get what you want, is that it?"

"No." He scowled at her, fists clenched. He saw her as so much more than that. She'd survived that darkness, built a life that at least appeared to make her happy. "I get where you're coming from."

"I seriously doubt you do."

"What? Because you're the only person who could ever have been fucked over?" He closed the distance between them until he loomed over her. He needed to stop this, walk away now, but she drew him in with those dark eyes that saw too deep. "I think you've got a chip on your shoulder you really need to brush off."

"I'm saving it for later. Thanks. The letters? Or should I go now?"

God, that mouth.

"Come on," he muttered.

She followed him to his Jeep Wrangler, which had seen better days, without another word spoken. He opened the driver's side door and reached across to the case file he started the day he took the letters to his lieutenant. It was also the day he'd been told to ignore the potential case. He laid it open on the seat and leaned against the door. The dome light provided enough illumination to see the ghastly creation.

"It's totally different." Emma squeezed in next to him, soaking up the page. Her disdain for him appeared to have been forgotten, at least for the moment. He closed his eyes and inhaled her fragrance again.

He cleared his throat and glanced at the letter. "I know. That's why I thought the first one was bogus."

The original TBK letters were done on copy paper, with glued or printed words, sometimes on ruled school paper. This letter was one huge image. A collage of graphics layered together with a wash of red over the whole thing. The text was printed as well, but the fonts for each word varied, as if imitating the cut and paste style. But it wasn't the same. It was like a work of art made in imitation. The text was white, with a thin black outline that made it pop on the red background.

Emma put the file box down to peer closer at the page.

"I will finish what my soul began," she muttered the first line of text aloud. "At least the bastard made it easy to read. What do you think these pictures in the background are?"

Did he tell her the truth?

"I think they're images of his learning kills. If he's a copycat, he probably experimented somewhere, and we haven't discovered the bodies. These could be images of those kills made to taunt us."

"TBK pieced magazine pictures together on a few of his letters." She shivered and took a deep breath. Though those images weren't as graphic, they were disturbing.

"A lot of the text doesn't make any sense. I think I'm missing a piece of it. Makes me wonder if there was a third letter or if he's fucking with me." He reached past her and tapped the first paragraph. "In the first one he talks a lot about finishing what his soul began, but he doesn't say what it is he's doing—"

"Why he?" she asked.

He flipped to the second letter and pointed to the first pronoun that caught his eye. "The pronoun usage is masculine. Whoever did this at least identifies as male."

"You can tell that from this?" She pointed at the page.

"Yeah. I mean, we could tell from the first TBK letters he was an educated man based on the grammar usage. This letter isn't as grammatically clean." He pointed at a second block of text. "There are no apostrophes or commas. I think based on the presentation, this person is more artistic. They sure as hell have more graphic skills than TBK ever did."

Emma snorted. "Tell me about it. What are you thinking? Copycat, wannabe, or what?"

He didn't pray much anymore, but he prayed that was all it was. For both his sake and Emma's.

"I'm hoping it's a dumb prick. What did you call them? Creepadoodles?" He chuckled.

"Yeah, it seems a lot nicer than calling them crazy fucks. What do the other cops say about this?" She crossed her arms and leaned against the Jeep, finally looking him in the face.

Jacob shrugged and flipped the folder closed. He'd seen those pages enough to visualize them when his eyes were closed. "Ignore it. There's no bodies, no one's dead, there are plenty of real crimes to solve."

He crossed his arms, mirroring her pose, and glanced at a car pulling into the lot. He was seeing things in the corner of his eye, and he couldn't shake the sensation of being followed, though he had no evidence of anyone stalking him.

Both Jacob and Emma had spent their lives in the shadow of TBK and what he'd done. He couldn't pretend to know what it was like for Emma, but he knew his father and what he'd been like.

Emma's brows drew down and she stared at him as if he were a puzzle. He was pretty good at reading people, but she was a mystery. He couldn't keep staring at her— memorizing the arch of her brow, the slight scar on her right jaw—and he was going to drive himself crazy with this misplaced obsession.

The parking lot was full of cars and relatively quiet. The muted sound of music from the restaurant and the occasional car going by were the only sounds to break the silence. What if they were being watched now? What if this wasn't an idiot getting their rocks off? What if they were facing a real copycat, or TBK himself?

"Hey."

He glanced at her, somewhat surprised to find her features softer, less stubborn.

Emma nodded at the box. "Anytime you want to look through the stuff, give me a call, okay?"

"Sure. Thanks." He nodded. That box of paper wasn't what he wanted from her, but he doubted their desires aligned.

Part of him wanted to pore over the pages just for an excuse to be near her, but that was a bad idea. He needed to walk her to her truck, say goodnight, and drive away. It was better to walk away.

"Hey, Emma?"

"Hm?" She jerked her chin toward him.

"Do me a favor? If you think someone's following you, give me a call? You're the only kin of the victims left here. If this is more than a few letters, you might be a perfect target." It wasn't like he could assign a protection detail to her because he had a bad feeling, and she wouldn't like cops hanging around anyway.

"Should I make sure to get an escort back to my truck?" She smiled and thumbed over her shoulder.

Wait—what? Now she was flirting with him again?

"You really should," he said with a straight face. She shouldn't play this game with him. Not now.

"Well, come on then, big protector." She picked up the box and waited for him to lock the Jeep before heading back to her truck.

They wound through the cars, Jacob following close behind her. She didn't like cops, and she didn't like him, but Jacob liked her. There was no good reason, but he did.

Her silver truck loomed ahead. It was one of those ridiculously tall ones, with big tires and lifted at least a foot higher. He'd have expected a man to drive it, but the pink stickers across the back window were a dead giveaway.

"If you were a guy I'd think you were compensating." Jacob nodded toward the truck.

"I like big things." She grinned at him as if the animosity weren't there. Women were confusing, flighty creatures, but Emma could probably give lessons.

"I can see that." He chuckled. "You'll let me know if you see anything out of the ordinary?"

"Maybe."

Maybe his ass. If it came down to it, he might kidnap her and stash her somewhere safe. Okay, he wouldn't, but she brought out all his protective urges, and she didn't even need them. Emma was the kind of woman who would face down her enemies on her own and win. But she was still human and breakable.

Jacob grabbed her arm and took a step toward her until she was completely in his shadow. "I'm not jacking around, Emma. Please, be careful."

The last thing he wanted was to find her dead, lifeless body. He'd seen enough to last a lifetime, and he didn't want that for Emma. She'd had too much pain in her life to pile on this too. He'd do whatever it took to keep her safe. From afar. She tempted him too much.

"You don't know me very well, detective." Emma shrugged off his hand. "I can take care of myself."

"I'm sure you can."

"Let me know if you see anything suspicious, Detective." She winked at him, pulling her bravado around her like a shield. "I could protect you."

Jacob planted a hand on the truck and leaned down a bit, so they were face to face. "Would you protect me from the big bad wolf?"

This needed to stop, now.

"If I needed to I could probably run him down in my big bad truck." She flicked a crumb from his shirt, her breath fanning against his skin. Nothing good could come of this, but damn she was tempting.

"I'd have to arrest you then. Vehicular homicide."

"Again with the handcuffs. You're a kinky one, aren't you?" She flattened her palm against his chest. Was she going to push him away? He'd let her, but he didn't want to give her space. This was going nowhere good, and he couldn't stop himself.

"I'm pretty sure I can do the job just fine on my own."

"And we're back to the compensating."

"Well you said you liked big things."

"Do you have something big to show me?"

She rose up on her toes the same moment he lowered his face. There was nothing soft or tentative about the way she set her mouth against his. He wrapped his arms around her waist, bringing her flush to his chest. Her arms were around his neck, pulling him down farther. Hell yes, he wanted closer. He wrapped her ponytail around his fingers and tugged, pulling her head back and breaking the kiss. Her gaze ate him up, driving sane thought out of his mind.

"You need to be more careful," he whispered, his voice low and rough.

"Shut up and kiss me."

He could do that.

Jacob pushed her back up against the truck and pushed his knee between her thighs. She shifted against him, wiggling on his leg. This couldn't go farther. She didn't need someone like him in her life. But he wasn't strong enough to keep from devouring her mouth.

This close, he could see the same shadow that haunted him deep in her gaze. They were cut from the same cloth. Two souls created from darkness, struggling in the light. He'd protect her, even from himself if he had to.

2.

HAROLD ESPINOZA flipped through his mail on his way into the kitchen. A few bills, some fliers for local businesses, and—ah, there they were. His permits for the upcoming LGBTQ parade. Every year the city turned out more support for the growing community in Oklahoma City. It was a far cry from what things had been like when Harold was coming out in his twenties.

Tomorrow was the first planning meeting for the Pride Week festivities. Local businesses and organizations who would never have considered such a move five years ago were turning up to support the movement. This year, he'd cracked the motorcycle community. On the weekends bracketing Pride, there were organized rides and even a dirt bike competition. They were doing a big push this year on the new acronym, QUILTBAG, which besides sounding like a new sort of insult was actually an inclusive representation of the community. Instead of just standing for Lesbian, Gay, Bisexual, Trans or Queer, QUILTBAG would bring all of the identifications together. It would be a while before it caught on, but Harold had hope.

Things were seriously getting better. He wished his brother from another mother had lived long enough to see this, but AIDS had taken Jose's life five years ago.

Harold dropped the rest of his mail onto the kitchen counter. The permits called for a celebratory drink. He poured two fingers of scotch into a crystal glass Jose bought him one year for Christmas.

"Jose, you'd be shocked to see how far we've come." He lifted the glass, saluting the picture of Harold and his chosen family on his refrigerator.

He swirled the amber liquid in the glass, watching the light refract off the crystal. Maybe he should whip up some cocktails tomorrow to kick the meeting off with a bang? He could do the sangria recipe that had been Jose's favorite.

A creak of wood sounded through the house.

He paused, listening for the sound again. Was that the back door?

Harold peered at his back door. The kitchen and patio were next for his renovations, which would cut down on the creepy noises at night. Nothing was out of place. Chalk one more up to things that go bump in the night. He shook his head, but caught a glimpse of something on the floor, past the counter, in front of the back door.

He crossed to the piece of paper.

"You're losing important stuff," he said out loud. It had to be one of the permit documents. He really needed to be more careful. Jose wasn't there to keep him on track anymore and the city offices weren't that understanding of lost paperwork.

Except, he stared at the piece of paper and couldn't make heads or tails of the orange hodgepodge of images. Was it a flier of some sort? He turned it ninety degrees and saw the text. He needed his glasses to read something that fine.

Now, where were his glasses?

JACOB PAYTON climbed out of his Jeep, a sense of dread settling in his stomach.

"Detective. Where's your partner?" One of the patrol officers crossed the lush, well-manicured lawn toward him.

"Morning, Aaron. Freeman's going to be out for a few days. It's just you and me. Some family thing." Jacob shook the officer's hand. "What do we have?"

Dispatch had only informed him of a dead body and a bad scene, but these days any dead body made him anxious.

"It's..." Aaron shook his head. He seemed a little green around the gills, which was saying something. Aaron was a seasoned officer who had been around it all. "I've never seen anything like it."

"Show me. Anyone else here?"

"EMTs and another patrol. We set up a perimeter."

"EMTs weren't able to help?"

"Fuck, Jacob, no one could help this guy." Aaron led him toward the house. "Elderly neighbors called it in. I guess he picks up their newspaper and has breakfast with them every day, and when he didn't show up they got worried. We knocked, no answer. Went around back and saw it."

"Who called the EMTs?"

"Dispatch had trouble understanding them, so they sent the EMTs out just in case. The husband's had a couple of falls. Guess they figured it was better to cover all the bases."

Jacob swallowed as they stepped over the threshold. He could hear the buzz of flies and smelled the nauseating aroma of human excrement mixed with the metallic tang of blood. He breathed through his mouth as Aaron led him through a very neat, well-kept home. At a glance he could tell the owner liked thrillers and non-fiction books on finance. There were a number of pictures of large groups of people—several of them displayed parade floats.

"He's in here." Aaron stepped through an arch into a long, rectangular room that comprised a breakfast nook and a kitchen.

"Fucking Christ," Jacob said before he could think better of it.

"I can't stay in here." Aaron pivoted and fled to the front of the house, leaving Jacob alone with the carnage.

In life, Harold Espinoza would have been of average height, maybe five foot ten, of Hispanic descent, and neat—much like his home. In death, he was an image out of Jacob's worst nightmares.

He waved flies away from his face and pulled out his cell phone, activating his recording app. He wouldn't step foot in the kitchen until the forensics team went over the scene. There was too much blood—everywhere.

"Victim is positioned in his kitchen, tied to what I assume is a ladder-back chair from the breakfast nook. Judging from the blood splatter throughout the room, the attack started near the back door. There was a struggle. Some kitchen utensils and things are broken. There's papers strewn around and some things are knocked off the kitchen counter. Canisters. A box of cereal. The victim seems to have been posed. He is tied with his palms up, head tilted back, and his eyeballs..." His mouth was dry. "His eyes are gone. Where's the fucking CSI team?"

He leaned as far over the threshold as he dared without disturbing the blood spatter. He wanted a closer look to see what manner of tools might have been used. If it was a frying pan and a meat tenderizer, he'd lose his shit. The posing, the brutality and especially the missing eyeballs. It was too coincidental.

Jacob paced into the living room.

Was he crazy? Was he looking for a copycat where there wasn't one?

He glanced over his shoulder, but he was alone.

The poor vic had experienced the three hallmarks of the notorious Oklahoma City serial killer.

Torture.

Blind.

Kill.

Jacob's head spun, pulling together a hundred different factoids about the murders from his father's time, building a case. It was the only thing he could do. Where did he start? How was this victim connected to their killer?

TBK had picked his victims from people he knew, or were on the fringes of his life. Two victims seemed to be kills of opportunity, but he'd tortured them all to the point of death, and in their final moments he removed the eyeballs as some sort of sick trophy.

If this murder was going to follow the pattern, that meant someone in Harold's life was a killer.

The letters, now this. It was too much of a coincidence.

Where was that damn forensics team? He needed to search the scene, see if this copycat left anything. If there was a letter.

It couldn't be the real TBK, could it? His father had arrested him, hadn't he?

He pulled out his cell phone, punching in a number he did not want to dial. He paced the living room, searching for anything that seemed out of place. Had anything been stolen? Was the murderer in any of the photographs? The victim seemed to be an excellent housekeeper, neat and tidy to the extreme. It should have been easy to tell if anything was missing, but nothing appeared out of place.

"Lieutenant Miller," a grating voice said on the other end of the line.

Jacob ground his teeth. "Hey LT."

"Payton. How's the scene looking?"

"Like a TBK copycat."

Miller sighed heavily. "Payton, we talked about those letters and agreed someone is fucking with you."

"The victim is bound in a similar fashion to the very first TBK victim. And, his eyes are removed." Payton paused in front of a wall of photographs, the ones with the floats. Warning bells went off in his head.

The Pride Parade.

"Do I need to take you off this case? I can assign someone else. Maybe you need to be on desk duty until Freeman gets back."

"I do not need to be reassigned, I'm just saying it's too much coincidence."

"No, Payton, you work this crime how it is. By the book. Relying on what happened in the past is going to blind you to what this killer did."

Jacob's vision hazed red and he ground his teeth together.

One...two...three...

"Yes, sir. I'll do that as soon as the forensics team gets here."

Four...five...six...

"Good. Brief me when you're done, I want this case closed in a week. We can't have any more open ones lying around. Now get to work." Miller hung up the line.

Seven...eight...

Oh who the fuck was he kidding? He wanted to deck Miller in that obnoxious, stubbed nose of his and break his teeth. It wouldn't fix things, but it would make him feel a little bit better.

Jacob turned back to the pictures, grasping for the strands of thought teasing his memory.

Harold was an activist for the gay community. It was all over this wall. It had never been proven, but TBK's first victim was suspected of being part of the lesbian community, which at the time was a much smaller and tight-lipped group of people. Was that the link between the kills?

Lt. Miller would never accept they had a copycat on their hands, because for some damn reason the man had this bullshit idea he and Jacob were in competition with each other. All because their dads had been cops. Miller was a tool to work for and the bane of Jacob's existence since becoming lieutenant. All he could figure was that Miller considered himself the victor in this one-sided game, while all Jacob wanted to do was catch the bad guys. He didn't play the system like Miller.

Which left Jacob with a predicament on his hands. He knew this was a copycat. The evidence might not be as solid as Miller would want, but the signs were there.

Footsteps heralded more people on the scene. He turned toward the door and felt at least some of the tension ease.

"My favorite CSI team."

Jacob shook the hand of the two-man geek squad before launching into what he could tell them of the scene.

Miller wanted him to work this like any other case? He could do that, but someone else was going to point to TBK, and when the chief of police heard it from someone else, Miller would be in a world of hurt. Not that Jacob took any joy in seeing his LT screw the pooch, but this time around he'd like to know he was right.

"What do you think was the murder weapon?" Jacob leaned against the archway, trying to contain himself as the forensics team got to work.

"Shit. All this blood came from him?" The lead shook his head. "I'm going to take a wild guess," he leaned over the sink and snapped a few pictures, "and say a meat tenderizer. A big one. I'm guessing our vic did a lot of cooking. This doesn't look like a cheap tool. Professional grade."

Jacob blew out a breath. "Hey, do me a favor and look at those papers there, on the floor?"

"Dude, chill. Can't rush the magic. Where's Freeman?"

"He ran off to Vegas with a stripper." Jacob crossed his arms across his chest.

"Vegas! Hey, did you see that news bit this morning about the creepy clown in Vegas?"

"Clown? No."

"Yeah, this guy's been seen in like, three cities in this clown costume, hanging out on street corners and busy intersections. Saw on Twitter he was spotted in Vegas a couple days ago. Clowns freak me out."

"Weird." Okay, Jacob didn't care about some clowns. He wanted those papers.

He rolled his eyes and waited, crossing and uncrossing his arms. If this was a copycat, there'd be a letter today at the police station. What would happen then? Miller would fuck up this case. Jacob wasn't sure if it was something he'd done, or a hold-over from Miller's old man, who had not gotten on well with Jacob's father, but there was no love lost between them.

"Here." The lead handed him the blood splattered papers. "Glad to see someone wears gloves at a scene."

"Thanks." Jacob took the papers. He leafed through the first few, which appeared to be a legal, city document and cover letter. The last page, that chilled his blood.

The "letter" was orange this time, but the rest fit the two Jacob had received. Images of bodies collaged together, and in the lower right hand corner—an eyeball.

This wasn't just a murder case anymore, this was something else entirely.

MAX HUMMED TO THE TUNE on the radio, resolutely ignoring the sensation of someone watching. It was all in his mind. He was alone. No one was behind him. If there was anyone, he could see them in one of the mirrors hanging behind his desk, but he was completely alone.

This was his safe haven.

He clicked over to the chat room and smiled when he saw someone had joined him.

```
Iron: Hi
```

For a few moments, Joker's icon didn't show any activity and Max almost gave up, then a pencil appeared next to the name.

```
Joker: Didn't think you'd be online.
Iron: Had a break. Hows it going?
Joker: Just getting ready to start my pro-
ject.
Iron: Cant wait to see it. You being careful?
Joker: Yes.
Iron: Good.
Iron: What city are you in now?
Joker: Vegas.
```

Max chewed his lip. He didn't have much interaction with Joker. He was the quiet one of their online group. Hardly ever spoke. Hell, this might be the longest exchange Max had ever had with the guy.

Did he tell Joker he thought he was being watched?

No, it wasn't like the guy could do anything through the Internet.

Max was on his own. Besides, it was probably all in his head.

EMMA STARED IN HORROR at the TV in the office of the garage. She'd been out in the shop working on oil changes all morning and hadn't seen the news until noon. Now, she couldn't tear her gaze away from it. The guys darted glances her way as they ate their burgers, and she knew what they were thinking.

They were her friends. Her teammates. And her co-workers.

"You okay, Em?" The shop owner, Simon, sank into the waiting room chair next to her. They all gathered in the relative coolness to watch the news. It wasn't like there was anything else on, not when the coverage was so horrible.

"Yeah. Fine." She swallowed hard.

The news crews weren't saying much, just that a man had been found murdered, his body posed. People were murdered every day, so that wasn't what caught her attention. It was the letter the news anchor flashed on the screen.

The image was similar to what Jacob had shown her last night, except it was orange. What did the colors mean? Did Jacob know? Why hadn't he told her? Probably because she was nothing but a source to him. It shouldn't sting, but it did.

He was right though. Not that she doubted him when he said it was dangerous, but she'd hoped whoever had sent him the letters would fizzle out into a lack of follow through. But the copycat certainly had acted on his plan.

"Some are saying this murder imitates that of TBK killer, Mitchell Black—"

"I need some air." Emma shoved to her feet and stalked into the shop. The heat wrapped around her like an electric blanket. Sweat beaded her brow, and her shirt stuck to her back within moments.

She wanted to kill the murderer. Was that wrong?

Did that make her like him?

Emma needed to know more. She couldn't sit here waiting for the news to tell her a watered-down version of the truth. She had to know what was going on. And wasn't it her luck she knew a detective?

But did she dare call him?

He kissed her like it was the most important thing in the world. No man had ever made her feel like that. It had left her off-kilter and reeling, not to mention hornier than a teenager.

If she called him, would he read into it?

Did she want him to?

Could she trust herself to ask the questions and not say, *I want to see you again?* She shouldn't. He was a cop. The son of the man who'd traumatized her father even more after the murder of her grandparents, but it wasn't like Jacob had been involved.

Whatever.

She wanted to talk to him, so Jacob would damn well talk to her.

Emma punched in his contact and hit dial.

The line didn't get through a single ring.

"Fuck, I meant to call you," Jacob snarled, and the vicious quality of his voice soothed her nerves.

"Is it your copycat?" Despite the heat, her skin was clammy, her palms cold.

"I can't talk about an open case."

"Fuck, don't shut me out like this. You came to *me*. You involved *me*. I have a right to know."

He didn't reply immediately. She heard rustling, the murmur of voices then the sound of a door clicking shut and silence.

"I can't talk about this right now," he said.

She would make him talk. She could figure out a way, couldn't she?

"Jacob—"

"You aren't hearing what I'm saying. Dinner. Tonight. My place. I can't risk talking about this to you here, or in public. Now, shit is hitting the fan. I've got to go. I'll let you know when to come over, okay?"

The tension eased, and she wasn't sure if it was because she'd get to see him again, or if it was because she would get answers. Why did the idea of being nearer to the badge-carrying cop make her breathe easier? She didn't want to think too hard about that one. Or her little fantasy last night starring a detective and the back of her truck.

"Okay," she replied after a moment.

"Are you still being careful?"

"Yeah." There was nothing more to say, but she wanted to talk to him more. Maybe then she'd understand the cosmic pull behind those intense blue eyes.

"Shit, I've got to go. See you tonight."

The call ended abruptly, but it didn't matter. She would see him tonight.

Emma stared at her phone.

"What are you smiling about?"

She jerked her head around, glaring at the owner of the voice. "What the fuck are you doing here?"

Her ex-boyfriend, Derrick, stood outside the open bay doors to the garage. He'd never been a fan of the grease, but he'd liked to watch her fix things. She'd thought it was kind of hot for a while, but now her skin crawled as his gaze slid over her body. Why had she stayed with him for so long?

"Wanted to check on you. I saw the news." He took a step over the threshold.

She threw up her hand. "Stop right there, asshole."

Derrick slowed to a halt, his petulant pout irritating her. She used to think he was cute when he didn't get his way. Now she wanted to shove a tire iron up his nose and kick him to the curb. He wasn't worth her time anymore.

The office door banged open and Simon entered, headed straight for Derrick. "I thought I told you to stay the hell away from here."

Shit!

"Simon, back off." Emma stalked toward her ex and grabbed the front of his shirt before Simon did something stupid. "I'll handle my own problems."

She loved the guys she worked with better than her own kin, but they could keep their noses in their own damn business. She was perfectly capable of handling a cheating ex-boyfriend on her own.

Derrick followed her out and around the corner of the shop. With at least a thin layer of privacy, she wheeled to face him, hands balled into fists. Derrick wasn't concerned about her. He wanted something. There wasn't a selfless bone in that man's body.

"I thought I told you to leave me alone," she said.

"I know, I just thought if I gave you some time to cool down, you might see that it's not that big of a deal." He edged toward her, that charming smile coming out to play.

"Oh stop that. We haven't had a real relationship in a long time. Why are you really here?"

"I saw the news, and I wanted to make sure you were okay."

"Please." She rolled her eyes. "If you cared about me you wouldn't have stuck your dick in a prostitute."

"It's not cheating if you paid for it," he whined. "Come on. You loved me."

"Derrick, seriously, get the fuck away from me. We're over. Done. That's it." She'd loved him, but he'd never loved her. She knew that now.

"Yeah, but it could have been love."

"No, it wasn't. You love yourself too much to leave room for anyone else. Just—leave." She stepped around him, feeling freer. She might actually owe Derrick a thank you for cheating on her. If she was still with him, she'd never have allowed Jacob to kiss her. And she wanted to kiss the detective again. But first, she wanted answers.

JACOB STEPPED OUT OF the interview room and into chaos.

Miller had all the detectives working the Harold Espinoza case. The phones were ringing, every available person was underfoot, and Jacob couldn't even get to his desk. The shit had really hit the fan once the noon news went live with their kill note.

He'd kept his head down after the telecast and the reporter making the same connection he had. It wouldn't do to give Miller an *I-told-you-so*, not when he wanted to stay lead detective on the case.

"Payton." Police chief Kevin Stevenson stalked through the bullpen toward the LT's office, dubbed the fish bowl because of the glass walls. "Miller's office. Now."

Fuck.

Jacob tensed and grabbed the files off his desk.

"Chief, I was about to come give you an update," Miller said as they entered his office.

"Close the door, Payton." Stevenson paced the length of the office. He glared at Miller then Jacob, sparing neither of them. "Why the hell didn't you warn me about this?"

"The murder just happened, sir—" Miller smoothed his tie, eyes darting around.

"And the letters?" He pulled a piece of paper out of his pocket. "I quote, 'Since my previous letters have gone without being heeded, I turn to the media.' What the hell?" The chief tossed the smaller collage letter onto Miller's desk.

Miller's jaw twitched, and he pointedly kept his gaze on Stevenson. "Payton did receive some unique notes, but that's all they were."

Stevenson turned his gaze on Jacob. His father and Stevenson had once been partners. "Is this true?"

"Yes, sir. I brought both of the letters I received in as soon as I got them." He avoided mentioning Miller's vehement statement that they were not dealing with a copycat.

"Show me."

Jacob opened the file he'd carried in with him and presented it to Stevenson.

"Shit. Why didn't you say anything?" He slanted his glare toward Miller.

"There was no proof we were dealing with a copycat. It could have been a prank. Some kid in a picture class wanking off and being stupid." He waved his hand around, his voice going up a few notes. This was not going to look good for Miller.

"And last night's murder? I've seen the pictures. It's a copycat job if I ever saw one." Stevenson planted his hands on his hips, lips pursed.

"We don't know—"

"Bullshit, Lieutenant. Someone doesn't go to this degree of detail without the intent to follow through." Stevenson glanced at Jacob, then Miller again, as if weighing his decisions. "I'm going to invite the FBI in on this."

Miller pushed to his feet. "But—"

Stevenson held up his hand. "The perp is obviously focusing on Jacob here, as the son of the man who put TBK behind bars. We do not have the objectivity to handle this. I will keep you notified if they accept our invitation or not. I also expect Detective Payton and all of the original TBK evidence to be made available to them, and the full backing of this department. Understood?"

Jacob kept his mouth shut. Miller's face was an ugly shade of red, and the man's jaw moved without sound.

"Payton, with me." Stevenson stalked out of the office without a care that Miller was fuming.

Jacob gave his LT a mock salute. *Take that, asshole.*

"Payton, do not screw this up or I'll have you on desk duty for a year," Miller said, his voice pitched barely above a whisper.

"Got to go. Killers to catch."

Jacob followed in the wake of the chief of police, who was already at the elevator, holding the door to an empty lift.

"Jacob, what the hell?" The doors had barely closed before Stevenson turned on him. "Why am I hearing about this from the news and not you?" He tugged at his tight-fitting collar. Though Kevin Stevenson could play the part of a suit, he was a pavement-pounding cop to the core. Kevin had been Jacob's father's partner for years, and part of Jacob's childhood.

Jacob blew out a breath. "I brought it to Miller. If I went over his head, he'd be taking it out on me for months."

Stevenson shook his head. "I wish you could play politics, son. I really do."

Jacob shrugged. He wasn't like Stevenson. He couldn't play nice forever. The only thing keeping him in line with Miller right now was that he'd been written up a few weeks ago for being overzealous in his investigations.

"Do you think the feds will come in on this?"

"I hope so. Miller's a good LT, but I'd rather this be in the hands of someone who can look at this objectively. We're going to end up with more copycats and TBK fanatics within the week if we don't nip this in the bud and catch him quick." They exited the elevator and made their way to the executive offices.

They were going to war, and as much as Jacob wanted to be the man to lead them into the fray, he could see Stevenson's point. Hell, he even agreed with him.

EMMA GLANCED IN HER rear-view mirror and frowned. The cars all appeared different. So why couldn't she shake the feeling someone was watching? It had started after her little chat with Derrick, then when she went to the gas station for drinks and now on her way to Jacob's. Was it Derrick? Was he being a sore loser and following her? Wouldn't surprise her, but they were over. Done with.

Besides, for some crazy reason she was actually nervous about her not-date with the hottie of a cop. It wasn't a date. At least, normal dates didn't involve getting together to hash out murder details. And yet it was going to be the best date she'd had in ages.

She turned onto a street lined with small, old houses that had to have been around since the Great Depression. Jacob wasn't kidding when he said he lived close to downtown. During the afternoon, the skyscrapers would practically cast their shadows over the neighborhood.

While the rest of the guys were going out for a dirt bike ride, followed by a bonfire BYOB party on a Friday night, she was going to talk about serial killers. It was an odd life she lived, but TBK had branded her with his darkness before she'd been born. She'd never escape his mark, and now someone wanted to fuck with what he'd done.

"Your destination is on the left," her phone announced.

The house was one of the better kept homes on the block. The exterior was painted slate gray, with blue shutters, trim, and door. The lawn wasn't a work of art, but it was obvious Jacob tended to it regularly. It didn't look much like a bachelor pad, but what did she know about houses?

Emma had never lived in a house, at least not one that couldn't be moved. She'd grown up in trailer homes, mobile parks, and RVs when times got really tough. The closest she'd gotten was her current lodgings, splitting a duplex with her friend, Amanda. It was a temporary situation, until Emma figured out what she wanted to do next. Whatever it was, she wanted to change things, get out of the hole she'd dug for herself while she was with Derrick.

Her hands were full, so she knocked on the door with her knee. Her nerves were buzzing in her stomach. The door swung open, and Jacob stood on the other side. The second she met his gaze, an electric shiver zipped down her spine and her heart beat heavier.

"Hey. Wow, what is that?"

"A peace offering. Wanna take it? It's heavy."

He stepped closer and scooped the metal sculpture from her arms. He stared at it, his brow creased in confusion. It was kind of a cute expression on such a confident type of man. She grinned. Yeah, it was weird to bring a present to the guy she'd told to fuck off, but something about Detective Jacob Payton had stuck with her. She wasn't going to fight it. Truth be told, she had too much merchandise on her hands right now from putting in long hours instead of hanging out with Derrick, so giving away one small piece would make room for another.

"Uh." He glanced at her. "I'm sorry. What is it?"

She tossed her head back and laughed. "It's a lawn ornament. You put it out front, people look at it, think it's pretty."

"Oh." His gaze traveled over her, and her damn nerves danced up and down her spine. "I only got you dinner."

"I like dinner." She shrugged.

"Let's put it out here."

She followed him to the lawn. He studied one side of the yard and then the other before finally deciding to position the sculpture in front of the large windows on the right side of the house and stood back to study it.

"What exactly is it?" he asked, still sounding a bit perplexed.

"I made the pedestal out of reclaimed metal. Those are all old mufflers. I wanted something to emulate clouds and dreaming. The crystal is supposed to absorb bad energy. Altogether it protects the house and residents from evil spirits, especially while you sleep." She shrugged. "I didn't have time to make a pig or a donut."

"Funny. Thanks." He cracked a smile at that. It transformed his face, from hot to dead sexy.

What do you know? He has a sense of humor.

"You're welcome. I figured I owed you an apology." She mentally pulled herself together. It wasn't fair that a guy flashing her a little teeth could knock her off her thoughts, but he had.

She might not trust cops as a whole, but he might be okay. At least when she searched his name on the Internet there weren't any viral videos of him beating people like other cops.

"Come inside." He placed his hand on the small of her back. The heat from his touch soaked into her skin, straight to her core. "I almost didn't think you'd come."

"Let me grab the stuff from the truck first."

Jacob followed her to the passenger side and took the box before she could pick it up. She opened her mouth to protest, but closed it before she said a word. Jacob wasn't Derrick. If a guy wanted to do something for her, she should let him.

His hand went back on the small of her back. That one spot had some magical property she would never understand. It was as if a hand there short-circuited the rest of her cognitive ability until all she could think about was the point of contact. This wasn't like her. She didn't do the flirty, simpering girl routine. She was straightforward, direct, a little bawdy even. But her response to him was so different, it had her off-kilter.

Jacob ushered her inside the house, through a man-cave of a living room in all brown leather and dark wood, and into a larger space that seemed to be a rec room of sorts. The country kitchen on her right was spacious and updated, while the corduroy sofas around the fireplace on her left looked inviting. There was also a pool table and a dining set that had that aged, hand-me-down look to it.

"Nice place." She shoved her hands into the pockets of her jean skirt and turned around.

"Thanks. It was my grandfather's. He left it to my dad, but Dad didn't need it, so I got it. It's been a work in progress ever since. Have a seat." He gestured to the bar stools lined up along the counter overlooking the kitchen. "Want anything to drink? Tea? Water? Beer?"

"Beer," she said as she slid onto one of the stools. A little liquid courage never hurt. Besides, it might calm her down a bit. Or something. She had the jitters bad.

There was something charming about the sight of Jacob in the kitchen, barefoot, his hair mussed and hands massaging a chicken breast. Hell, the idea of a man in the kitchen doing anything except making a mess was a miracle. She was almost afraid to make a sudden movement, or he might bolt and leave it to her.

She took the beer he offered her and sipped it. "Anything I can do to help?"

"Um, not right now. I think I've got everything going."

"Aren't you a Mr. Crocker, handling your meat so well?"

"I handle meat just fine, thank you very much. You'll like my meat." He stroked the chicken while giving her that come-hither stare.

She took a deep swig of the beer to keep from telling him what else she'd like him to do with his meat. What had gotten into her? Not him, but something. She was losing sight of why she was here, which was to hear about the TBK copycat case. Instead, she was starting to strategize how she could get into his pants.

"It's my way of getting stress and shit out after work." Jacob glanced up at her once more, his expression a little sheepish.

"What? Cooking?"

"Yeah." He shrugged. "I've had anger issues."

"Anger issues? Like beating people?" The distrust crept back into her voice. What kind of a cop was he?

"No. Never that. Cops like that...they wouldn't want me on a jury of their peers. I deal with my issues." Jacob drew in a deep breath, his knife poised above the chicken.

"Yeah?" Emma's voice broke through his thoughts.

"What's happening lately...in the news?" He shook his head and trimmed the meat. "It's unacceptable. I took this job to protect people. I don't care what color someone's skin is, what side of the tracks they live on or whatever. As cops we're supposed to protect people. I get so pissed off..."

The knife slipped on the glass cutting board and he slammed the handle on the hard surface. This was an anger she could understand. And appreciate.

Jacob shook his head and picked up the knife again. She could almost feel him refocusing his energy, pouring it out through the knife and into what he was doing. Here was a man self-aware of his shortcomings and how to handle them.

"I took an anger management course a while back. They suggested finding a healthy way to work out frustrations."

"And cooking was it?"

"No, my mother was it."

"No." She laughed at the idea of an older, graceful woman with his eyes twisting Jacob's ear and sitting him in a corner of the kitchen. Was it possible the cop was human after all?

"Yeah. Dad had passed away and I was losing my shit. Snapping at people, I was rough with a suspect once, not physically. Verbally. It was a child molester. I hate those cases. I didn't handle a situation the best. I was going downhill, and I started the classes as a way to show my LT that I was trying to get my act together. But as soon as I finished the classes I'd go get trashed at some dive. It started with her picking me up from a bar, totally wasted. She'd bring me home and make scrambled eggs to soak up the liquor. One night, I passed up the bar entirely and went to the kitchen. The rest is history."

"You must be really close with her." Emma's heart squeezed. Her mother had always been addicted to Daddy, and Daddy was addicted to the bottle. It hadn't left much room for her.

"Yeah, we are."

"She's not jealous you're passing up dinner with her tonight?"

"Mom moved to Florida a few years ago. Just me now."

He slid the chicken into the oven and wiped his hands off while he studied her. She resisted the urge to fidget. God, she wanted to kiss that mouth again, but that wasn't the reason he asked her over tonight. What did he see when he looked at her like that?

3.

GOD, SHE WAS BEAUTIFUL.

Jacob cleared his throat. He was staring when he needed to be talking.

"The chief is bringing in the feds to handle the case tomorrow. They're flying down tonight to take over," he said as he washed his hands, trying to get his mind back on why he'd asked her over. Which was not to leer at her amazing legs.

"What the fuck? No." Emma slapped her hand on the countertop.

"It's actually a good thing."

"How is that a good thing? They're taking your job from you."

"Not really. Come over here for a minute." He gestured toward the corduroy couches set up around the fireplace. "My LT is a good face for the media, and he knows how to play department politics, but he's not the best detective. I'm actually relieved we're bringing someone else in. They'll handle it ten times better than he or I would."

There. He'd said it out loud. As much as it chapped his ass to not be in charge, it was the best decision.

They settled on the couches, beer in hand, and the files he'd brought home with him spread out on the coffee table. He shouldn't show her these, but she was the only other person who got this like he did.

Emma studied him, her brow furrowed and mouth screwed up into a puzzled expression he wanted to smooth away with his mouth, to tease a smile from her. He might have forgotten how to smile, but he could enjoy the way she lit up a room with one. He was in awe of her. She'd built a life for herself out from under the shadow of what had happened to their parents. To them. He didn't know if he could be half as strong as her, were he in her shoes. Life was hard enough where he was now.

She was still staring at him with that odd look on her face.

Right, they weren't talking about her.

They were talking about the case.

Jacob knew his decision didn't make a lot of sense to others. He should want to stay lead on the investigation. It would be a career-changing opportunity. But he'd never put much stock in moving up the ladder. He didn't want to be promoted to a desk, playing nice with crooks in suits. All he'd ever wanted to do was put killers behind bars. And if that meant bringing in the feds, well, he'd play chauffeur and babysitter if that's what it meant. Besides, he'd be close enough to the action, and profilers were a different creature entirely. He could learn something from them.

"So...what happened? Why are they saying it's TBK?" She sipped her beer, brow still marred by those lines.

"Body posing. Removal of the eyes. The letters." He ticked off each on his fingers, but took a deep breath before laying the last item out there. "Sexual orientation."

"What?"

"TBK's first vic was a woman suspected to be part of the lesbian community, but it was thirty years ago. No one talked about that. Today, our vic runs the OKC Pride Week. I mean, he had—"

"Harold?" Emma gasped.

Jacob went still, every fiber in his body screaming. "You knew him?"

She set her beer down and turned to face him, her face a little pale. "Not really. I mean, I met him once. He came out to the track to talk to some of the guys that run the local motocross series about doing a special Pride Week thing. We talked a little. What? Why are you looking at me like that?"

"Nothing, I'm just—tired." He glanced away, his thoughts whirling away. Harold was a people person. It shouldn't surprise Jacob that Harold would know someone in about every circle of people. Jacob was grasping for straws where there weren't any. It was coincidence that Emma had run into Harold once, nothing more.

"But it is a copycat?" she asked.

"I think so. It's not a serial killer investigation—yet—but I'm afraid it's going to become that soon." He eased back onto the cushions, letting the age-worn sofa cradle him.

"What qualifies a serial killer? Is there a test? A quiz?"

He chuckled. "I would have thought you knew these things."

"Hey, I'm not the cop here." She leaned against the arm of the sofa, her legs stretched toward him and smiled. He had a feeling she knew the power of her looks, which was why he didn't feel quite so lecherous admiring her.

"How'd you start doing that lawn ornament stuff? I saw your website." He sipped his beer, enjoying the view.

"Such a stalker." She shook her head, but the smile was back. "Shop class in high school. Someone gave me a blow torch, and I found out I could do something besides drive really fast. When did you have time to find out so much about me?"

"Before our date."

"Is that what we're calling last night now, a date?"

"You did let me buy you dinner."

One side of her mouth hitched higher. "And you did kiss me."

Yes he had, and he wanted to do it again. He tightened his hold on the bottle. He knew what her hair between his fingers felt like, what she sounded like when she panted for breath, and he knew how her lips tasted. And he wanted more.

They stared at each other, and he had to wonder what she was thinking. She said she didn't like cops. Hell, she'd all but run from him, but now she was back of her own free will. What secrets was she hiding? Did he want to know them?

The aroma of baking chicken, herbs, and cheese wafted through the space, but nothing else existed between them.

Emma tucked her feet under her. He held his breath as she crawled across the cushions like some sex kitten until she invaded his space, one arm braced on the side of the sofa. He didn't move, wanting to see what she would do. She studied his face, so close now he could see flecks of gold in her brown eyes. She'd come to him. Last night he'd promised himself he wouldn't bother her.

Not unless she came to him.

He threaded his fingers through her loose hair, but it was her who leaned in, closing the distance between their mouths until he felt the whisper of air on his skin. He'd thought about her mouth, her lips, and kissing her again last night and all through the day. He curled his fingers in her hair, tugging her closer.

The timer in the kitchen screamed the second her lips brushed his. She smiled against his mouth. He pulled her closer. One touch of skin on skin wasn't enough. He could eat her up all night long, given the opportunity, but then he'd burn the whole house down.

She sat up, grinning while he glared.

"Tease," he muttered.

"Hey, I don't lack follow-through."

Her laugh followed him all the way into the kitchen.

Jacob pulled the chicken out of the oven and paused to adjust himself. What had he been thinking when he suggested she come over? Oh right, having a nice, private discussion about an ongoing investigation, which he was not supposed to do. But, there weren't a lot of people who understood the draw of this case, how it had changed his family. Hell, Emma might not really get it, but at least she understood why a copycat bothered him so much.

In a matter of a few minutes he had the chicken parmesan plated and served at the dining table.

He could feel Emma's gaze on him, as if she weren't undressing him with her eyes but stripping away layers, leaving him on edge and slightly raw. He wanted to push her onto her back, kiss her, and forget the meal. If she knew what he was thinking, she'd run from him.

"Smells amazing." Her foot bumped his leg under the table as she twirled the pasta on her fork. "Anger issues, huh?"

He paused, utensils in hand. Anger was the tip of the iceberg. He learned control, tricks to manage his short fuse, and to never initiate intimacy unless he was calm. Emma stirred insistent needs in him that weren't controllable. But she didn't need to know that.

"Yup." He focused on cutting his chicken into neat, precise bites.

"I called Daddy today. Well, I called, and my mom answered. Their TV antenna's down so they haven't seen the news. I told her to make sure they didn't fix it. The last thing anyone needs is Daddy on a binge." She sighed and took a dainty bite.

"I thought they were off the grid completely?"

"Yes, and no."

He shrugged. The less he knew the better.

"How was that? Growing up with him, I mean? Mom said it changed Dad." He shook his head. "I don't remember, of course. I was still a baby by the time TBK got really going on that last spree."

"Daddy's pretty fucked up in the head, but he and Mom were together before it all happened. I think she thought she could save him, which is why she's stayed with him through the cheating and the drinking."

"Did he ever get physical with her or you?"

"Oh yeah." She shrugged it off as if it were okay her father had laid a hand on her.

"What?" His vision hazed red, and he gripped his fork tighter than was necessary.

"Look, it wasn't like he beat us or anything. I'm not saying it's okay, but every now and then he'd get really drunk and start in on something. We knew to stay out of his way—"

"Your file. It was his fault you got arrested, wasn't it?"

Emma sat up a little straighter and stared at her plate.

"Shit." He dropped his fork and leaned back, crossing his hands behind his head.

"Do you look to see if all your dates have records?"

He pursed his lips. "Yes."

"You must be a blast to date. Do you get reports whenever your girlfriend get a ticket?"

"No."

"Lighten up, sheesh." She blew out a breath and propped her chin on her hand. "You told me last night you knew. I don't like thinking about that. And yes, the only reason I was driving drunk was because he tried to put a bullet in me. We were all drinking that night, but he got it in his head he'd do me a service and kill me before someone else did. Cops got me a few miles down the street. I got off light, all things considered, especially since Dad was firing his gun and causing a stir with the neighbors. Cops had more than a crying girl to deal with. What I did was wrong. I knew it then, and I know it now, but all I was thinking about was that I needed to get away. Fast."

Jacob nodded. He'd known that, but it was different hearing her say it instead of reading the report for himself. Her parents had lived in Oklahoma City still, and she'd barely been past twenty-one. Hell, her mug shot made her look all of sixteen. Emma was hell on wheels. Nothing would keep her down.

"You know my less than desirable history, and I know you struggle with anger management issues. We've both survived families branded by a killer, and we are now reliving their nightmare. What other topics should we hit on tonight? Politics? Religion? Take your pick. Might as well get the other touchy topics out of the way."

He chuckled. "I don't side with either of the major political parties."

"Me neither. They're almost the same thing now, just different stances on what they spend tax dollars. Religion?"

"I'm...spiritual. Parents were Baptists."

She shrugged. "I guess I'm spiritual, too. Never been big on church, but I think there's got to be something—bigger—out there."

He nodded. "I agree."

Emma smiled slowly as she chewed. "There, all the awkward topics are off the table. Unless you want to talk about sexual partners? I mean, we can hit all the tricky stuff at once."

Jacob laughed despite the absurdity of the conversation. "I'm practically married to my work."

"I'd believe it. I can smell the stress on you. You should lighten up a little. Maybe take up boxing? Or MMA. Those little shorts those guys wear are hot. I bet your ass would look really good in them."

"You've been checking out my ass?"

"Hell yes, just like you've been looking at my boobs."

"Guilty."

"Hey, my boobs are pretty great, so I don't blame you for looking."

Jacob found himself relaxing, which was unexpected.

She placed her fork and knife on the plate before pushing it away from her a bit. She sat up a little straighter, folding her hands one over the other, and leaned forward, her gaze full of mischief. What was she up to?

"I have to use the restroom," she announced.

That was not what he'd expected.

"Hallway behind me, first door on the right."

He watched her sashay away from him. She was a free spirit and rough around the edges. They had little in common besides TBK. And yet, he was drawn to her, which made no sense at all. At least not until his cock factored into the equation, and then there was no question what he wanted from her.

EMMA STARED AT HER reflection and blew out a breath.

What the hell was happening here?

She braced her hands on the counter and hung her head forward. She didn't need to pee. She needed to clear her thoughts.

When Jacob had asked her to come over, she'd expected two things. The first was to discuss the copycat. The second wasn't a guarantee, but she wouldn't turn down sex. Now, with all their cards on the table, her palms were damp, her pulse was too quick, and she couldn't tear her gaze away from the way he put food in his damn mouth. She wanted that mouth back on her. And not in a one-time-only kind of way.

Desire was something she embraced, but this level of lust was burning her up from the inside out. She almost wondered if he drugged her food, but considering he was a rule-following type, she doubted he'd do that. Then again, he didn't need drugs to get in her panties. She'd throw them at him if he wanted her to. And he was a cop!

It made no damn sense, which was how she found herself hiding in the bathroom.

What kind of a date included talking crime scenes and serial killers? She choked out a bitter laugh. Of course TBK would touch even this part of her life. Hell, even for a few years, whenever she raced, people called her "that TBK girl." But she was more than her family history, and so was Jacob.

She ran warm water over her hands to chase the chills away.

If only she'd met Jacob another way, another time, maybe things would be different.

But who was she kidding? A man like him had no reason to want her for anything other than a good time. He had a career, probably went to school, and he had his shit together. She was living out of boxes, had barely passed high school, and all three of her jobs depended on her physical abilities. They were completely different people. Totally wrong for each other. But they had two things in common: a shared history, and a lust as palpable as the meal she'd eaten.

Emma was hard-wired for relationships. It was a fact. There was no fooling herself about the future here. A night, that's all this was. The banter was just talk. There weren't more dates, he wasn't interested in her beyond what she could give him, and really, she didn't need another boyfriend right now. She needed to be on her own.

Emma shook the water droplets off her hands and dried them before exiting the bathroom. The table was cleared off, and Jacob was in his cozy, country kitchen, leaning into the refrigerator.

One night. That's all this was.

She added a little sway to her hips as she rounded the bar, and Jacob turned to face her.

The dishes from dinner were gone, the counters cleared except for a gallon of Blue Bell ice cream and a spoon.

"Hope you like vanilla." He dug a spoonful from the carton and held it out toward her.

"Mm." Emma leaned forward and wrapped her lips around the chilled metal, holding Jacob's gaze as she slowly licked the frosty treat off the spoon.

His gaze narrowed, focused on her lips. She licked them just to see what he'd do.

Jacob's lips compressed into a tight line and he spooned up another bite of ice cream, shoving it in his mouth before neatly selecting a smaller bit and offering it to her. Blue Bell had to be about the best ice cream on the planet. It melted on her tongue all rich and creamy, which made it completely understandable to groan in the sheer pleasure of tasting it.

He stabbed the spoon in the gallon and captured her face between his hands.

About damn time.

He pressed her back against the island, his hips pinning her in place. Though his hold was fierce, he slowly lowered his face to hers. Was he giving her an out? Or slowing down?

She strained toward him and finally—finally—their lips touched. The ice cream flavored the kiss and his hot mouth warmed her cold lips. She twined her arms around his neck, through his hair.

He lifted her and set her on the counter with ease. She liked a man who could toss her around like that, it was a definite turn-on. She wrapped her legs around him and pulled him back against her body, letting her hands rove over him.

"You should tell me to stop," he whispered against her cheek.

"Why the hell would I do that? Am I going to catch something from you? Any unwanted party favors?"

"What? You mean a STD or STI?"

"Yeah."

"No."

She shrugged. "Lucky for you I got my latest results in. Clean and on the pill. I'll ask again, why should I tell you to stop?"

"You should." There was a tortured twist to his voice that tugged at her heart.

"Then you shouldn't have invited me over, because I don't run." She slipped her hands up under his shirt, relishing the feel of his hard body under her palm. He'd taken her by surprise last night, and she hadn't been able to really appreciate him.

"Damn it, Emma, this isn't a good idea." He pushed himself backward, breaking her hold on him.

"What the fuck?" He had to have known, after last night, what would happen if they were in the same room again.

He gripped the edge of the countertop as if it were his life-line.

She shoved off the island and planted her hands on her hips.

"I really didn't invite you over for more than food," he said.

"Okay, lie to yourself if it makes you feel better." She rolled her eyes and walked toward the dining table and her purse. She wanted him, but she wouldn't beg.

"Wait." He caught her by the wrist, stopping her in her tracks.

"What, Jacob? You want me, then you don't. Shit. I don't play these fucking games." She twisted her arm in his hold, and he actually let her go.

"I'm sorry."

"For what? You're pretty damn confusing for a dude."

"I know." He gripped the counter again, his gaze searching her face for—something.

Emma couldn't tell what was going on in his head. Something bothered him, but she didn't know if it was her, or them, or maybe it was just sex. Some people were weird about it.

For some crazy reason she wanted to ease this burden weighing him down. Give him a reason to smile. But if he was determined to wallow, that was all on him.

"Look, it's not you—"

"Oh please, don't give me the 'It's not you; it's me,' line." She rolled her eyes.

"Emma."

"What? What is so damn bad about me? Or are you that complicated?" She stalked to the table and snatched up her purse.

Jacob followed her, blocking her path. His gaze was shuttered, lines bracketing his mouth and marring his brow. She wanted to reach out and smooth the imperfections away, kiss his mouth until he smiled again because he didn't seem to do that enough, but he wasn't her responsibility. She didn't have to care about him, even though she wanted to for some fucked up reason.

"I don't...want to—hurt—you."

She stared at him, running the sentence through her head. Well fuck.

"Is this about the anger management issues?"

He nodded.

"So what? You get angry during sex and smack a girl around or something?"

"No, nothing like that," he blurted, slashing his hand through the air.

"Then what? What's so horrible you're pushing me away and lying to yourself? You knew this would be more than dinner. You're a smart guy. At least I think you are. Even you should be able to feel chemistry."

"Fuck." He shoved a hand through his hair.

Was he going to pull it together? Or should she leave now and figure out where her vibrator was?

"You said that already." She crossed her arms over her chest.

"I get—rough."

Rough sex? That was what this was about?

"Is that it?" She dropped her purse on the table. "You do know I'm a mechanic, and I race dirt bikes, right?"

"Yeah."

She closed the space between them and looped her arms around his neck. "I don't know what kind of girls you've been with before, but I don't mind a few bruises if the sex is good." She kissed the corner of his mouth, lingering until she felt him relax a bit.

"I've scared others," he mumbled.

"Did they tell you to stop?"

"No."

"Would you have if they told you?"

"Of course." He jerked back as if she'd slapped him.

"Hey, I'm just asking." She pulled him once more into her embrace. "I don't know what kind of porcelain dolls you've been fucking, but I think you need a new type, Detective."

"What type would that be?" He dropped his head until their brows rested against each other.

Me.

The whisper in her head was her voice, but it scared her. She had no business being with a man like him. Her edges were rough, but so were his.

She laid her finger over his mouth. "You talk too much, anyone ever told you that?"

He shook his head.

First time for everything.

Jacob moved so fast that one moment she was standing, the next he'd picked her up, crossed to the dining table, and sat her down on the edge so hard her teeth clicked together. A surge of adrenaline flooded her system, and for a second she hovered between the edge of fear and excitement. He loomed over her, hands around her wrists, holding her palms to the table.

Oh, hello there.

She chuckled, the sound deep and husky in her throat. Someone's bad side was coming out to play. She let her flip-flops fall to the floor and curled one leg around his thigh.

The hard lines on his face hadn't eased, but neither had he moved. Was he waiting for her to fear him? Was this his attempt to intimidate her? She hadn't been lying when she said she didn't run. Besides, scary wasn't the word she'd use to describe him right now.

Emma arched her back and strained against his hold, but he remained out of her reach. He held her there for a moment, completely in control. She wasn't the kind of girl who craved a man to dominate her, but there was something about a hot, in-control guy that pressed all her buttons.

He let her wiggle her hands from his grasp. She grabbed the hem of his shirt, tugged it up, and worked it over his head and shoulders without his help. He seemed frozen to the spot, which was fine by her. There was plenty of him to explore and touch.

She kissed his cheek and down his neck while she acquainted herself with the dips and curves of his chest and all those sleek muscles. He had a body honed from use, not one of those muscle-bound gym bodies. Later she'd have to become more intimately introduced. Now, she needed to give him a little motivation.

He wanted to play rough? Well, she could do that.

Emma gently bit the juncture of his neck and shoulder as she dug her nails into his pecs and raked them down.

Jacob sucked in a deep breath. She let go and smoothed her hands over the nail tracks. He dug his hand into her hair, wrenching her head back and taking her mouth. He nipped her lower lip and thrust his tongue into her mouth. The flavor of the ice cream was a distant memory, but she moaned at the taste of him.

Her pulse thundered in her veins and her nipples tightened, not to mention the state of her panties.

His stubble rasped over her cheek as he pulled her head farther back, exposing the column of her throat. He supported her weight with his other hand under her back and bent over her, lavishing her throat and shoulder with kisses and little nips of his teeth. Slowly, he lowered her to the hard surface.

Jacob stared down at her and she glimpsed some of the wildness in his gaze, but she was fluent in wild and crazy. It was his lucky fucking day.

He grabbed the neck of her tank top and pulled, and the fabric came apart as if it were tissue paper, ripping straight down the front. She gaped at him, but he was already pulling her bra down, freeing her breasts and palming her.

Okay, that was hot. She'd never had her clothes literally ripped off her before.

He massaged her breasts, capturing the stiff peaks between his fingers and rolling them. She hissed and arched her back, hooking her other leg around him. He pushed her breasts together and licked one nipple, then the other. She groaned and threaded her fingers through his hair, giving it a little tug. He growled against her skin and scraped his teeth over her sensitive flesh as he switched breasts.

"Oh, fuck, do that," she muttered. Teeth and boobs—who would have known that felt good?

He bit down harder, and her internal muscles clenched.

"Mm, yeah." She scraped her nails over his shoulders, arching her back.

The man had a talented mouth, that was for sure.

She reached between them and palmed the front of his jeans. His whole body went rigid, and for a moment he didn't move. She could feel his breath against her breasts, but he didn't move, so she pressed harder.

He grabbed her wrists and pinned them to the table once more, surging up over her body to press her flat and kissing her so deeply she could barely breathe.

"I want to be in you," he said in a ragged whisper.

Jacob released one of her wrists, but she still felt the implied command in her bones.

Don't move.

His fingers dragged over her ribs, down her hips, and between her legs. He panted against her lips as he pushed her panties aside and plunged a finger into her channel.

"Christ," he groaned.

"Mm. Condom?"

"Fuck," he snarled.

Emma groped for her purse, which had been shoved down the table. She grabbed the strap and pulled it closer, fishing out a condom from the side pocket. People could call her a slut if they wanted to for carrying her own protection, but she was a woman with needs that were about to be met.

Jacob chuckled and kissed her cheek as she ripped the package open. "You are an angel."

"No, I'm just horny."

She tabbed his jeans open and lowered the zipper, careful of the erection straining toward her.

"Are you going to put it on me?" he asked.

"Do you have a problem with that?"

He flashed her a too-brief smile. "No."

He shoved his jeans and underwear down, kicking out of his clothes until he was gloriously nude. The glimpses she got of his body proved that he was a man of action, with the scars to back up what he did. Another time she'd ask him about them, kiss each one.

Jacob grabbed her skirt and panties and tugged them down. She lifted up enough for him to divest her of the hindering garments and shrugged off the ruined top and bra herself. She grabbed the condom and reached for him. He braced himself with his hands on either side of her thighs.

It was happening too fast for her to be nervous. There was a deep, driving need pushing her, urging her on.

She grasped his cock, pumping the smooth, velvety flesh in her palm.

Jacob grabbed her chin and kissed her, thrusting into her hold. He broke the kiss, leaving her gasping.

Emma lost no time in rolling the latex on his hard length. She'd enjoy this.

He pushed her hands away and passed the head of his cock through her folds, coating himself with her arousal. She planted her hands on the table and let her head drop back on her shoulders, surrendering herself to the sensations. Her body trembled—it had been too long since she felt a man's touch, even longer still since she'd enjoyed it.

"Emma," he whispered.

She lifted her head and met his gaze, staring into the black pits. It felt as if she could see straight through to his soul, that tortured, battered beast inside of him that he thought needed to be contained, controlled. It looked an awful lot like her own inner darkness.

Jacob grasped her hips and thrust. They each gasped as he slid inside of her. He pressed deeper, and she gripped the edge of the table as her body stretched and adjusted around his girth.

Fuck, he felt good.

He dug his hand back into her hair and kissed her as if his next breath depended on the connection. He withdrew and thrust, sending little shivers of pleasure up her spine.

So good.

He laid her out on the table, bending over her, lavishing her mouth with kisses. Her lips were swollen and sore from his teeth, but fuck if she cared.

She locked her ankles around his waist and slipped her arms under his, where she had free rein of his back with her nails. Each scrape over his skin seemed to fray his precious control a bit more, so she laid into him, digging her nails in and creating long tracks.

He braced himself on his forearms and shoved deep, driving the breath from her lungs as sparks went off behind her eyelids. He growled something she couldn't understand and grasped her thigh, pushing her open wider.

Jacob's gaze had gone nearly black—there was the tiniest bit of blue around his iris. It was as if she could stare into the darkness he carried inside.

He reared up, holding her thighs spread, and pistoned in and out of her. He tilted her pelvis so each thrust stimulated her clit, but she could feel him everywhere. On her skin, the tender places on her breasts and neck, her mouth, in her pussy—and inside of her where their darkness merged as their souls twined together.

Her body shuddered as desire coiled tighter and tighter within her. She grasped his forearms, digging her nails in, spine arching.

"Come on," he muttered.

The table groaned as it inched across the floor.

He shook off her hold and placed his hand above her mound, flicking her clit with his thumb.

"Oh, God," she moaned. "Jacob. Don't stop. Harder, okay?"

She felt the tremor through his muscles at her words, but he didn't hesitate giving her what she asked for. One hard thrust after another. Her vision hazed and the muscles around her ribs constricted, making it difficult to breathe.

"Fuck," Jacob roared.

He pulled out of her and she whimpered at the loss of him. He flipped her over until she was face down on the table with her toes barely touching the floor. He gave her no warning before thrusting deep once more. His hands grasped her hips so tight she thought she might have individual bruises from his fingers tomorrow. Her very own tangible reminders this wasn't another fantasy too good to be real.

He drove into her, pounding her harder than before. She clung to the table, barely able to move with him for how tight he held her.

He placed one hand on the back of her neck, applying the barest pressure. It was a possessive hold.

"Oh, Jacob." She squeezed her eyes shut—*so close.*

His nails gently scored her skin. He dug the other hand into her hair and tugged, ever so slightly, but it was enough.

The tight spring coiled within her released. Her orgasm shot her up over the moon. She squealed and grasped the table tight, kicking one of her legs as Jacob continued his sensual assault and fucked her through the orgasm.

She was vaguely aware of his groan of release. He came forward, draping his body over hers and nuzzling her cheek. She relaxed, exhaustion and tension leaving her utterly spent, not to mention the sheer pleasure of it all.

Had she ever been fucked like that?

Hell no.

For several long moments they didn't move, not that she was capable of doing more than laying there, between the boneless quality of her limbs and Jacob's weight holding her in place.

He moved before she'd quite recovered, pulling out and running his hands over her. She arched into his touch as he traced lines on her back.

Jacob picked her up and carried her to the couch, where he settled her with a light afghan while he cleaned up.

He'd been intense, but he'd never intentionally hurt her. It was something she knew.

When he joined her on the sofa once more, the openness was gone from his gaze and his defenses were back up. She missed that connection, felt the ache in her chest.

Well, Emma wasn't having any of that. She crawled across the sofa to him and pushed him back against the armrest, draping the blanket over both of them. He needed rough sex, well, she had her own needs, too.

"I have a secret," she whispered. He'd turned off most of the lights, leaving them in the gentle glow of a lamp.

"And that is?" His fingers drew lazy swirls on her shoulder.

"I like to cuddle. Don't tell anyone, okay?"

He snorted and kissed the top of her head. Well at least he could be humored.

"Was that—okay?" he asked after several moments.

"Better than okay, though you owe me a new shirt now."

"I shouldn't have done that."

"Why not? It was damn hot. I'm glad it wasn't a shirt I liked though."

"But I wasn't too rough?"

She sat up, taking his face in both of her hands. "Detective, I'm considering kidnapping you just to keep you in a creepy basement somewhere so you can do that to me every day."

He snorted. "Is that a threat?"

"Only if you feel threatened."

She pulled him back, bringing him up over her so he lay on top of her, blanketing her body with his. He smiled then, the first true smile she'd seen from him that reached his eyes and deep inside him, and her heart broke a little.

That's right, she wasn't good at one-night stands because her heart loved too freely, and Detective Jacob Payton, with his demons and barefoot cooking, was easy to care for.

4.

EMMA TIPTOED DOWN THE hallway, her clothes clutched to her chest and Jacob's phone clenched in her hand.

She shouldn't do this.

It was wrong.

Totally and completely wrong.

But she couldn't help herself.

That was a lie. She didn't want to stop herself. She wanted to see things for herself.

She dressed hurriedly in the den, tying her butchered tank-top into some semblance of a shirt and put it on backwards. Vent holes were a trend now, right?

Her body was deliciously sore—everywhere. Jacob hadn't been too rough, but with the controlled force and the power of his grip, she could completely understand how he would have scared a gentler woman.

She peered through the open archway and strained to hear any movement, any sign Jacob had sensed her leaving his bed.

Nothing—silence reigned supreme.

Guilt ate at her, but this was how it had to be. She couldn't allow herself to fall for Jacob. That was a world of hurt waiting to happen.

She tapped the power button on his phone and the screen lit up. What were the chances it wasn't password protected? She swiped the unlock button across the bottom, and a page full of apps flickered to life.

Holy shit, the man really needed to password protect his stuff.

She stuffed her guilt deep down and clicked his texts first. It only took three tries before she found a text trail with an address. It would have been sent that morning. What were the chances this was the location of the copycat's kill site?

For some reason, she couldn't shake the idea of needing to see it for herself. It was a wholly irrational drive, but she felt it in her bones. If she saw the site of the murder, she'd know it was a copycat. Wouldn't she? Who knew TBK better than her?

She forwarded the text to her cell then erased the evidence on his phone before placing it in the kitchen. He could realize her deception, which sucked, but it wasn't like they had something that was going to last. He might want her body, and they might have stuff to talk about with the murder investigation going on, but there wasn't much beyond that which connected them. It was better she got out now before she got hurt. A serial monogamist like her didn't do casual well.

The temperature outside had only dropped a few degrees. Moonlight bathed the street well enough she didn't need a light to pick her way down the stairs or across the yard, though her feet were coated in dew by the time she reached her truck.

Should she go to the murder site now? Or wait for the sun to rise? Considering this was Oklahoma, someone might get trigger happy and think she was the killer coming back to take her jollies out on the victim's home once more. Waiting for daylight would be safer.

Earlier she'd considered asking Jacob to take her there, but from the sound of it he already had enough marks against him. Asking him to bend the rules for her would be too much. Besides, she doubted he'd allow it, and what he didn't know wouldn't hurt him.

At least those were the lies she was buying into. The truth tickled the back of her mind and spurred her into flee-ing in the middle of the night.

Emma liked him.

A cop.

It couldn't end well.

She opened the passenger side of the truck and stopped.

Hadn't she locked the truck? Her keys were still in her purse, so she couldn't have unlocked it.

Emma set the file box in the floorboard and stepped up on the metal running board along the side of the truck to peer into the cab.

A piece of paper lay in the driver's seat, bathed in red.

Her heart leapt into her throat, pounding so hard it was difficult to breathe. She glanced around, but nothing moved on the quiet street. She grabbed the paper.

I see you.

I will finish what he began.

TBKiller

The images behind the text were in hues of red, but the pictures she knew well. They were her grandparents. Her fucking *grandparents*.

How dare he.

How fucking dare this son of a bitch threaten her with the atrocities that were done to them. The sick bastard probably thought he was going to scare her.

No.

Now she was seriously pissed off.

Mitchell Black had killed himself, denying the families he'd wronged justice.

This one, this copycat, he couldn't get off so easily.

Emma had to find this guy, even before Jacob. She didn't know what she'd do, but she had to find him. He wouldn't fuck with her the same way he killed her family.

She'd...she didn't know what she would do, but she wouldn't let this happen. Not again. Not to her.

"Emma?"

She grabbed the door handle and peered over her shoulder.

Jacob leaned out the front door, pajama pants low on his hips. Where had those come from? She could barely make him out in the shadows.

She stuffed the letter under the passenger seat and climbed down out of the truck as Jacob crossed the lawn to her.

"What are you doing up? It's like, two in the morning." His hair stuck up every which way and his features still had that relaxed ease from sleep.

"I—uh—didn't think you'd want me here when you woke up."

"Why would you think that?" He stood close, almost toe-to-toe with her.

"I don't know." And she really didn't. He wasn't the kind of guy that shoved a girl out the door a few minutes after orgasm. He'd actually tucked her in bed and snuggled her after round two on the couch, which was how she fell asleep in the first place when she meant to go home.

"Come back inside." He took her hand and tugged her toward the door.

"One second." She pressed the lock button on the truck and closed the door.

She was certain she'd locked the truck to begin with, so the only other way for someone to get into it was with her spare key. She went to the back fender and reached up to her customary spot next to a bump in the metal.

But the key box was not there. She felt to the right and left, but still no box. She found it shoved so far up the fender she could barely reach it.

Someone—TBKiller—had moved her spare key.

She should be frightened. Terrified. But she knew what was out there. She'd be prepared from now on.

She pried the magnetized box off the fender and pocketed the whole thing.

"Something wrong?" Jacob asked.

"Yeah, I think my key fob has a short in it or something. It's not unlocking every time. I'm going to switch them out in the morning."

"Okay. Make sure you get it taken care of. Could just be the battery. Come on."

Jacob took her hand once more and led her back into the house. Her heart didn't know if it should pound in anger or desire. What exactly was she getting herself into?

LAURA WINTHROP circled the truck stop, key in hand for the bathroom. She had a long haul ahead of her to get to Houston, but it would be worth it to see her babies again. There were some serious downsides to being a truck driver, but she couldn't deny the pay was better than anything she'd get working at the corner grocery store or driving a delivery route.

After this trip, she'd be able to take a four-day weekend. Maybe drive her babies down to the beach for a little fun before she had to get back on the road for a few weeks. She had a plan and everything. They could rent bikes, fly kites, maybe even camp out on the beach.

She clung to that thought as she slid the key into the lock and held her breath. You could never trust these run-down gas stations to do any upkeep on the bathrooms. Hell, if the toilet flushed she considered herself lucky. She opened the door and flicked on the light.

Another dingy, blue tiled bathroom. At least the diesel was cheap.

She stepped in and flicked the lock before going about her business. Exactly as she'd expected, there wasn't any toilet paper on the roll, which was why she never got out of her truck without some in her pocket. She'd learned that trick on her first haul. It was almost a bonus there was soap in the dispenser and the water worked.

She hummed the tune to the latest catchy song and unlocked the door, ready to get back on the road for a few hours before she caught a little sleep.

The door jerked open and out of her grasp. She had the impression of a figure dressed in dark clothing the second before something hit her in the face, directly between her eyes. It felt like an ice pick straight to her brain. Laura stumbled back, holding her nose and howling in pain.

The door clanged shut as her brain screamed at her.

Fight.

Run.

Bad things happened to women on their own out on the road. She'd had that lesson drilled into her. Never, ever give up without a fight.

She charged the man, throwing her weight into it. She wasn't a big person, but surprise was on her side. She hit him in the side and stumbled.

He shrugged her off, tossing her back against the wall with the sweep of an arm. Her head bounced off the tile, and her vision swam. If she couldn't force her way out, she needed someone else to come in. The gas station was empty besides her and the cashier.

"Help!" she yelled. The bathroom was a cinder-block box, and all the sound did was resonate through it.

"Go ahead. Scream." He swung his arm at her and caught her in the shoulder. She bounced off the adjacent wall, her back to the corner.

"Somebody, help!"

He came at her again, but this time she was ready. She balled her hands into fists and punched him, as hard as she could, just like her boss had taught her. Her heart hammered against her ribs, adrenaline giving her strength.

The man knocked her blows aside and wrapped a hand around her throat. He shoved her back and squeezed, cutting off her air. She got a look at his face, only to see the plastic visage of a cartoon character staring back at her.

"You have lovely eyes." He squeezed her throat tighter, until she saw dark spots.

She kicked out, trying to hit him in his balls, his knees.

Oh God, her lungs burned. She couldn't breathe. The fight was leeching out of her. Would she see her babies again?

"Usually I like to take time for these things, but not tonight."

The world went dark.

MAX LET THE WOMAN drop to the ground. He would never tire of the way human bodies went from these vivacious sacks of life to glorified chum.

He turned the lock on the door to ensure they wouldn't be disrupted. This was a perfect kill room. There was a single vent to the outdoors and two layers of cinder-block between the restroom and the back of the gas station. It was completely possible to stand in either of the restrooms, scream, and be unheard inside the gas station.

The tricky bit was tracking Laura's route across the Midwest and aligning her schedule with everything else. Planning for tonight had required a bit of creativeness on his part, but everyone had their routines. Even the transient truck driver.

Everything was falling into a pattern. It was beautiful.

He bound the woman's wrists behind her back and her ankles together. That task accomplished, he could slow down. Savor this kill a bit.

He placed the bag slung across his body down in the sink and pulled out his first, most important utensil. The required camera. He set it on top of the toilet and adjusted the viewfinder so he could ensure they stayed in the frame. He hated this damn mask, but it was important he wear it. The record button blinked, capturing these all-important moments.

Behind him, the woman started groaning.

Good. He liked a live one on film, it made for a more enjoyable watch later.

Besides, his audience loved to hear them scream, and no one could scream like a woman just before she died.

THERE WERE BETTER WAYS to start a Saturday morning than re-interviewing potential witnesses in preparation for the FBI's arrival later that morning. Jacob would have preferred to spend it in bed with Emma going for round three, but they both had to work.

Thinking of her eased some of the tension in his shoulders. For once, he hadn't needed to explain himself. His only explanation was that she understood that darkness in him because it had touched her, too. Which made it all that much more complicated.

Emma was a remarkable woman, but last night shouldn't have happened. She was potentially part of this case, and getting involved with her was a first-rate horrible idea. Except it had felt so right. But he couldn't risk her life on account of how she made him feel. Chances were he had a target on his back due to his father's involvement with the original TBK. But Emma, the copycat seemed to have left her alone. Could he be drawing attention to her? It wasn't like she tried to hide her connection to the Ration family survivor.

Harold Espinoza's house was still taped off with yellow caution ribbon. He'd go there next, but first he wanted to have a chat with the elderly neighbors, the Kelleys. Hopefully they would be less rattled today and able to answer a few questions with greater detail.

Jacob parked his Jeep Wrangler along the curb. Both Harold's home and the Kelleys' had lush lawns. A far cry from the simple sod he'd thrown down a few years ago. Emma's lawn ornament looked awfully lonely out there. Maybe it was time he planted a few things, find out if he had a green thumb or not. Some hedges at least would improve things.

He knocked on the door and waited. There was a TV on inside and the sounds of human life. A figure bobbed toward the door through the frosted glass panes before the door swung open.

"Hello." An elderly man blinked up at him, eyes magnified by his glasses.

"Mr. Kelley, I'm Detective Payton."

"Oh yes, I remember you."

"Would you have some time to talk to me about Harold?"

"Yes, yes. Come in, we were actually sitting down to talk about him now. Join us." Mr. Kelley waved Jacob into the house. "Irene, we have another visitor."

"Oh, what's that?" A woman in a pink velour pantsuit stood in the doorway from the sitting room to the rest of the house.

"Get another coffee for the detective," Mr. Kelley said at a near-yell.

"Oh, good. Come join us on the porch. I'll get another cup."

She shuffled into the kitchen as Mr. Kelley led Jacob through the quaint old house.

"She can't hear nothing these days," Mr. Kelley said over his shoulder. "My hearing's still sharp as ever though."

Jacob chuckled but kept his comments to himself. He'd called Mr. Kelley yesterday and the old man hadn't understood a word Jacob had said. He might be able to hear better than his wife, but he doubted Mr. Kelley had the hearing of his younger days.

"Good timing, dropping by right now. One of Harold's parade friends stopped by. Cute girl." Mr. Kelley led Jacob out onto a deck overflowing with carefully tended flowers. A white wrought iron garden set for four already had coffee for two.

"Who else did you say was here?" Jacob asked. He'd need to go through Harold's family, friends, and acquaintances. Chances were their copycat knew Harold. Now that they had a victim, Jacob could parse out the language from the first letters to see if there was anything that pointed to Harold. Not to mention the images behind the words, which might be clues themselves.

"I think her name was Erica or Emily something," Mr. Kelley muttered.

Jacob's gaze snapped to the figure of a blonde woman trying to peer over the privacy fence separating the two properties. The scratch marks on his back burned in memory of her touch.

What the ever loving fuck was she doing here?

Emma dropped back to her feet and glanced over her shoulder like a kid caught with their hand in a cookie jar. Except this was far more dangerous. He grit his teeth and stared at her.

How had she known where Harold lived? The man had been a public enough figure, maybe she'd found it online? Whatever her reason for showing up here, it wasn't good—at all.

"Here we are." Mrs. Kelley emerged with two more cups of coffee.

"Want to come join us?" Jacob called out.

That seemed to start Emma out of her deer-in-the-headlights moment. She turned and strode toward them. Her clothes were different— jeans and a t-shirt—but he'd be willing to bet she hadn't had time for much else in order to beat him here.

"Detective Payton." He extended his hand toward her.

She winced and took his hand, but still had the gall to meet his gaze. "Emma."

He wanted to wring her neck. Didn't she know this was dangerous? And even potentially incriminating for her?

"How would you like your coffee?" Mrs. Kelley asked, breaking the tense moment.

"Black is fine." Jacob sank into the chair offered and glanced at Emma.

"The same." She scooted her chair a little ways from him, and when she sat, she leaned away. Her whole demeanor screamed guilt. Good.

"What?" Mrs. Kelley blinked at them.

"Black. They want it black," Mr. Kelley said in his near-yell.

"Oh, okay. You don't have to yell so much."

Mr. Kelley shook his head and glanced at Jacob as if to say, *See what I deal with?*, but the way he smiled communicated years of love. He glanced at Emma and found her watching him from the corner of her eye. Of course, the moment their gazes met, she busied herself with the coffee.

"I don't know what else we can tell you, Detective. We never heard a thing the other night." Mr. Kelley sighed and sat back with his coffee.

"What about cars? Did you notice anyone parked on your street that you didn't recognize? Anyone walking around who doesn't live here?" Jacob asked.

Mr. Kelley shook his head again. "Not a soul. It's real quiet around here. We would have noticed anyone new."

"Actually, the mailman was sick about two weeks ago, and there was a new boy on the route. He wasn't very friendly," Mrs. Kelley chimed in.

"Do you know what his name was?" Chances were slim he was connected, but there were too few clues at the scene.

"Mitchell something. Not very polite. He wouldn't tell us how Jerry, our usual mailman, was doing," Mrs. Kelley answered.

"Mitchell?" Emma sat forward. "Did his last name start with a B?"

Mrs. Kelley frowned. "I can't recall."

Emma glanced at him.

Mitchell Black was TBK's real name. Was it a coincidence there was someone who happened to fill in on the victim's mail route before the murder? Was this their copycat scoping out his first kill?

Jacob sipped his coffee and kept his questions to himself. It was his nature to see deception where there wasn't any, but with her it was everywhere. What had she been doing outside at two in the morning? Was last night some kind of game? An act? Disgust curdled his stomach. For a little while he'd thought they understood each other, but had he been wrong?

He didn't know what game Emma was playing at here, but he wasn't going to be part of her file box of TBK memorabilia. Had she come to him last night to add more to her collection? Was that what he was to her?

He honestly didn't know.

EMMA WAVED GOODBYE to the Kelleys, hyper aware of Jacob at her back. He'd not said a single word to her during their chat with the elderly couple. Not a single word. Hell, he'd barely glanced at her, and could she blame him?

This was bad. Really bad. She should never have come here. It was a horrible, awful mistake.

And she'd known it—from the second she committed to coming here, she realized it was wrong.

The Kelleys' front door creaked shut and the second the door thudded into place, Jacob grabbed her elbow and jerked her around.

"What the fuck are you doing here?" His voice was low, practically a growl. Last night this voice had urged her to orgasm. Now, she stared into the gaze of a man with barely contained rage. The tendons on the side of his neck stood out, a vein protruded on his forehead, the muscles at his jaw bulged from clenching his teeth, and his skin was tinged red. He let go of her as if she'd burned him, which for some reason hurt worse.

She gulped and held up her hands. "You're angry. I totally get that."

"Hell yes, I'm angry." He loomed over her, fists clenched.

She couldn't tell him about the letter, not now that she'd kept it from him. The rest, she could tell him that. The truth was always the best policy, wasn't it?

"Jacob, you get what it's like having TBK part of your life, don't you? It's something you can't shake. I just—I just want to understand."

"Come on, we don't want to make a scene." Jacob paced down the drive, away from her, his gait stiff. He half-turned.

She was parked in the other direction around the corner, but it was better to do what he asked of her. They walked down the sidewalk to the next house, the one that had been all over the news.

"I own that getting involved with you right now is a bad idea. I shouldn't have invited you over last night. At least not until we catch this guy. I accept my mistake, but then for you to show up here? How did you even know where it was?"

Oh, she couldn't tell him that. Not with his rage pants on so tight.

"The house was all over the TV. Google maps gives you a street view of everything. News tells you a neighborhood. Number's on the house. Just go street by street, putting in the number until it comes up." Okay, so she'd done that once, the first time Derrick cheated to find out who he'd been with.

"Fucking Internet." He rolled his eyes and tipped his head back for a moment. "What makes you think coming here is a good idea?"

"I didn't really think. I needed to see it." She shrugged. Being the center of Jacob's wrath was not a fun place to be.

"Seeing it on the news wasn't good enough? You can't go inside. It's still a crime scene." He gestured toward Howard's house.

Emma held her tongue and didn't dare ask if she could see it with him. She already knew the answer there was, *Oh, fuck no.*

"I didn't know you'd be here. I thought I could come here, see the house, then the neighbors came out and invited me in once I told them I knew Harold."

"I thought you met him once."

"Yeah, I didn't tell them that part." Her insides squirmed. She hated Jacob's anger turned on her. She didn't even know the guy and he had his hooks in her. It wasn't fair—not at all.

His phone beeped and he pulled it out to glance at the screen. She resisted peering at it, but only barely. She might hate being the object of his regret, but this TBK copycat was all she could think about. While she might want to see the guy dead, she didn't want to be the person to pull the trigger on him. At least not when she was rational. Last night, well, she'd been emotional. She'd rather see the copycat suffer in prison, which meant he needed to get caught.

"I've got to go." There was no emotion in Jacob's voice, which was worse than the anger seething through his teeth.

"No, wait." She grabbed his arm before he could circle his Jeep.

He stopped, but didn't bother looking at her.

"You have every right to be angry with me." *You don't know all the reasons.* "I'm sorry, okay? I just—I need to understand this, and I thought maybe I'd get something if I came here. I knew you couldn't show me, and I didn't want to ask in case you'd consider it. TBK might as well have killed my daddy. I think leaving him alive was crueler than letting him live, and I can't wrap my brain around a person like that. I thought...I don't know...I'd see something that would help me. Be angry with me, but don't shut me out, okay?" She let go of his arm and took a step back.

He pivoted toward her, his head tilted to the side. God, it felt like he saw straight through her.

"I'm trying not to."

"Okay." She nodded.

Yeah, she'd never hear from him again, which was probably for the best, anyway. She didn't need her heart getting tangled up with someone who was unobtainable. She might not be educated, but she could see all the reasons they couldn't work out, and she was beyond the appeal of something that was merely a flash in the pan.

Jacob took two strides, almost bowling her over. Instead, he slid his hand into her hair, cupped the back of her head, and crushed his mouth against hers. She fisted the front of his shirt, lifting up on tiptoe to get closer. It might be the last time he touched her, and she wanted to commit it to memory. The kiss was rough, bruising, and short.

"I have to go," he said against her mouth.

"Okay." She kissed him back, short and sweet. God, she shouldn't do this.

He wrapped his arms around her, burying his face in the crook of her neck.

"He killed again," he whispered into her hair.

Shut. The. Front. Door.

Emma hugged him back, unsure if she should be scared or sad. The more kills, the more chance there was this guy could get caught. And what were the chances Mitchell the postman was their guy?

"Go get him for me, okay?" She squeezed Jacob harder, then released him.

He backed away from her, his gaze still hard.

"We aren't done," he said.

She hoped not, even if she knew they should be.

Jacob climbed into his Jeep, and she stayed rooted to the spot. She didn't want him to know she wasn't in her truck right now.

She knew following him was a bad idea, but she would do it anyway.

To catch a killer you had to be a killer, or at least understand how one thought, and she was pretty close on that point.

I'm coming for you, TBKiller.

JACOB GRIPPED THE STEERING wheel so tight his knuckles were white.

She'd lied to him.

Emma Ration was a liar.

She was sneaky, but she wasn't sneaky enough. His phone was department property, and everything was backed up. And since he couldn't shake the feeling something didn't ring true with Emma's story, he'd checked the logs. The messages were there.

He wanted to punch something, so he'd feel anything except the rage burning him alive.

There was no denying that he was a sucker. He'd known her story, painted her as the victim, another casualty like himself, all the while ignoring the truth. For a few brief moments, he'd thought they'd clicked. That she got him in a way most women ran from. But it was all too convenient.

He didn't know if he'd confront her about it, if it was worth facing his own foolishness, but he'd have to figure that out later. For now, he had a case to work, and the Behavioral Analysis Unit from the FBI to meet.

Jacob pulled up to the ancient gas station off Interstate-35, south of Norman. This far out, there wasn't much except pastures and hills. The small brick building must have been around since the sixties, if not earlier. At one time it had probably been a crucial fueling stop, but now it was run-down, and the only patrons were either locals or long-haul truckers.

There were a couple of patrol cars, two black SUVs, and the forensics van blocking off most of the lot designated for eighteen-wheelers. Only one big-rig occupied the space. Yellow tape roped off a large portion of space, including the rig. Most conspicuously, there was a cluster of suits that had to be the FBI.

"Detective Payton?" A tall man with close-cropped blond hair and a hard stare walked toward him.

"I am. Are you Special Agent Brooks?" He offered the agent his hand.

"Ryan Brooks. Brooks is fine. We were waiting on you to begin." He tipped his head back. "Some weather you have here."

Jacob chuckled. "Yeah, you might want to do without the jackets. Has the CSI team started?"

"Yes, we cleared them to begin photographing the scene." Brooks gestured toward the other agents. "Let me introduce you to my team."

The introductions were made in brief—names and specializations only. There were two dedicated profilers, a PR guy, a young woman who had so many letters behind her name he wasn't sure what she really did, and Brooks.

"I'd like my guys to talk to the attendant on duty," Brooks said and gestured to two men in slacks and sports coats. There was a deadly air around the two that made Jacob glad they were on the same side.

"Sure. You don't have to ask my permission for anything. Chief asked you to come in and chose me to work with you as liaison because of my connection."

"And you're cool with that, mate?" Connor Mullins, one of the profilers, asked. He was a tall, lean man, with the body of a swimmer. His accent wasn't exactly American made.

Jacob opened his mouth and closed it. He couldn't say that his LT was an incompetent asshole with a grudge against him and this case, so he shrugged.

"Politics," he answered. "I want this guy caught and put behind bars. Bringing your team in seems to be the fastest, most economical way to make that happen, and I will do whatever it takes to catch him."

"Well we'll do that." Connor glanced at the other man and nodded toward the gas station. "Shall we?"

The duo strode off to begin their part of the investigation as a news truck rolled in.

"That's my cue." The black agent buttoned his jacket. "Police haven't confirmed they are working on a copycat, correct Detective?"

"That is correct, but the news is spinning it that way," Jacob replied.

"I can work with that. Should I know anything about the current racial climate?"

"What?" Jacob blinked at the man.

"I'm a black man about to go on TV. Is that a good idea?"

"Yeah. Sorry, I'm a little one-track minded right now."

"It's all good. Just want to know if I should put him on the camera instead." Benjamin thumbed at Ryan and grinned.

"Take care of it, Ben." Ryan nodded at the camera crews.

"I'll keep them busy." Benjamin strode toward the camera crews.

Jacob turned to the remaining two. "All right, where would you like to start, Agent Brooks?"

"Patrol said the eighteen-wheeler belongs to a Laura Winthrop." The red-headed woman gestured to the truck. "She was a long-haul trucker who made regular stops at this station for the last ten months, but only on her return trip."

"How do you know that?" Jacob blinked at the woman's near-emotionless face.

"I read her driving log."

"And she only stopped at this station on her return trip. Why?" Brooks asked.

"There was a note from nine months ago. She couldn't navigate into the station at night due to a lack of visibility. She likes the homemade pies the owner's grandmother sells here. There were six of them in her truck when it was searched."

"And you read the whole log?" Jacob asked. They couldn't have beaten him to the scene by more than twenty minutes.

Brooks chuckled. "Speed reading. Agent Perez is nothing if not economical."

"Yo, Payton." They turned toward the lead forensics guy. "It's all you. Just don't touch anything, okay? And if you need to throw up, do it in the garbage cans. We still might find something out here."

Jacob and the two agents circled the back of the gas station. The stench slammed into them like a wall. He swallowed hard and breathed through his mouth.

The three of them clustered around the door to the women's restroom. The forensics team had placed plastic milk crates upside down to create a walk way so as to not disrupt the evidence.

"So much for having a clean scene," Jade Perez muttered. "Don't show this to Lali. She'll scrub her hands until they bleed."

"What do you see?" Brooks asked.

Jacob swallowed the bile he could taste at the back of his throat. Good thing he hadn't had more than a glass of water and the coffee at the Kelleys', or he might lose it. He'd seen a few ugly crime scenes in his life, but this was the worst.

Laura Winthrop lay on her back, bound and gagged. They wouldn't know the cause of death until after the autopsy, but he could take a guess.

"Bludgeoned to death, like the others. Christ." Jacob shook his head.

"The others?" Brooks asked.

"The old TBK cases, and the first copycat TBK victim." He wiped his mouth against his forearm.

"The marks on her face and chest indicate the suspect used something with weight to it," Jade added.

"The patrol officer who responded found a bloody wrench on the sidewalk." Brooks replied.

Jacob shoved down his annoyance that such a major detail hadn't been relayed to him. But, he wasn't the case officer anymore. He was the detective gopher for the FBI. It was a tough pill to swallow, even if it was the best decision.

Jade leaned over the threshold, her long, red ponytail swinging over her shoulder. "The gag appears to have been an afterthought. It looks like it's torn from a shirt or something. TBK never gagged his victims."

"Probably from the acoustics. Can you imagine how loud her screams would be in here? I bet he didn't think through that. He's probably younger, still figuring out who he is." Brooks asked.

"There might be trace on it. He doesn't gag his victims, so he would have had to improvise. It could be the suspect's shirt. Do you notice that spot on top of the toilet? There's a void." Jade pointed at the blood-splattered toilet, and the spot that was still relatively white.

"We have a deviation from the plan and a void," Brooks mused.

"There was a similar void at Harold's house," Jade said.

"I'm wondering—could he be taping these?" Jacob glanced at the two agents. He was too used to talking through a scene to keep his comments to himself.

Brooks and Jade stared at him.

"It's just an idea." Jacob shrugged.

"No, no, it's brilliant," Brooks said.

"It would make sense, judging by the positioning." Jade scrutinized the place, gaze narrowed, lips tightly compressed.

"This had to be planned. He picked this location." Jacob turned to survey the expanse of wilderness that backed up against the gas station. There wasn't anyone to see the crime. "I don't think it's chance that the room is practically sound-proof. Someone had to see him. Last week, last month. He's been here before. I interviewed Harold Espinoza's neighbors this morning, and they mentioned a substitute mailman who said his name was Mitchell. TBK's real name was—"

"Mitchell Black," Jade blurted.

"Good point, Detective," Brooks said. "I want to call Lali and get her working on that." He stepped away, pulling out his phone.

"Do you think she was still alive when he started cutting out her eyes?" Jade asked.

He glanced at the woman, more than a little disturbed by the question. What would it be like to have your eyeball dug out of your skull?

"Pre- or postmortem will tell us more about his psyche," she explained.

"TBK. Torture. Blind. Kill. She was alive for this. What does that say about him?" Jacob wasn't sure he wanted to know the answer.

"The eyeballs are his trophies, we know that much. Or at least he perceives them as trophies. They might not be his trophies, as in this TBK's, they could be part of the ritual."

Jacob blinked at the woman. She stared at the body, hardly blinking, as if she saw something not evident to his gaze.

"The original letters you showed us were signed TBK." Perez shifted her attention to him. "The new ones are TBKiller. It's his identity. Is he taking the eyes because TBK did, or is he taking them for himself? What kind of a relationship does our copycat have with the original killer?"

"I...don't know."

"Neither do I. I need to go over the files from the corre-lating TBK case. There might be something there."

"Like what?"

"An identity. There's a difference between TBK and TBKiller. Those differences will be more pronounced the more kills our copycat makes because he's finding his identity. It's like cooking. The first time, you follow the recipe. After that, you sort of improvise to get the results you want." She smoothed her hand down over the long tail of red hair. "I really want a donut. Do you think they're still selling stuff up front?"

"I have no idea."

"Hm. I'm going to go check." She pivoted and headed around the side of the building.

Jacob glanced from Jade to the victim, unsure which was more unnerving. Jade recited these things as if she were a robot, dry facts, no emotion or physical reaction. It made him think of the TV serial killer, Dexter. In a way, the lifeless corpse was a more settling companion.

His phone chimed with an incoming message. He hovered over the delete button when he saw who it was from.

Emma.

Was he a fool for wanting her?

I really am sorry. Let me make it up to you tonight.

The next message was an address and a picture of a dirt bike. She wanted to make up by allowing him into that part of her life? Was that what this was? He didn't know, and honestly there wasn't time to figure out the intricacies of a complicated woman. He blew out a breath and pocketed the phone.

His brain needed to be here. In the moment. With the vic. If the copycat was evolving, he was going to screw up. That was how they'd catch him.

Jacob knelt, leaning toward the body. Her hair was bound in a braid, her head thrown back. They hadn't identified the victim by her face, between the bludgeoning and the lack of eyeballs, they'd trusted her license and the owner of the freight company that owned the truck in the parking lot.

There would be another letter today. The media coverage at the station was going to be crazy, but that was now the domain of the FBI. In a way, it was nice to not have to deal with those details. He might only be playing a supporting role, but he could expend all his effort on finding the killer.

5.

E MMA TOOK HER FOOT off the gas as Jacob's Wrangler exited the highway some distance ahead of her. She'd kept her distance as much as she could and still tail him.

I shouldn't have followed him, she thought for the hundredth time.

It was too late to turn back now, despite what her conscience said. The car she'd borrowed from Amanda was running on E.

Jacob was getting out of his Jeep at the station by the time she coasted down the ramp onto the service road. She slouched in her seat on the off-chance he'd glance her way, but he never did. The little store was clogged with people from one side to the other, most in uniform or with a news crew. Two vans bearing the emblem of TV stations rolled down the ramp ahead of her. Word was getting out fast. The bad part for her was that there wasn't anywhere else to stop for gas. It was one of those exits to nowhere, with one station and what looked like a livestock supply store across the street operating out of a shed held together by duct tape and bailing wire. There was another truck at the pump, so at least she could get gas. Eventually.

The influx of reporters could entertain the officers while she got gas and hightailed her ass out of there. If Jacob caught her at this scene, he might never forgive her, and that was becoming unacceptable.

She wanted to see the scene with her own eyes, even if she knew it wasn't going to happen. The next best thing was being near it. Killers often came back to their crime scenes to relive the kill. Maybe she'd see him.

Then what?

What could she possibly hope to learn from this?

"I'll get gas, and go. It's not a crime," she muttered to herself.

Jacob was never going to forgive her, and she had no one to blame except herself.

She clung to her decision to leave as soon as she could as she cruised down the service road. The cars and people were little flecks in the distance, growing larger as she approached.

Somewhere between sex and cuddling, she'd begun to fall for the man, against her better judgment. But the heart never listened, did it?

Emma rolled into the station and took the farthest pump from the action. She killed the engine and glanced around, but Jacob was nowhere to be seen. The front of the store appeared to be business as usual, so maybe she didn't have anything to worry about. The only pumps roped off were those for the long-haul truckers.

"Get your ass in gear," she told her reflection in the rearview mirror.

Emma pumped gas, keeping her head down and minding her own business. There was no way Jacob would see her. He had way too much going on to pay any attention to random people pumping gas. Except the skin between her shoulder blades prickled, as if she were being watched.

Glancing over her shoulder, she only caught sight of the news vans. No Jacob. No one that appeared out of place.

And yet, if anything, she felt the sensation even stronger.

What the hell was going on?

She peered around, trying to appear casual, but no one seemed to be taking any interest in her. There was one other person pumping gas, some suits in the gas station. Across the street at the feed store a couple of trucks were clustered together. No doubt the locals gathering to rubberneck and talk about each other. There was also a car up on the overpass. Maybe it was broken down, or maybe they were curious locals. That was it. Nothing too out of the ordinary.

Whatever. She needed to get her happy ass out of there.

Emma filled up the tank as a thank you to her roommate and sped out of the station, relieved more than anything else she hadn't seen a single thing of note. She didn't breathe easy until she was headed north once more. Sitting at the red light she pulled out her phone and texted Jacob a quick, "I'm sorry," message to ease her conscience.

He didn't need to know her transgressions, but she had to make this right. She'd keep her nose in her own business from now on.

Okay, that was a lie. She'd still be curious as hell, but she wouldn't follow Jacob to another scene. That was right out.

THE ROOM JACOB HAD set up to run his investigation from had a whole new look. The FBI had taken his dry erase board for Harold Espinoza and begun one for Laura Winthrop.

"Detective Payton, Stevenson said you had a theory about the first victim," Brooks said as they entered. "I'd like to hear it."

The FBI agents turned almost as one toward him, their gazes falling on him and hanging like weights around his neck. He was a good detective—it was born into his blood—but these guys lived and breathed serial killers. What did he know they wouldn't?

"Yes." Jacob cleared his throat and approached the first board.

"Your father arrested TBK, correct?" Brooks asked.

"He did."

"Sir?" The red-haired woman, Special Agent Jade Perez, held up her hand.

Brooks gestured to the woman.

"Thank you." She nodded at her supervising officer before turning toward Jacob. "Before we look at that, I'd like to establish that we are not looking for the original TBK, and that we are—in fact—looking for a copycat. I think this will help us with the profile." She turned to him. "The original signature, will you show it to me?"

"Does this need to happen now?" Brooks asked.

"Yes, because I know what you're going to ask, and that's if the correct person was convicted of being TBK. I have a theory. Please, give me a moment?"

Brooks nodded and gestured for Jacob to continue.

The contents of the original evidence boxes he'd retrieved were spread out on a table against the wall, as far from the window as you could get. He appreciated the deference shown for the older documents, already yellowed from age.

Jacob leafed through the box until he came to the folder containing the documents. "TBK never sent in anything in his own handwriting. It was typed on an old typewriter, one of his letters was done at the public library, he even cut and pasted words from a magazine. The only thing handwritten was the signature."

"The new signature isn't hand written. Was that detail made public?" Perez followed him to the table, her intense gaze nailing him to the spot. She had no concept of personal space. Hell, if he wasn't careful he'd knock her over.

"Not at the time of the murders. Dad told me they didn't tell anyone for fear of exactly this. A copycat."

"But people know this now?" Perez's gaze was intense, unwavering. She gave him the fucking creeps.

"I would say it's highly likely. There have been letters from TBK uncovered since the murders that were sent to the victims pre-murder and to the families postmortem that were never given to the police."

"Where are these documents now?" Brooks asked.

Jacob rubbed his fingertips together. Well shit.

"In a private collection," he replied.

"What are the chances we can see those? To determine if they're real?" Perez asked.

Fuck, but that was going to piss off Emma, and he couldn't decide if that was a good or bad thing. He should want to push her away, make her angry enough to refuse to see him ever again.

He cleared his throat and pushed the uncomfortable knot of emotions aside. He had to focus.

"I think I can make that happen. Here are the originals." Jacob laid the documents out on the table. He could almost recite these word for word.

Perez immediately bent over them, her nose almost pressed against the paper. "Can I see the new letters? Do we have the letter from Laura's truck yet?"

"No, forensics hasn't finished with it," Jacob answered. They'd found it in the trash can at the station, wadded up with other fliers Laura might have picked up along her route.

Mullins shook his head and brought the documents over. The smothered smile spoke volumes. Perez was the kind of officer—agent—who only saw the case. Jacob could relate.

Mullins laid the print next to the first generation letters.

"Here, in the first set, they are signed as TBK. This signifies his MO, which was to torture his victims, take out their eyes and then kill them. It was assumed the removal of the eyes was to steal or preserve that experience for the killer. The eyeballs were his trophy—"

"Perez," Brooks barked.

Jacob folded his arms tightly over his chest, gripping his arms with both hands. He'd heard all of the theories. Every damned one of them.

"The point?" Brooks prompted.

Perez blinked at him, clearly taken by surprise. "Oh. Right." She glanced at him, her cheeks growing pink. "Sorry, the point. The original killer was TBK, the man your father arrested and the same one who died in prison. This one," she gestured to the new letter, "he signs it as TBKiller. It's both a copycat and a killer trying to find his own identity. There are probably more bodies out there we don't know about. His learning victims, while he was trying to figure out how to reproduce the kills."

"Mullins, call Lali and get her to look up bludgeoning and any murders to do with the orbital cavity. She might be able to find those. Let's keep this piece to ourselves. I'd like to mitigate what the public knows. I want to control his public image. It will enrage the suspect to hopefully make a mistake." Brooks leaned over the documents, examining the differences.

Jacob blew out a breath.

It was a copycat. He'd known it in his gut, but hearing the FBI confirm his suspicion was all the confirmation he needed.

TBK was dead. Who was the new person? Where had they come from? And when would they kill again? Was Emma in danger?

"Uh, Brooks?" The agent in charge of PR, Benjamin Johns, stared at his phone, gaze growing wide.

"Yes, Ben?"

"I think you should see this." Ben grabbed the remote and clicked the power button on the TV mounted on the wall. The noon news flickered into view—with Lieutenant Miller on the PD steps.

Miller was decked out in his full uniform, giving the cameras his warmest *trust me* face. The lying bastard's ability to spin stories was what got him the LT job in the first place.

"We want to settle our citizen's fears," Miller said. "These TBK-style murders are not the same person. We are dealing with an incompetent, lowlife copycat—"

"Damn it. Ben, get out there and fix this. Get him off that microphone," Brooks snapped.

Ben hustled out of the room while Jacob grabbed his phone and dialed the chief's cell.

"I turned the news on," Stevenson snarled on the other end of the line. "Do the feds know?"

"They're working on it now," Jacob replied, his vision hazing red. He should have known Miller wouldn't go without a fight. "Fucking cocksucker."

"I'm going to have his head over this. Tell Brooks I'm dealing with it." Stevenson hung up. Jacob hoped the chief tore him a new asshole.

"Mullins, Abraham." Brooks turned toward the two men. "I want you two to work on our copycat. He's going to react to this statement. I want to know how. Also, have Lali look into the mailman Detective Payton said the first victim's neighbors saw. I don't buy it for an instant he happened to be named Mitchell." Brooks glanced at Jacob. "Go over the details of the old cases. Look for connections, a pattern we might not have considered before. TBK picked his victims out far in advance. Our copycat will mimic that, and we might be able to narrow down who the next target is."

"Excuse me." One of the mousy receptionists danced in the doorway with Mullins. The agent stepped back and allowed the woman into the room. She peered at Jacob.

"What's up?" he asked, ambling toward her. She held a large pastry box.

"This was delivered for you, Detective." She set it down on one of the empty tables.

Jacob frowned and flipped the lid open.

Inside was a dozen strawberry-frosted donuts with donut holes in the center of each, dipped in white frosting and painted to look like an eyeball. In the center of the box was a letter, and on top of the letter—a finger. A human finger.

A present, just for you, Detective.

IRON: I HAVE NEW STUFF UPLOADING.

Mercy: Can't wait to see what you got.

Iron: How are the others doing? Havent had time to check the logs.

Mercy: Good, as far as I can tell. Joker is having storage issues.

Iron: Hes a prick.

Mercy: That's not very nice.

Joe: How do you get blood out of a white shirt?

Mercy: ...you don't

Iron: Dude, burn it already. Remember the rule? No evidence left behind unless you mean to.

Private Window

Mercy: You have to be more careful about what you say in the group, Max.

Iron: I know I forget.

Mercy: You can't fuck up. She'll kick you out of the club, and you know what happens when people get kicked out.

Iron: I dont know, but I can guess.

Mercy: I'd hate for that to happen to you.

Iron: Yeah at least not until I get to meet you.

Mercy: Seriously?

Iron: Yeah I mean I was.

Mercy: Iron...

Mercy: I don't think that's a good idea.

Mercy: If we start meeting up, it'll draw attention to us.

Iron: Yeah, I guess youre right. It was stupid.

Mercy: No, it's not. I like you, I just think what we're doing—it's bigger than us, you know?

Iron: Yeah.

Iron: I think I can hear him.

Mercy: Who?

Iron: Mitchell Black.

Iron: I can hear him speaking to me.

Mercy: What does he say?

Iron: To kill the girl. Finish what was started.

Mercy: Are you sticking to your plan?

Iron: To the letter.

Mercy: Good. I always thought your plan was one of the best.

Mercy: Hey, got to go. Rounds are starting soon.

Iron: Me too. Want to try to do some scouting tonight.

EMMA KEPT HER GAZE on the top of the hill. She revved the bike and it shot up, up—she hunched down and at the last possible second, kicked out of the seat—she soared over the last hill before the designated stop of the course. Adrenaline pounded in her veins, and her heart thundered in her chest. There was nothing like those brief few seconds she was airborne to really make her feel free. Like she could do anything.

She put the back wheel down first, then the front, and shot forward, not easing off the accelerator until she'd gone over the white chalk stripe. Or what was left of it. As soon as the guys hot on her tail had passed, she cut across from her inside position toward the boundary and her truck.

The light was fading, and she'd burned enough gas and energy for one day. She'd needed to drive some of her guilt away, and riding her bike always gave her a fresh perspective.

She might have screwed up with Jacob to the point where it couldn't be fixed, but she would still figure out a way to apologize. He might hate her, might never trust her again, so all she could do was be honest with him. Tell him she was sorry, that she regretted it, that she missed his damn scowling face, and she barely knew him.

God, she had it bad for a *cop*.

A figure unfolded from the lengthening shadows near her truck and began ambling toward her. She pushed the face shield up and peered at him. The sense of being watched had never faded, and if anything, she was more on edge.

She knew that face.

Jacob.

She blew out a breath, torn between relief, joy, and dread at seeing him again.

Emma came to a stop near the tailgate of her truck and pulled off her helmet, half-afraid to look at him.

"That's a nice look." Though Jacob's words were easy, his posture was tense, as if he were a coil about to snap.

"Thanks. Helmet hair is all the rage these days." She leaned forward on the handlebars. Sweat trickled down her spine, her chest, everywhere really. This was not how she'd expected to see him. "How'd you find me?"

"Called the shop. Simon told me."

"Ah." Now that made sense. Simon was more than ready for Derrick to be out of her life, and if that meant throwing another man at her, Simon would do it. Wasn't the first time.

Jacob stared, scrutinizing everything about her. Was this what it felt like to be a suspect? She didn't like it.

"Too bad you didn't get here earlier. We could have done the flat track. Ridden a bike before?"

"Yeah."

"What kind?"

"Motorcycle."

"A road bike, I'm guessing?"

"Yeah."

Well this was like pulling teeth.

She swung her leg over the side of the bike and toed the kickstand into place. Whatever came next, it was bound to be the least fun she'd had all day. And here she'd thought it couldn't get worse than standing in the Kelleys' yard with Jacob angry at her.

God, she'd done that to him. Pushed him right to the edge of being that enraged—and she knew he had anger issues. It was so her fault. Could he forgive her? Not if he knew she'd followed him to the second scene, but she couldn't keep secrets like that from him.

She crossed to the tailgate, took off her long-sleeved jersey, and started unzipping her impact rig. It was essentially a long-sleeved sports fabric shirt with crash pads for her upper body attached to it. She'd seen enough riders seriously injured on the track to never get on a bike without more than a helmet. Hell, she was kind of attached to breathing.

Prying the gear off was another matter altogether. She wiggled out of it, leaving her panting, her skin damp and her sports bra sticking to her. She peered out of the corner of her eye at Jacob and found him watching her still.

What did she say to him? How did she proceed?

He seemed willing to wait her out.

She grabbed a bottle of water from a cooler she'd stashed in the bed of the pick-up and faced him while she sucked down the chilled liquid, trying to come up with something else to say besides, *I'm sorry.*

"The FBI ever get here?" she asked for lack of anything else to say to him.

"Yeah, they're working the case now."

"Oh." She bit her lip and sat on the tailgate. Fuck it. "I really am sorry about today."

Jacob merely watched her. She wanted some reaction from him. A flicker of emotion. But all he gave her was a dead-pan stare.

"Why are you here, Jacob? You have every right to be pissed at me." She didn't have the energy to coax anything from him. If he was going to hate her, he might as well get on with it.

"You texted me."

"And you never replied. I thought that was it."

"I was busy all day." He sighed and sat on the tailgate next to her. "Miller shit on us all. Then we got a letter in a fucking donut box with someone's finger in it. The print was burned off, and it doesn't match our last two victims. That means there's a third out there. This guy is screwed up."

She opened and closed her mouth, not sure how to re-spond to that. There was a third victim now? One they hadn't found? That was unlike TBK, but they were dealing with someone new. She wanted to ask him questions, crawl into his brain and get him to tell her everything, but that wasn't why he was here. If it was, he'd be asking her ques-tions, telling her more.

Jacob needed a safe place to land. This case was fucking with him, probably more than her, and he'd come to her. Was there hope? Did she dare try to mend the bridge?

"The finger—are they looking for them?"

"Yeah." Jacob nodded. "They told me to go home, get some rest."

"Instead you showed up here, a track in the middle of nowhere?"

"I told you. Simon said you were here."

"And you couldn't call me?"

He didn't say anything for a moment.

"I didn't know if I would come," he said finally.

Ouch.

"Because I betrayed your trust?" she asked.

"Something like that."

She bit her lip, a little voice whispering, *He knows.*

"I followed you this morning," she said. "After Harold's house."

Silence.

She wiggled her toes in her boots and took a long pull from her water bottle, waiting for him to yell at her, to rage or something. When he didn't, she wasn't sure what to do with herself.

"Are you going to say anything?" She turned toward him. Anger would be better than silence.

"I know you followed me. I saw you." He twisted to face her as well. "Would you prefer if I yelled and screamed about it? Had you arrested?"

"I'm more used to the yelling, screaming, and hitting than the silence." She tried to laugh, but it died on her lips. Her chest ached. This was some kind of twisted, goodbye-and-thanks-for-the-sex chat, wasn't it? "I'd prefer to not be arrested, though I'm not against the use of handcuffs."

Jacob's lips were a thin, white line.

"Did he yell a lot?" he asked.

"Yeah." She glanced away.

"Dad did sometimes. Not often. The silence was worse."

"I can imagine."

"They had a picture of you at the gas station. That's how I knew you were there."

"Am I in trouble?"

"No, it's not a crime to go to a gas station, but it doesn't look good. Did you leave at all last night, Em?"

She blinked at the shorted version of her name. "No. I went out to the truck to leave, but you followed me. You don't think I did this?"

"No, but I have to ask."

"Now you've asked." She pushed off the tail gate.

She couldn't even pretend to be angry, because he had every right to ask.

"Emma, there you are."

Shit, couldn't he leave her be?

"Derrick." Her lips curled, and not in pleasure. "I thought I told you to fuck off."

Derrick closed the distance between them and reached for her. She pushed his hands away and shoved at him.

"But, baby—" He'd left her voicemails all day.

"She said to fuck off." Jacob came out of nowhere, shouldering between them and planting Derrick firmly on his ass with a simple shove to his chest.

Emma would have laughed had she not been shocked. In a split second she wasn't at the track anymore. She was in a dirt driveway, clinging to her daddy's arm as she held him back from kicking ass.

"Jacob, no—don't!" She grabbed his arm. "He's not worth it. Derrick, get your ass out of here, now."

She cupped Jacob's face and stared into the depths of his eyes. He practically vibrated with rage. With all that was going on with the investigation, it was no wonder he'd have a short fuse.

"Jacob, look at me." She heard Derrick stomp off, which was for the best, since he was out of his league here.

Jacob's gaze flicked to her and back over her shoulder. "Who the hell is that?"

"My lying, cheating ex-boyfriend. He must need money right now or else he wouldn't be bothering me."

"You deserve better than that." His gaze narrowed, glaring over her shoulder.

"Yeah, well, lonely is lonely, and for all of his faults, Derrick was okay company. But he's out of the picture now."

"Is he?" Jacob finally looked at her, those sky-blues focused on her, pinning her.

"Yeah." She splayed her hands on his chest. "He's out of my life."

"Good."

Jacob bent toward her, and she held her breath as he gathered her close. She expected a crushing, bruising kiss, but he treated her with care, his lips whispering over hers.

Her heart felt as if it stuttered to a stop. She couldn't move, couldn't breathe for fear this was just a dream.

To: BLACK WIDOW
From: Mercy
Subject: Loose Cannon

I wouldn't say anything, but I'm worried. Iron thinks he hears the voice of Mitchell Black speaking to him. I know Iron is one of our more eccentric members and he believes in reincarnation, but hearing him talk like that concerns me.

He also thinks that someday he and I will meet. I know you said to stay close to him and watch him, but I don't think we should encourage this kind of a connection. I still think Iron is going to end up getting caught. The cat and mouse game he has planned with the police is too much. If he showed up here while the FBI is still looking for him, that could turn them on to what I'm doing.

Also, you might want to check the chat logs. Joe is still trying to get blood out of the white shirt he was wearing in that first video. He's either going off his rocker or something else is going on. I'm sorry to dump that on you, but I'd rather tell you than you be unaware.

In the end, I'll do whatever you say. I'm here to uphold the rules of the club and be a team player. I want you to know what Iron is up to right now. He's at a crucial part of his plan. The third kill, but I think he's too focused on the one who got away from TBK.

—Mercy

JACOB STALKED INTO THE duplex behind Emma, pausing to take his boots off. He was being an ass, and he couldn't stop himself. There was this crazy, senseless chant running through his head he couldn't silence.

Mine.

They had a history born from the same horrors. She soothed the monster inside of him with a touch, a glance. There was nothing but acceptance in her gaze when she looked at him. And, she made him smile. It wasn't a big thing, but when so much of his life revolved around the dead and dying, smiles were hard to come by. He'd almost forgotten how one went about it. She cut through all that and touched him.

The last task of the day had been to call Laura Winthrop's family, and he'd taken it upon himself once she'd been positively identified. The grandmother couldn't hear, so he'd had to tell her children. Her goddamned children.

He had to catch this guy, if for no other reason than to let those kids sleep easier at night. They would have a better life than he had.

"Amanda's not here this weekend. Or next week, for that matter. Want anything?" Emma turned to face him. She wore a paper thin t-shirt with the sleeves cut out. He could still see her hot pink sports bra though the fabric. Her nipples were two hard dots.

You.

"No."

She seemed confused about his presence, but if she was looking for him to tell her his intentions, too bad. He didn't know why he was here, except he needed to be near her. He could no more leave than cut off his own balls.

"Okay, I'm going to take a quick shower because I'm pretty sure I smell disgusting, then we can, I don't know, watch a movie or something. If you're still hungry, help yourself to something in the fridge."

"Thanks."

Emma studied him for a moment longer before shaking her head and turning into what must be one of the bedrooms. Maybe she was waiting on more of a comment from him? She'd chatted away nervously to him while they grabbed burgers, and he'd kept his replies monosyllabic. The truth was, he hadn't had anything to say. He'd soaked up her presence, calming himself by simply being around her.

He made a slow circuit around the room, examining decorations, pictures, taking the measure of the mysterious Amanda, who had let Emma crash here.

For some reason, Derrick had taken him by surprise, though he shouldn't. A woman with Emma's looks and personality had to have a string of exes on one side, and a line of potential boyfriends on the other. How did he measure up to the rest of them? She seemed to have forgiven him for being a cop. But anything else? It was a mystery to him.

Amanda appeared to be a nurse of some sort. There were many pictures of her with her face smushed up against another, smiling at a camera. Emma was in a few, and in those the girls were making silly faces. He picked up one from a shelf where Emma and Amanda were in lawn chairs at what appeared to be a bonfire. They were leaning toward each other, mouths open, twisted into ridiculous expressions. He had no idea what the story behind the picture was, but he bet if he asked Emma about it she'd laugh first.

Jacob wanted to laugh like that, but couldn't remember the last time he had.

He finished his circuit of the house, checking windows and doors to make sure they were locked. When Emma first mentioned staying with a friend, he'd been relieved. Someone else around to deter a single attacker from targeting her. Two people were harder to handle. Now that she was alone in a house, he wasn't as thrilled. Anything could happen to her here by herself.

Despite her actions, his gut said he could trust her. Anyone else looking at her as a suspect would think otherwise. He was traversing a slippery slope, and he knew it. But he couldn't walk away from her.

The sounds of her shower echoed through the small house. He peered through the doorway she'd gone through, and saw the bright rectangle of light cast across the bedroom floor. Steam billowed through the opening, and if he listened hard enough, he could hear her humming.

He blinked, and suddenly the bathroom was opening up before him. He couldn't remember crossing through the living room or bedroom. It was as if a rope were tied to him and he was being reeled in.

Emma's figure was a blur on the other side of the opaque, blue shower curtain. She stilled under the spray of the water.

"Jacob?"

"Yeah." His voice sounded rough.

"Everything okay?"

"Yeah, doing a walk-through, checking windows and doors."

"Okay." She turned, lifting her arms and stretching.

Did she know he was watching?

He should back out, leave now. Maybe go home.

Instead, he reached out and pulled he shower curtain aside. Emma glanced over her shoulder, not a shred of surprise on her face. She dragged one of those shower poofs over her skin, white suds sprinting down her body.

"Coming in?" She turned to face him, and he nearly swallowed his tongue.

He'd touched pretty much all of her, but she still took his breath away. Pert, firm breasts, a generous swell of her hips, and the longest legs he'd ever had the pleasure of having wrapped around him.

Jacob stepped into the shower, and she laughed, that gorgeous smile tugging her lips. There were marks on her body, ones he hadn't seen but felt last night.

"Aren't you going to take your clothes off?" she asked.

He didn't care about his clothes, they weren't important. He reached for her and she dropped the poof, letting him tug her closer. Her touch settled him, but not as much as the feel of her mouth against his.

He pushed her back against the shower wall, pinning her with his body. She stared back at him, not a shred of fear or hesitation in her gaze.

In fact, she seemed to say, *Come and get me.*

He slid his hands down her sides until he could cup her ass. She arched her back a bit, and one side of her mouth hitched higher.

You'll come, again and again.

6.

JACOB PULLED EMMA'S PELVIS forward, rocking against her. There were a hundred reasons he shouldn't be here, not the least of which was that she'd lied to him. And yet here he was, with no desire to be anywhere else. He hoped she was sorry, that she wasn't lying to him again, because if she was, then he was the real fool. But right now, he needed her as much as he needed his next breath.

She sucked his lower lip between hers and gently bit down. He'd never had a lover bite him before. It was primal, raw, and it drove him crazy. He groaned and leaned into her harder. Despite his conscience telling him to be gentle with her, she seemed to like pushing him to the edge of control. It was as if she liked it when he was rough.

The spray of the shower didn't even register to him anymore. Nothing but the taste of her lips and the feel of her ass in his hands.

She grabbed the tail of his polo shirt and peeled it away from his skin. His clothes were completely soaked, but he couldn't find it in him to give a fuck. Not when Emma's nails traced his spine. She'd left scratches on his back that had reminded him of her constantly, and he wouldn't mind adding to them.

He leaned back enough to grab the fabric and pull it up and over his head. It hit the bottom of the tub with a heavy *slap.*

Emma wiggled her hands into the waistband of his jeans, struggling with the tab. She had this determined expression on her face, brows down, gaze focused, teeth clenched, and her lips parted. There wasn't an ounce of fear or hesitation about the way she touched him. Every time he thought he should maybe pull back, she reeled him in closer.

The waterlogged denim wouldn't cooperate, but he was sure enjoying her efforts. Her fingers wiggled against his abdomen, and every now and then she scratched him as she lost her grip on the tab. He planted his hands on the wall on either side of her shoulders and nuzzled the crook of her neck. He'd make this good for her, too, so she'd want to come back to him. If he could brand himself on her, maybe she wouldn't walk away from him.

Jacob kissed his way up and down her neck, tasting her with his tongue and letting her feel the scrape of his teeth while her fingers slipped and tugged on his jeans. If he weren't so focused on the little gasps and growls she made, he might laugh at her frustration at his zipper.

"Ah-ha!" She grinned like the cat who got the cream, all heavy-lidded seduction, as she won the battle with his jeans, spreading them open. "Stay right there, okay?"

What exactly did she have in mind? He wanted to find out.

Emma kissed his shoulder, over the scar from his patrol days. A would-be car-jacker had stabbed him, only grazing his skin. Lower, her lips trailed across his ribs, abs and stomach, lingering over the marks and scars that would never go away, until she settled on her knees.

Oh fuck.

His vision hazed, and his pulse kicked up as his heart began to beat in double time. He didn't know if he could handle this. The control it took to stand there, it might be beyond him, but he'd sure as hell allow the lady to do as she wished.

She tugged his jeans down past his knees and held the denim while he stepped out of them. It was a relief to be out of the confines of his jeans. He'd been sporting wood since she'd peeled that motocross gear off and stood back-lit against the sunset in her damn sports bra.

Emma settled on her knees and wrapped a hand around his cock. There was nothing hesitant about the way she touched him. She was a woman with confidence and no shame about what she wanted. Maybe she was right, and he'd been chasing the wrong type of woman all along. She didn't flinch away from his harder side. He'd left bruises on her last night she'd laughed about this morning—even thanked him for. Right now, he'd have to trust her, because he couldn't trust himself.

She pumped him several times, root to tip. Her grasp was firm, and her talented fingers sought out the most sensitive places. The thick vein on the underside of his cock, the area under the mushroom cap. She played him like an expert. If he allowed it, she'd drive him mad like this. Hell, she seemed to be smiling in anticipation.

"Don't test me, Ems." His voice was so low and rough, he hardly recognized himself anymore.

"It doesn't feel good when I do this?" She massaged his balls and stroked his length once more.

"It would feel better in you."

One side of her mouth hitched higher. "In me? Like this?"

She didn't tease him. No, she opened her mouth and took him in until the head of his cock bumped the back of her throat.

His throat constricted until it was hard to breathe. His vision hazed even more, and he tried to dig his fingernails into the grout between the tiles to keep his hands off her.

Fuck, she was amazing.

Her tongue was even better than her fingers. She rubbed the flat of her tongue on the underside of his cock as she bobbed up and down, treating him like some erotic lollipop. He tossed his head back and squeezed his eyes shut. His whole body felt as if it were on fire, both inside and out.

He should tell her to stop. To back off. How long could he keep his hands off her?

Unlike other women, Emma didn't relent after a few pumps and call it foreplay. She sucked down harder, twisting the hand at the base of his cock, working all of him. He felt the whisper of her teeth against the mushroom cap, and his whole body tensed. How he wanted to thrust into her, hammer away, but he couldn't.

He groaned and grit his teeth, his muscles screaming for relief. Even watching her was out of the question. It would test his control, and he couldn't lose it with Emma. He couldn't live with himself if he saw even a hint of fear in her gaze when she looked at him.

Her nimble fingers worked his balls, tracing the seam between each testicle, back to that tender, erogenous zone behind his sac. A tingling sensation began at the base of his skull and radiated out through his limbs, pleasant, pleasurable, but nowhere near enough. He rocked up on his toes as she continued back farther. She circled his anus with her finger. His jaw dropped and he gaped at her, too shocked to move.

He felt the rumble of her chuckle through his cock. She glanced up and winked at him.

Her hand slid back to his balls. Was she baiting him? His thoughts were too hazy to muddle through her intentions. All he could think was, *Want. Now.*

The urge to thrust, to move inside of her was overpowering. He leaned back and arched his hips, just a bit. The pure ecstasy of it, moving together, feeling her touching him, it brought a deep shudder up through his body.

Oh hell no. He would last longer than this, and there would be a hell of a lot more pleasure.

He grabbed her by the shoulders and hauled her to her feet. She wavered, blinking at him with a dazed, unfocused expression. He crushed his mouth over hers, clenching her to his chest.

Jacob needed to be inside of her, to feel her and see her all at once.

She muttered against his lips, something he couldn't understand.

"Condom," she said louder.

"Where?"

Emma pushed past him and reached out of the shower and retrieved—an open condom. Her grin widened a bit. "Like I said, I was expecting you. What took you so long?"

She rolled the latex on him and backed up against the wall once more, like she understood this was how it had to be. This time. He hooked his arm under her leg and she wound hers around his neck, as if it were a choreographed dance and they each knew their parts. He had to bend his knees a bit, but he found her pussy and guided his cock to her entrance. He wanted to go easy on her, but his thrust was hard and deep.

Emma's back arched and she tossed her head back and forth. He froze, watching her, feeling her body stretch to accommodate him.

God, she was beautiful like this.

He withdrew and thrust, driving into her just as hard.

"Oh, yes," she moaned, easing some of his worry that it was too much.

Trust, he could trust her.

Jacob's muscles quivered and he relinquished a little more of his control. She thought he'd been rough with her last night? Hardly. He dug his fingers into her thigh and hip, thrusting harder. Her breath left her lungs in a whoosh as he pressed his body against hers and the shower things rattled on the edge of the tub. Her moans increased in pitch and volume, spurring him on harder. He held onto her with all he had, pistoning into her body. Her nails scraped over his shoulders, digging deeper than before until they stung, adding new tracks to his skin, new marks to remember her by.

A prickling sensation started at the base of his spine.

No, no, not yet.

Jacob couldn't stop the tidal wave of release rolling up through his body. He tightened his hold as his thrusts became unrestrained, his orgasm shredding the last bits of his control. He groaned and let his head sag forward against her shoulder, spent but sure as hell not sated. Not even a little bit.

EMMA'S BACK HIT THE mattress, and her towel slid down around her waist. She laughed as Jacob came down on top of her. He was so stern, so serious. Had no one ever showed him how fun sex could be? Well, she doubted that lesson would come tonight. But another night, she'd make sure he smiled.

"I'll give you something to smile about," he muttered in her ear.

"Oh yeah?" She stretched, wrapping her arms around his neck and spreading her thighs to accommodate him.

He supported himself on his forearm and slid his hand between them. She knew where this was going and she still gasped when he slid his fingers inside her. It wasn't his cock, but it felt good as he rubbed all those sensitized nerve endings.

"Your smile is amazing." He kissed her cheek.

Words escaped her. Her brain was too scrambled, her body screaming for one thing—release—for anything else to make sense.

"Stay right there," he said.

Where the hell did he think she'd go?

Jacob scooted down her body and she reached for the spindles on the headboard.

Oh, yes, please.

There was something wickedly satisfying about how he moved her around like a rag doll, as if she didn't weigh an ounce. In the shower, on his table, and now here. He draped her legs over his shoulders, shifted her hips. He made her feel small and petite, which no man had accomplished in at least the last ten years.

He spread her labia with his fingers and licked over her sensitized clit. She gasped and shifted her hips, or tried to. He had her pinned, completely at his mercy. He was in complete control. There was no moving unless he allowed it.

"What do you like the most? Clitoral orgasms?" He flicked the nub with his tongue, rubbing it back and forth.

Her spine arched, and she dug one heel into his back. Hitting that spot shut down all rational thought.

"Hm. Or do you prefer vaginal?" He thrust two fingers into her pussy and pumped them several times, as deep as he could go. Her body relaxed, and her eyes nearly rolled back in her skull.

She shuddered and blew out a breath. This teasing business could easily be turned back on him. Next time, she wouldn't be so nice.

He curled his fingers deep inside her and pumped.

"What about your g-spot? Is that the way to go?"

He stretched her a bit, rubbing all those nerve endings in her vagina—but then he hit something else. A deep pleasure center in her body. Her muscles constricted and her toes curled as sensation shot up and down her body.

"What if we do these two together?"

Oh no he—

Jacob stroked her g-spot and wrapped his lips around her clit. Her jaw nearly came unhinged and she gripped the headboard tight. It was too much, all at once. She tossed her head back and screamed as her orgasm rushed over her, sharp, bright, and immediate, robbing her of her senses. She babbled words, thrashed under his hold, but he continued to stroke her for several moments, drawing it on and on. Her body felt as if it rippled, and her muscles went completely lax until there was no fight left inside her.

After several moments he eased up, giving her some respite. He kissed her inner thigh and she jumped. She was too spent to chuckle. He eased out of her and crawled up to lay beside her.

Emma didn't even have the energy left to cuddle, but he gathered her against him, nestling her head under her chin and stroking her side.

"You," she poked his shoulder, "are an evil, evil man."

"Didn't I warn you?"

"No, you left that part out."

"I'll make sure to add it to my resume next time."

"Good."

He chuckled and she wished she could see his face, if he was smiling or not. Even that was beyond her.

Jacob's hands roved over her body. There was no rhyme or reason to where his fingers went, but she enjoyed the simple sensation of being held and touched. There was a level of intimacy between them she hadn't expected. This didn't feel like two people hooking up for some random sex. She felt a burning connection in her chest, as if there was a thread tied to her that attached to him and it hummed with the energy of their coupling.

Damn if she wasn't emotionally invested in this man. She was already thinking about next time and what she'd do to him then. That was getting way too ahead of herself, which was dangerous, since they weren't anything to each other. Not really. She fell into relationships quick, but even this might be a record breaker for her. Except she doubted Jacob wanted the same thing.

There was no denying in her mind that a long-term thing between them was impossible. They were from different sides of the tracks. Different worlds. Besides, she had a record. A cop couldn't be with someone like her, could they? But it wasn't like she needed the happily ever after and the white dress right now. Couldn't she enjoy what they had for however long it lasted?

She smoothed her hand down his chest, the scar on his shoulder staring back.

Life was so short to pass up on what might or might not work out. If he wanted her, if she brought a little joy to his life, and if they worked, even for a week or a month, she wanted to be with him. That was the certainty resting in her chest.

"Who was she?" Emma asked.

"She who?"

"The woman you scared so badly you think you can't be yourself."

Jacob was silent for several moments. It wasn't hard to figure out that there must be a reason, a story why he thought his sexual appetite was wrong.

"Yeah. There were a few, actually. The first told me when she was breaking it off with me that I became someone else when we were—together. I kept a pretty tight leash on myself with the next one, but even that wasn't enough, I guess."

"Do you go fishing for a certain type or something?" She propped her chin up in her palm.

"Why do you want to know about them? Aren't you supposed to not want to talk about my exes?" The ever-present frown deepened.

She shrugged. "Their history is part of yours. Besides, I'm not stupid. I know you've been with other women, just like I'm no virgin. What's the point of being upset about some woman I've never met before?

He shook his head and pulled her close once more. "The last few women I've dated all broke up with me because I wasn't emotionally available enough to them."

"Hard to be when you aren't being honest with them."

"Are you my shrink now?"

"Do I get to charge you if I am?"

"No."

"Well, my unprofessional advice is to find a new type, Detective Payton." A type like her? Yeah right, but she could dream.

"What was that—finger on my ass—business about?" He sounded truly befuddled.

She couldn't help but laugh and roll away enough to peer at his face. He looked even funnier now, brows down, eyes a little large, and mouth open. He really didn't get it.

"You were just standing there. Either you were the kind of guy who'd be into a finger up your ass, or it would startle you into at least doing something. Shit, I might as well have been going down on a dildo for as much as you seemed to enjoy it."

"It was fucking awesome." He stared at her as if he didn't understand what she was saying.

"Yeah, I'm pretty good." She studied him for a moment. "You know you can let loose a little, don't you? You don't have to be so in control all the time. It can't be healthy."

His fingers traced a spot on her hip.

"They aren't from him, if that's what you're looking for." She peered down at the crescent-shaped scar. "That was a bike accident. That's why I wear every piece of safety gear I don't have to."

"And yet you're still covered in scars. This is a burn mark." He tapped one on her arm.

"Yeah, remember I also do metal sculpture? You can't work around hot metal and a blowtorch without fucking up every now and then." She cupped his face. "Seriously, I'm not as fragile as you'd like to believe. Or is this what you do? Coddle your girlfriends while keeping them at arm's length until they leave because you're emotionally unavailable?"

"Who's the detective now? The FBI could use you as a profiler."

"Now he makes a joke." She waggled her finger at him. "You're deflecting."

Jacob sighed, his gaze still on the burn mark. If he met her gaze now, would he see too much?

"He never left a mark on you? Ever?"

That wasn't a question she wanted to answer, but she'd kept so much from him already. Was still keeping the letter from him. If she told him about that the letter, he'd have her bundled up and away from this so fast.

"He did, but they were temporary and accidental." She held up her hand. "I know, I know. It sounds like I'm making excuses for him, but not really. Yes, Daddy left bruises sometimes, but it was an accident. I know what it sounds like, but he's a sloppy drunk. He'd flail an arm and catch me. He wouldn't set out to intentionally hurt me."

"But he didn't stop drinking, did he?"

"No."

"Is your brother the same way?"

"You read the file, you tell me."

Jacob pursed his lips for a moment, his gaze harder. "The case was fucked up. Travis should never have removed his friend's kid from the mother's house."

"That's what a SEAL does though. They protect. She was trying to stab her own son." Two years and the case still made her furious. Travis had gone to see his best friend's baby momma because the woman was sending crazy texts. The two men had arrived and found the mother trying to kill her son. Travis had grabbed the son, while his friend calmed down his ex-wife. Once cops and lawyers got involved, the blame of it landed on Travis. It was a federal offense to kidnap a child, despite the fact if it weren't for Travis, the kid would probably be dead.

"I know." He dropped his gaze. "I would have done the same thing. Fuck the laws, she would have killed that kid if it weren't for your brother."

"Thank you. Did you know she's in prison now?"

"No."

Emma nodded.

"She killed the kid's father six months later. Thanks to a lunatic my brother will be branded as a felon his entire life—for protecting a child." She blew out a breath. "He's not a bad person."

"I know. I've looked into him, too."

"Are you sure you aren't stalking me?"

One side of his mouth kicked up. "Maybe I am."

"Prison changed Travis. All things considered, he got a short sentence. He never comes home anymore."

"Right now, that's probably a good thing. What is he doing now?"

"He works for a private security company, the Aegis Group. It's all former military. Several of his SEAL buddies work there. No one cares about his record, but it's dangerous work."

"He landed on his feet. Plus, he has you."

She nodded, but she had to wonder if Travis wasn't doomed from the beginning. They only shared a father, but that was the link that branded them.

She scooted closer, soaking in Jacob's comfort. She and Travis had never been very close. His mother was always jealous she wasn't the woman Daddy chose to be with. But they'd gone to the same school,s and Travis had spent time at her house at various points over the years. They were all the family they had. And for now, she had Jacob, too.

AMANDA PEERED up and down the street.

No truck.

No Emma.

Christ, she was a horrible friend, but she and Derrick had had this arrangement since before Emma had even met him. Amanda had tried to steer Emma away from Derrick. She'd really tried. But Derrick was a god of sex and Amanda couldn't give him up. Even if she really didn't like him, she had a thing for his cock.

It was an addiction, really. She was an addict. Her drug of choice happened to be dirty, nasty sex with someone she didn't like. It was psychological. Hell, she was a nurse, she knew this stuff. She had all the hotlines and specialists she could ever want at the tip of her fingers, and yet here she was, over and over and over again, at Derrick's doorstep. At least now her needs didn't have to revolve around Emma's schedule.

One more glance around to be sure the neighbors weren't watching either.

Coast was clear.

She grabbed the bag she kept in the car specifically for these little get-togethers. The last thing she wanted was to leave Derrick's place smelling like him or Emma's soap. But, Emma and her soap were at Amanda's place, so technically that wouldn't be an issue anymore. Thank goodness Emma had finally dumped Derrick. It left Amanda guilt-free to continue these little meetings.

The front porch light was off, as normal, to deter the neighbors from snooping too much.

She took a deep breath and loosened the belt on her coat. From inside she could hear the thump of feet. She put her hand against the frame and smiled. Tonight would be good. There was no more reason for guilt.

The door swept open, and Derrick stood on the other side of the glass, naked and semi-erect.

It was that kind of night?

Well, she'd wanted hot and dirty.

"House call," she said and opened the glass door.

"About time you showed up." Derrick's scowl wasn't his usual sexy smile, but she could work with that.

"Hey, I texted you and said I'd be late." She dropped the bag on a table near the door and shrugged out of her coat, leaving her in the naughty nurse outfit. Every Halloween she stocked up on a few models. This one was a thigh length sheath that zipped up the front, complete with a silly little hat she'd pinned on. She'd foregone a bra this time because she was that needy.

"Yeah, I know." He grabbed her by the shoulders and pushed her up against the wall. "I hate waiting." His mouth crushed hers. She could taste cigarette smoke and beer that curdled her stomach.

Amanda pushed him back, shaking her head.

"Gross—you started smoking again?" She held her hand up, keeping him at arm's length.

"Hey, it's a free country." He had that angry pout thing going on.

"Is this about Emma?" she asked.

"If it weren't for you, she'd still be here, and I wouldn't have to get some hooker to suck my cock."

Emma hadn't really cared for oral, or maybe not with Derrick. Amanda avoided all sexual topics as a rule with her friends. No one needed to know where her preferences ran.

Amanda rolled her eyes. "Is that what this is about? Your cock is lonely?"

"Yes."

Dear lord, this man was disgusting and ridiculous, but she still got hot and bothered thinking about going down on him.

"Well, if that's all, I have just what the doctor ordered. Keep your ashtray of a mouth away from me, okay?" She flattened her hands against his chest and slid lower, over his pecs and abs. She peeked up at him through her lashes. "Did you miss me?"

"No. Why would I miss a dirty little slut like you?" he spat.

Amanda settled on her knees, smiling up at him. She'd learned in her formative years that the best sexual experience contained more than a little dirty talk. Most of the time what Derrick said to her was flat out degrading. And she loved it.

She grasped his cock and stroked it. He shifted his stance and the old floor groaned under his foot. Except—the floor didn't normally creak there.

"Did you hear something?" she asked.

"I don't hear you sucking my cock and moaning like the cum slut you are."

Fuck whatever she thought she heard. If he was calling her a cum slut already, tonight would be amazing. She wrapped both her hands around his cock.

"Come on, bitch. Stop dragging your sorry ass." He grabbed a handful of her hair and pulled her face toward him.

The glass door creaked open.

"Derrick—"

"What the—"

Thwack.

Crunch.

Derrick's body hid the intruder from her as he slumped to the ground. It all happened so fast, she couldn't even process what was happening.

"Emma—no—wait!" Amanda threw up her hands. It was too dark to see who it was, but it could only be Emma, right?

Derrick rolled to his side, groaning.

The dark figure—why the hell weren't the lights on?—leaned toward her.

"I'm not Emma," a man said.

Amanda scrambled, crab walking away from the man. She slipped over Derrick's arm and landed on her side. She rolled and crawled, trying to kick off her damn heels. What was this, a stupid teenage horror dream? This couldn't be real.

"Oh now, don't go leaving me. We're getting started."

The man grabbed her ponytail, and she screamed. The sound barely left her mouth before he shoved a wad of cloth between her teeth, muffling the sound. She scratched at his hand, his arm. She twisted until she could jab her heels at his legs.

"Fuck, ouch. Bitch!"

He hauled back with his other arm. The light from the kitchen glinted off silver metal.

A tire iron.

She saw a patient beaten almost to death with one of those last week.

DERRICK GROANED. The last thing he remembered was Amanda going down on him. That bitch had a great mouth. Except he couldn't remember coming.

Where was he?

He tried to lift his head, but the room spun. A woman whimpered nearby.

"Manda?" It was hard to move his tongue. Part of it was swollen, as if he'd bitten it. Why did his head hurt so bad?

He tried to lift his arms to cradle his aching head, but they were too heavy. Had they binged instead of fucking? That wasn't normal at all. Usually Amanda fucked and left. She wasn't too big on chatting if the words slut, bitch, or cum weren't involved.

"Come on, wake up." A man patted his face, one side and then the other.

Pain blossomed wherever the man touched, lighting up his face. He spat curse words and tried to move, but he couldn't. His head was secured to something.

"If I would have known what a wimp you are, I'd have used my fist instead of the iron." The man bent over him, filling his vision. "Smile for the camera, will you?"

The man grabbed Derrick's face and pushed the corners of his mouth up, as if he were smiling.

"Cheese! Say hi to the rest of the Killer Club. Hi guys." The sicko actually waved at a hand-held camera taped to the kitchen counter.

"What the hell? You're a sick freak. Let me go." Derrick tugged at his bonds, but he hurt—everywhere.

"Derrick here was dating Emma. You all know Emma. She's the granddaughter of the Ration family, who I killed before I was caught about thirty years ago." The guy stood, talking to the camera.

Why did he look familiar?

Derrick couldn't even process what the man was saying. Where was Amanda?

"Now, Derrick here," he grabbed Derrick's leg, digging his fingers into his hair and pulling. "Derrick was keeping secrets from Emma. Remember Amanda? The girl I didn't really let talk a whole lot? Well, it seems that these two have been having a rip-roaring affair together behind Emma's back."

"How do you know that?" Derrick demanded.

"Shut up. No one wants to hear you speak." The guy scowled at him. He couldn't be more than twenty-five, still with the pudgy cheeks of youth. Derrick had seen that same scowl aimed at him before, but where? His attacker turned back to the camera. "Now, when I realized what was going on, well, I had to make room for them in my schedule. I couldn't let these two live."

Live? What was going on here?

"Where's Amanda, you sick fuck?" Derrick tried to kick, but his legs were tied down.

The man glanced down at him. "You want to see Amanda? I'll get Amanda."

He took two steps and reached into the shadows next to the refrigerator. He grabbed one of the dining room chairs and pulled it closer.

"Oh God. Oh God. No. No!" Derrick tried to push backward, but his legs were restrained. He jerked against the bonds even though every movement hurt.

"Don't be like that. Always with the screaming." The man crossed to Derrick and stood behind him. He shoved a wad of cloth into his mouth and pushed the chair forward, toward the gruesome sight.

Derrick tried to turn away, to not see what had happened, but the man held his face.

"Look. Look at what you made me do to her," the man said through clenched teeth.

Amanda was tied to one of the kitchen chairs. A two-by-four had been slid between her and the ladder back of the chair, creating a head support. She was taped and tied into place, a wad of cloth in her mouth as well. Her body hung lifeless, her soul gone.

Blood coated her, streams of it here and there. She'd been hurt, and for what? Getting her satisfaction from him?

The worst of it was her face. He almost couldn't look at her.

"Do you know why I took her eyes?" the man whispered.

Derrick groaned. He was going to be sick.

"Some people say they're the window to the soul. You know what I think?" He paused, as if Derrick would answer that. "I think they contain lifetimes of knowledge. We're all reborn, Derrick. And now, I'm going to free you to live again, and I will take your eyes, so hopefully, next time you become a better person."

The man circled him until he stood in front of Derrick, a broken and bloody table leg in his hand.

The gas station near Simon's garage. That was it.

"Your future self will thank me." He smiled, and it was terrifying.

MAX STARED AT THE two sets of eyes studying him from inside their new glass homes.

What had he done with the eyes in his previous life?

He couldn't remember, and those little details were starting to annoy him. Did he eat the eyes to ingest and absorb the history of those other lives? Did he keep them as trophies? What?

The souls weren't going to speak to him now, not since he was so close to their former husks. He sighed and put the two jars into his bag. It was the last thing at every scene he did before leaving. Those souls needed to know they were at rest. They'd found a friend. In him.

Behind the house, he stripped out of tonight's clothing and changed into another nondescript set of track pants and a hoodie. He'd burn everything eventually.

Max took the woman's keys—Amanda—and left the house the way he came, except this time he wouldn't be on foot.

His phone vibrated against his hip, but he didn't pause to look at it now. No doubt it was Mercy or Black Widow emailing him again. Joker had reached out to him, cautioning him against deviating too far from his path, which was ridiculous coming from him. They hadn't heard from Red in months after Black Widow moved them to a new server and demanded three weeks of net-silence.

He drove a mile to the twenty-four hour market in Amanda's car and picked up his second vehicle. It was a stolen hatchback he picked up a few hours before his date with Amanda and Derrick. He watched that house for months, keeping tabs on everyone who came and went. Installing the hidden cameras made it easier once he was able to hack the neighbor's Wi-Fi. When he realized how often Amanda and Derrick had their dirty little trysts, he'd known he had to stop them. Emma deserved better. She was so much better than those two.

Yes, it was deviating from his plan to take them at this point, but it was necessary.

Max drove the streets, staying a few miles under the speed limit, taking an indirect path across town to where he'd stashed his truck behind a rundown, boarded-up house that had been raided a week before for drugs.

It was a long trek, but he made it all the way to his truck without being noticed or raising an alarm. Only when he was in his own vehicle did he finally check his phone.

```
From: Black Widow
To: Iron
Subject: Concerned about you.

Iron,

You're doing great work. I've watched all
your material with joy. You make TBK proud. I
understand your reasoning from deviating from
```

the plan, but I caution you from getting caught up in the moment too much.

Our mission is to pay homage to those who have come before us.

Once your job is done, go forth and do your own work. But remember, membership in the club is dependent on carrying out your killer's murders.

Think it over. I'm here for you.

BW

7.

JACOB STARED AT THE two bodies, and his stomach rolled. It had been a long time since he'd lost it at a crime scene, but this was beyond anything he'd ever seen. It stretched from wall to wall on every surface of the kitchen, even the ceiling.

"This isn't TBK's style," Jade said. It was the first thing any of them had spoken since the forensics team had cleared them to enter the kitchen.

"No fuck?" Mullins shook his head. "What's she supposed to be doing? Giving him head?"

"He's defacing the bodies. This is more personal than the others. There's rage here. Coroner said the penis was removed postmortem." Jade tip-toed closer to peer at the woman posed with her face resting on one of the man's thighs.

Whoever she was, it would be a closed casket funeral now. The eyes were gone and much of the skull appeared to be crushed. She was completely unrecognizable.

"Any ID?" Brooks asked.

"Nothing," Jacob replied. "House is registered to a Pearl Jones, who died a couple years ago. They're still searching the house for something that will tell us who these two are, but it's kind of a dump." And that was before someone had splattered the kitchen with pints of blood.

"He prefers areas with hard surfaces," Mullins said. When the man concentrated, a slight brogue slipped into his voice. "They were attacked in the living room. I'm guessing they were getting it on, killer knocked them out then dragged them in here."

"Clean up?" Jade suggested.

Brooks shook his head. "He doesn't bother."

"Flat surfaces." Jacob gestured to the same blood void they'd found at the two previous scenes. "We think he's filming these, right? Well, he needs a flat surface to put the camera on."

Jade, Mullins, and Brooks stared at him, similar blank expressions on their faces.

"Fuck, that's good, Detective." Mullins wagged his finger at him. "The living room is trashed. The lighting is bad. He drags them in here to get a better shot on the camera, and no one lets their kitchen lights burn out because how are you going to make toast without light?"

"Toast?" Jade blinked at him.

"Throwing out ideas, love." Mullins patted Jade on the shoulder.

"Lali hasn't been able to track down the footage since we told her Payton's theory," Brooks said as though he were simply thinking out loud.

"Maybe it's a trophy?" Jacob suggested. He really should keep his mouth shut. These were the profilers, he was just a detective.

"Perhaps." Jade shrugged. "The eyes follow the TBK MO, but he's evolving. He's finding his own identity."

"We're treating TBK and TBKiller as two separate people now?" Jacob asked.

"Yes, I think it's safe to say that though TBKiller is inspired by TBK, he's found himself. The question is, what is he?"

"You know, I haven't seen any letters around here." Mullins paced into the living room and back. "Have you?"

"Once TBK hit the media he eased off sending letters to the victims ahead of time. There were notes and hints of who he would go after in the letters he sent to the police and newspaper, but that was it." Jade shrugged.

"Neither of these fit the clues in the last letters, though. It doesn't make any sense." Jacob stroked his chin.

"You're right. What if these two weren't on his radar until something else happened?" Brooks scooted past Jacob to stand with his back to the blood void on the kitchen counter, facing the victims. "What if he was supposed to kill someone else? The first scene was neat, almost as if each blood splatter was intentional. The second kill—something happened there. He got violent. Or maybe it was the sound? I need to see the second kill photographs again. Something changed with that scene to lead to this."

But what?

And how could they figure it out before it was too late?

EMMA LIFTED HER WELDER'S mask and glanced around. Sunday at Simon's garage was a ghost town. Usually the guys tinkered on their own bikes or a friend's truck, but everyone had somewhere else to be. It was just her, the latest sculpture, and a blowtorch. Normally welding was soothing. She could get out of her head and let the metal and flame speak to her, but today she couldn't shake the sensation that someone was watching.

Since Jacob had left to go to the station that morning, she'd decided to try to get some more work done. The break-up with Derrick had interrupted her production schedule and she needed to make up some ground on custom pieces she'd promised clients.

If Jacob knew she was out here, he'd be pissed beyond belief. He only suspected the copycat might be interested in her. He didn't know she was firmly in the cross hairs.

Maybe she should tell him?

She took a swig of water before lowering her welder's mask and starting the torch up again.

If she told him, her ass would land in protective custody. She'd suffocate with that many cops crawling up her ass.

The skin between her shoulder blades crawled. He was there. Somewhere. Watching her.

She glanced in the reflective surface of a tinted car window, but nothing was behind her. Nothing was out of place.

Her phone vibrated in her back pocket. She was too distracted to get much more work finished, and besides, the sun was reaching its zenith. From there it would be too hot to work with the torch.

She shoved the mask up once more and hurried to get her glove off to press the flickering answer button.

"Hello?"

"Hi, Ms. Ration?"

"Yeah?" Who the fuck called her Ms. Ration?

"My name is Ryan Brooks. I'm with the FBI. We'd like to see your collection of TBK documents and ask you a few questions, if you don't mind."

"This about the copycat?" Shit. Did Jacob know this was happening? Hadn't he mentioned an Agent Brooks at some point last night?

"I'd rather not say. Do you think you could come in?"

"Yeah, it'll be a little bit, though. I've been out working, and I need to clean up a bit."

"That's fine. Could you be here around, say five o' clock?"

"I can do that." She didn't want to, but she would. The truth was, as much as she wanted to understand this copy-cat and the senseless violence of it all, she wasn't going to be the one who took him down. That was a job for the cops. But fuck if she didn't want to give the asshole a black eye.

It took her most of an hour to clean up and put her latest sculpture back in the shed Simon had said she could use until she found a new studio space. By then, her nerves were clamoring so hard between being watched and her impending date with the feds that she couldn't even pre-tend to be hungry. She headed out to the station early to at least get it over with.

The quicker she wrapped the meeting up, the sooner she could be hungry. Hell, maybe Jacob would like to go have dinner with her and take a break. He was getting in too deep with this case and she knew how much it could stir up the darkness inside.

She focused on Jacob during her drive to the downtown station in Oklahoma City. His smile. The blueness of his eyes. The scars that told the story of a man so intent on getting his guy, sometimes he used his own body as a tool.

He was also a target. Or maybe it was because he was a cop that made the copycat reach out to him. TBK had liked an audience and he'd flirted with the authorities for years before they caught him.

She parked her truck and took the file box with all the precious history inside the station. An attendant signed her in, put her through a metal detector, and showed her back into the bowels of the building. There was no way she'd figure out how to get out of here on her own.

"Ms. Ration?" A clean-cut blond man approached her. He couldn't be a local, not in a long-sleeved shirt and a flashy pink tie.

"Emma, please. Ms. Ration sounds like my mother."

"Emma, then." He had a smile that didn't reach his eyes. "This way, please? I'm sorry we aren't having this chat in the conference room, they're all taken."

He led her into one of those interrogation type rooms she saw on TV. She hesitated near the doorway, her gut churning. She'd sat in one of these once before, while she'd recounted the story of what had happened the night Daddy chased her away. Lovely memories all around.

She took a deep breath. They wanted to see the collection.

Where was Jacob?

She glanced over her shoulder, but didn't catch sight of him. Were they a secret? It hadn't occurred to her that maybe Jacob hadn't mentioned their involvement. It stung a bit to think he might be keeping her in the closet, but it wasn't like she was cop-wife material anyway.

"What did you want to see?" Emma pasted on her brightest smile and went to the table.

"Have a seat?" Ryan gestured to the seat facing the door.

She set the box on the table to her right, the one-way glass on her left and tried to keep her focus on the man across from her.

"I wanted to ask you if you knew any of these individuals." He pulled four eight-by-tens out of a folder and laid them in front of her.

Emma gasped and her stomach clenched. If she'd have eaten, she'd have lost it all in that moment.

They were pictures from crime scenes. Close-ups of the victim's eyeless faces, their features destroyed to the point they didn't even look human. She gripped the edge of the table and sucked in deep breaths of air. She'd never seen pictures of the bodies that weren't heavily blurred. They were the one thing that had been kept from the public, and she could appreciate that now. It would take a lifetime to burn those images from her mind.

"Emma? Emma, do you know who this person is?" Ryan tapped the picture on her left.

She shook her head. "No."

"Are you sure?"

"I mean, that has to be Harold Espinoza, but I don't recognize him. Not like that. Oh, God." She slapped her hand over her mouth.

"How do you know that? Do you know him?"

"Christ." She flipped the pictures over. "Once, okay. He came to a race. He wanted to do a motocross thing for Pride Week. He liked my pink jersey. Fuck." She rubbed the heel of her hand over her eye, willing the image out of her mind.

"What about her?" He flipped the second picture back over.

That one was worse. Not only were the eyes gone, but there were tear tracks in the blood and a gag in her mouth. Just looking at her made it hard to breathe.

"No. Fuck. What's this about?" She shoved the picture across the desk as the desire to deck the smug bastard grew.

"Her name is Laura Winthrop."

"What?" she shrieked. She couldn't be more socked if he'd smacked her in the face with a steel pipe.

"Laura Winthrop is the ex-wife of your boss, Simon, correct?"

"Y-yes. She's dead?" Emma hadn't known the woman well. When she met Simon their relationship had been fizzling, but she'd liked Laura well enough. She was a ballsy, hardworking woman who wouldn't take Simon's crap. They hadn't been able to make the love last.

"Yes." He laid another picture out in front of her. In this one, her face was in sharp focus as she pumped gas into Amanda's car. "Why were you at the scene?"

She opened and closed her mouth. How did she answer that and not implicate Jacob?

"Harold's neighbors also said you stopped by. Can you tell me why?"

Well shit. This was really bad.

She dug her nails into her palms. The truth was a flimsy foundation in this case. No matter what she said or did, it was going to look bad.

"I wanted to understand, okay?" She flipped the picture of her over as well, stacked the images together and shoved them at the agent. "I didn't do this, if that's what you're trying to say. I've lived with this nightmare my whole life, and some sick fuck wants to get his rocks off recreating the murders? I don't get it. I don't understand. I thought going there, seeing the crime scenes, might make me understand, but I don't. I can't get what makes someone kill another human being." She was yelling now.

"Do you know who these two are?" He pulled the last two images out of the stack and pushed them back toward her.

Had there been more deaths? Had someone else died? It hadn't hit the news yet.

"Christ. No. Shit." She shoved them away and stared at the wall.

"This is Amanda. I believe you're staying at her house and were driving her car yesterday. And this is Derrick. Am I to understand you broke up with him a few weeks ago?"

"What?" She gaped at the horrid pictures of her best friend and ex. "No, that's not true. You're lying." Her chest hurt. The muscles constricted so tight she couldn't breathe.

They were dead.

Amanda was gone. It was too much to take in. It couldn't be true. There was no way Amanda could be gone.

"Emma, where were you the last few nights?"

His words began to register and she stared at him. Was he serious? Did he think she would do something like this?

FUCK.

Jacob turned to the chief and agents lined up, watching Emma getting grilled. He'd been left out of the loop on this plan. Did they know he was involved with her? Were they keeping this suspicion from anyone local?

"Sir?"

"Not now, Payton." The chief waved him away.

"Sir—"

"Not now. She might be our killer." His mouth was set into a hard line. And why not? He'd been the arresting officer when Emma was taken into custody for her DUI.

"I didn't do it." Emma's voice was thin and high over the intercom. Everyone was watching, hardly breathing.

He wasn't going to leave her in there to fend for herself when he knew good and fucking well he'd been with her at the time of at least two of the murders. Three, since the last one was a double.

Jacob stalked around to the door and yanked it open.

Brooks turned, scowling at him. "What's—"

"She couldn't have done it," he said, his gaze locking with Emma's tortured eyes.

"And that would be why, officer?" Brooks asked.

He could hear Stevenson swearing around the corner. Jacob could kiss this case goodbye.

"She was with me Friday and Saturday night." He grit his teeth. "I'm asking to be taken off the case. My involvement with Emma compromises my objectivity. Especially if you're considering her as a suspect, and I am her alibi."

"Jacob..." Emma stared at him, her beautiful smile nowhere to be seen.

"I'm at a loss for what to think here, Detective." Brooks spread his hands. "Would you enlighten me?"

"Yes, sir."

He grabbed a chair from the corner and dragged it to the table, keeping his gaze away from the window. Sure, he couldn't see the people on the other side, but he knew they were there. He could feel the weight of their stares. To them, he'd made an error of judgment, but he didn't regret it. There was nothing about his time with her to regret.

He cleared his throat and settled at the corner, near enough to Emma. "Thursday night—"

"This last Thursday? The night Harold was killed?" Brooks asked. His pen hovered over the pad of paper, his gaze locked on Jacob's face.

"Yes, this last Thursday night I had arranged to meet up with Emma to discuss the original TBK case. Like I told you, she has a number of documents that were never handed over to the police. I wanted to see them so I could get a feel for what had been sent to me and how to gauge the severity of what we might be dealing with. Emma and I had dinner around seven. We were at the restaurant until almost nine. The coroner puts Harold's death between nine and nine thirty. There is no way Emma could have crossed the city that fast and committed the crime before the time of death, even allowing for a margin of error."

"What if she drove really fast?"

"Agent, please." Jacob shook his head. "Emma is a strong woman, but the person we're looking for has to have more muscle than she does. In order to create the kind of damage to the bodies she'd have to use heavier weapons, not to mention stand on top of something to get the right swing for impact we saw with the blood splatter. At best guess our suspect is around five eleven to six three. Emma, what are you?"

"Five seven," she replied.

"See? She's not tall enough."

"And the last two night's murders?" Brook's gaze flicked between the two of them.

Jacob licked his lips. "She was with me. Both nights. We're...involved."

"Fuck." Brooks scrubbed his face.

"I realize that my relationship with Emma has compromised me, and I willingly take myself off the case." It hurt saying those words, but they needed to be said. The FBI was leaps and bounds ahead of his ability to catch this killer, but his gut said Emma would be involved at some point, if she weren't already. He didn't have anything to go on at this point except a feeling.

Someone knocked on the door.

Jade leaned in, her face even paler than normal. "You're going to want to see this."

They left the interrogation room, nearly scrambling for the door. One of the other agents had a flat screen turned on, but they weren't looking at the news coverage. They were getting the direct camera feed from what looked to be the mobile bomb unit's robot. The arms moved in slow, smooth motions, peeling the brown paper back from a box.

"What happened?" Emma asked.

Jade gestured to the screen. "Someone dropped this box in the courtyard in front of the courthouse. They've cleared the area, evacuated the buildings, and sent in both the robot and a bomb tech."

"When did this happen?" Brooks asked.

"A little bit before she got here." Jade nodded toward Emma.

"Did they take x-rays? What did they show?" Brooks asked.

"Yeah, the tech had an x-ray machine. Pipes. Some wires. That's it." Mullins shrugged.

A killer and now a bomb threat. Just what they needed.

It was a bold, ballsy move.

"What are the chances this is connected?" Brooks asked.

"It would be another alteration in the MO," Jade said.

"TBK left a victim at the courthouse," Emma said, and the room stilled. She blinked at the sudden attention, but didn't cower or try to hide. Instead she stood a little straighter. She knew her shit, and he was proud of the way she pulled herself together.

"Gideon Cross—TBK killed him at his home, but when no one found him in a week, he got the body and dumped it in front of the courthouse with a note nailed to the man's throat." She gestured at the screen. "From the newspaper clippings, I'd say it's about where that box is now."

"Someone identified his car. That was the lead police needed to figure him out," Jade chimed in. The two women studied each other. Sizing the other up, maybe?

"This could be TBKiller's version of Gideon Cross?" Jacob asked.

Emma shook her head. "It's too soon. There's at least four more killings between this one and Gideon's."

Jade held up her hand, like a kid in class. "His MO is changing. We don't know exactly what he will do. It's obvious from the lack of preparation last night that he's off his plan."

"Uh, he'll kill people. That's what the sick fuck does." Emma stared at the redhead, and Jade stared back.

"Look." Mullins elbowed Jade as the package was opened.

Jacob settled his hand at the small of Emma's back. A small touch, but it put him more at ease. Hell, after the scene this morning he could shut himself up far away from everyone. People were horrible creatures sometimes.

The black and white camera feed showed two unconnected pipes and a coil of wire shoved into the bottom of the box. No charge. No detonator. Not even any explosive material of any kind. This wasn't a bomb at all.

"Is that paper rolled up in the middle?" Jacob asked. He pointed at the white cylinder on the screen.

"I want to know what it says," Brooks said. He stalked through the office. Some of the agents followed him, others scattered.

I killed them, was printed in large, block letters against an image of two people in chairs. The overlaying images were too distorted to make out more. Fuck, he wanted to stay on this case, to understand and really know what was going on.

Emma turned toward him. "What now?"

He shrugged. "I'm off the case."

"No, you can't be. If we stop seeing each other—"

"Don't even say that." He snapped more than he meant it, but he couldn't help a surge of possessiveness. She wasn't about to get rid of him that easy. "Besides, that's not how this works."

"Okay, it was an idea. I mean, if we weren't...whatever we are, you could still be on the case, right?"

"No, it doesn't work like that. My personal involvement with you skews my objectivity on this whole case."

"I'm sorry." She grimaced.

"What for?"

"If I'd told you no, you'd still be on the case."

"Yeah, don't worry about it." He didn't consider himself off the case. There was more than one way to tackle a problem. Besides, he wasn't sure he'd do anything differently given the opportunity. Emma was a special kind of woman. The type that didn't come along too often in a person's life. His mother had taught him that much growing up. He wasn't likely to let her walk out of his life.

"But—this is the case your dad worked on." She gestured to the conference rooms where they could see the boards with the victim's information and a timeline set up. "It's important to you."

"And we'll still catch him. I won't be an arresting officer. Do me a favor will you?"

"Hm?"

"Go get your stuff together in the interrogation room. I'm going to stick close to you until they catch him, okay?"

"Why?" She frowned. "Do you still think he might come after me?"

"Maybe."

"Maybe? That's it?"

"Yeah."

"Fine." She frowned, not that he expected her to like his decision.

Jacob followed in the wake of the agents and found Brooks with Stevenson. They had a radio between them. Jacob approached slowly and strained to hear what they were listening to, but it appeared to be over.

"Thanks for that. Bring the letter up here as soon as you clear it," Stevenson said in reply to whatever they'd been told.

"Another letter?" Jacob asked Brooks.

"Yeah, they're gathering all the security camera feeds now. Someone must have gotten a shot of this guy." Brooks handed the radio off to Mullins. "We're going to get him. Hey Mullins, call Lali and get her on this footage, now."

"What color is it?" Jacob asked before Brooks could walk away.

"They didn't say. Why? Got another theory, Detective?" It was a little unnerving to have the agent listen to what Jacob said so intently. Miller usually had one ear on the phone or hands on his keyboard when Jacob spitballed theories at him.

Jacob licked his lips and pressed on. "The letters I received were red. The second victim's were orange and the third yellow."

"It's a god damned color wheel." Brooks slapped Jacob on the shoulder like he did his agents. "Good eye."

Brooks called to two of his people and headed back toward the conference rooms, no doubt to work the new angles.

Stevenson turned toward him, the shuttered expression not boding well.

"Sir, I can—"

"I don't have time for excuses." Stevenson held up his hand. "You're off the case, but you already knew that."

"Officially, yeah. I understand. I want permission to take a few days off so I can watch Emma. I really think she's going to be a target."

"Then put her in—"

"She won't go. Plus, if I'm there, and we make sure a patrol comes by every half hour, maybe we'll catch him. I can put this time to good use, going over what she knows of the first victims. We can profile them. I think this is an idea with merit."

Stevenson's lips were tightly compressed. "Is being with her in your best interest, son?"

Jacob shrugged. "You have a problem with her?"

Stevenson glanced away and sighed. "Your dad and I kept an eye on the Ration boy. He was never right after what happened to his parents."

"She's different."

"I hope she is. For your sake. Let me know if you find a connection, but you're doing this on your own time. I'm putting you on leave immediately. Have you heard from Freeman?"

"No, why?" Jacob wasn't all that close with his new partner, but he would have expected the man to be back soon.

"While Miller is on administrative leave, I'm handling Homicide personally. Freeman should have been back this morning, but he hasn't reported for duty."

"Want me to swing by his place? Check on him? I thought he was going to be out longer."

"He was, but plans changed. Now I can't get hold of him, and we need everyone we can get here. I'll have patrol check on him. Maybe plans changed again." He slapped Jacob on the shoulder. "Keep me updated."

"Yes, sir."

Now, to protect a woman who wouldn't want to be protected.

JADE SHOOK HER HEAD and repeated herself for at least the tenth time. "She's not our suspect."

"You don't know that." Mullins paced the room, back and forth.

Why was it he always second-guessed her? Mullins was a damn good agent, but he could be an obnoxious prick sometimes. She gritted her teeth and waited for one of the other men to chime in and validate her theory, since that was the only way Mullins would ever believe her.

Brooks had warned her before joining the BAU that it was the ultimate men's club. Besides support staff like their tech, Lali, there were only two female field agents. Half the other agents took her as a joke, what with her history, despite her resumé and exemplary marks at the academy.

"What if they're doing this all together? Payton and Ration?" Mullins wheeled around. The man was really grasping at straws if he was even thinking about suggesting Detective Payton as a suspect. "They're each other's alibi."

"Connor," Brooks barked at Mullins. "Knock it off."

Jade opened her mouth to point out the obvious, but thought better of it. Connor Mullins' track record with questionable women was long and legendary. It was no wonder the man was a jaded jerk. He was a good agent, but even he had his flaws.

"It makes for good fiction, man, but Payton and the girl, this ain't them." Dmitri Abraham rose and stretched, tossing a wink her way when no one was looking.

Jade frowned, but he only smiled wider at her. She'd asked him to stop doing that. Flirting, even if it was for fun, was highly unprofessional, and it was hard enough for the boys in the club to take her seriously. She didn't need rumors that she was dating one of her unit members to complicate things further.

"Perez, take us through the profile, please," Brooks asked.

She nodded and cleared her throat. "We're looking for a young, white male, approximately six feet in height with an athletic build. He's artistic, but not as educated as TBK. After evaluating his grammar usage and lack of punctuation, he probably did not graduate high school. He's picking victims that are similar to those of the original murders, but so far there isn't a solid enough connection between the four."

"Except for Emma," Mullins interjected.

"She spoke with the first victim once. That's a pretty flimsy connection," she replied.

"It still counts."

She sighed.

"Fine, one possible connection is Emma. There's motive for Emma to be the killer on the last murder, but not on the first two. Besides, she doesn't fit the victimology. TBK never killed any single, white females. He targeted either family units or people on the fringes of society, and even then those were crimes of opportunity."

"Enough. Mullins, Abraham, I want you to go back to Harold's house and talk to his neighbors. See if you can get a better description of the mailman. He's our best target right now."

"Yes, sir." Mullins pivoted and walked out of the room, followed by a more relaxed Abraham.

Jade sighed and let her shoulders fall.

"Don't let him get under your skin," Brooks said, though he hadn't glanced at her once.

"Maybe I should be moved to a different unit." She didn't want to, but having Mullins constantly second guessing her was exhausting. It wasn't enough for her to know the cases forward and backward, she had to anticipate questions or she simply wasn't pulling her weight.

"I wouldn't recommend it. You fit here."

"Do I?" She turned toward the pictures of the victims, but it wasn't TBK's she saw.

"It's not hereditary. You can't catch it." Brooks spoke quietly, as if he sensed she wasn't quite there with him.

"I tell myself that every day, but it doesn't change the fact that sometimes I wonder if it is." She shrugged and turned away before she saw too much of her past on those walls. "I'm going to get some air, clear my head."

She didn't flee from the homicide department, but she kept her eyes on the ground and didn't acknowledge anyone else as she headed outside. The sweltering Oklahoma heat wrapped around her lungs, soaking up every bit of moisture in her skin. If she wasn't careful, she'd burn in a few minutes, but she didn't plan on staying out here long.

Detective Payton had marched into that interrogation room like a badge-wielding knight. Not quite the armor of dreams, but he hadn't flinched away from going to Emma's rescue.

Jade sat down on the stairs in a bit of shade cast by a tree and allowed herself to wallow for a moment. No one could love a person with her past. She wasn't even sure if she was capable of expressing love. It wasn't as if anyone had ever demonstrated the emotion to her personally. But she knew it when she saw it. Like Jacob and Emma. The signs were all there. As a profiler she picked up on the clues. The way Payton had moved to put himself between Emma and Brooks. How he'd given her his left hand, keeping his dominant right free to ward off a threat. And Emma had bent to Jacob's direction when Jade didn't think the woman was used to taking orders at all.

Did they know?

Probably not. Emma was an independent woman who would turn a blind eye on her feelings until she was smacked in the face with reality. Jacob, on the other hand, she was willing to bet was closer to accepting it. He'd given up the case of a lifetime to become her fierce protector. The only person who'd ever tried to protect *her* was a child services representative, and Brooks to a lesser degree.

Jade allowed her attention to turn inward and prodded the cold, dark corners of her mind. Brooks always said that killers chose their path, but was he right? What if her fate was written in her genetics? What if she was born to be like her parents?

EMMA PULLED UP AT Amanda's duplex and stared hard at the little two-toned green house with its red door. She'd been friends with Amanda for years. Once, ages ago, Amanda dated a guy on Emma's race team. They'd broken up, but Emma and Amanda had clicked. Since it was hard enough to find other women she liked, Emma had gone after that friendship. It had been easy to have fun with Amanda. How had it come to this?

The idea that both Amanda and Derrick were dead made her numb on the inside. She hadn't been able to process it or think through what that meant. How long had they been together?

A patrol officer knocked on her driver's side window, startling her.

Emma shook her head and opened the door.

"Yes, officer?" She grabbed her purse and paused, perched on the driver's seat.

"Chief said you were on your way, ma'am. I'm to escort you inside."

"And what then?" She arched her brow at the man. If they thought they were going to keep her out of the house, then they had another thing coming to them.

"Your safety, ma'am."

"Fine, whatever, come on." She rolled her eyes and slid out of the truck, dragging the box after her.

Emma unlocked the house and pushed the door inward. She paused on the stoop, almost expecting to see Amanda pop out from her room, a smile on her face and the scrub set of the day still on. But she'd never be there for Emma again.

"Ma'am, would you like me to check the house first?" the officer asked.

"No, thanks." She shut the door in his face.

The stillness of the duplex settled around her.

Amanda had asked her before she left to visit family if she wanted the move-in to be official. Emma hadn't been ready to make a decision, and they'd put it off until next week. She'd shifted so much of her life into Derrick's crappy trailer, but at least there she had the big backyard lot to work in. Here, she'd have to get a studio space, and that was a whole other set of costs. It was too much to think about, and she'd put it off.

Her mind circled around the fact that Amanda was gone, but refused to accept it. It couldn't be true. There was no way Amanda could really be gone. This wasn't happening.

Emma put her purse down next to the door and toed her shoes off, like Amanda would have wanted. Emma sighed, shoving her hands through her hair, and wandered into the living room.

Something was wrong.

She glanced around, sure that something had been moved, but she couldn't put her finger on it. She went to put her cell phone on the coffee table, and that's when she saw it.

The coffee table was completely cleared of knickknacks. The candles were gone, the bowl of pointless gold balls cleared away. A single sheet of red paper lay on the glass surface.

I did it for you.

She read the single sentence over and over again.

For her?

She'd never have done that to Amanda or Derrick. The idea that their death was in some way a gift to her was ridiculous and offensive. Anger boiled in her stomach, so bitter and vile it burned the back of her throat. She grabbed the paper and ripped it to shreds, a deep, tortured growl rising up out of her as the bits of paper fluttered around her.

"Where are you?" she yelled.

Emma stalked into Amanda's bedroom, but no one was there. She went into the bathroom they shared, and still no sign of a trespasser. Emma's room, it was impossible to tell. She hadn't exactly been keeping things as tidy and neat as Amanda. Emma's clothes were in a pile on the floor until she got hangers. Most of her things were in boxes or a few suitcases.

"Emma?" Jacob knocked on the front door as it creaked open. "Emma, you okay?"

"Yeah." She scrubbed at her face.

The letter.

Fuck.

She scurried back into the living room, her heart throbbing in her throat.

Jacob knelt over the shredded mess of the letter, a piece of twisted paper in his hand.

"Why didn't you call me?" he asked, voice hard.

"It was just there," she blurted.

"Okay." He held up his hand and pulled his cell phone out with the other. He snapped a few pictures, no doubt sending those off to his FBI friends, who would now be completely up her ass. Just what she needed. They'd probably say she did it herself.

Jacob got to his feet and closed the distance between them. He cupped her shoulders and peered into her eyes. What did he see in her?

"I should have called you, I know." She pushed his hands away, needing space. All these people were starting to suffocate her.

"Yes, but that wasn't what I was going to say." His expression was unreadable. Solid stone.

"Then what? What do you want to say to me?"

He licked his lips, brow drawn down, and his blue eyes darker than normal.

"I was going to say it's okay to be angry. Your friend is dead, she might have been cheating with Derrick while you were with your ex, and you got accused of being their murderer all in about half an hour. Now this." He thumbed at the letter she'd foolishly left lying around.

"I am angry." She pointed at the letter. "I'm angry at him."

It was hard to breathe. She gasped and her eyes prickled. Oh fuck, was she crying, too? This TBKiller had killed too close to home, and he thought he was doing it for her? Emma could take care of her own problems. So what if Amanda wanted to fuck Derrick? She could have handled that, or at least ignored it. Her one true friend was now dead.

Her legs gave way and she sat down heavy on the tile floor.

"Go on, cry it out," Jacob muttered.

He folded his body around hers, pulling her against his chest and rocked her from side to side. She leaned back, resting her cheek on his shoulder.

"I want him dead," she said between sobs.

"Me, too. Me, too." He kissed the side of her head.

Did he really? Did he really get it?

In all the world, he was the only person who might understand the torment her soul went through, and even then she didn't know if he really understood. Maybe no one ever would.

8.

JACOB LEFT EMMA DOZING in her room. He cracked the door so he could check in on her without disturbing her.

He couldn't imagine the kind of torment she must be going through. She was holding it together well enough. At least she wasn't afraid, though once the anger burned out of her she might be.

His phone vibrated, right on time.

Jacob tip-toed barefoot through the living room, scooping up the clear plastic gallon-sized bag he'd gathered all the paper bits into and his boots. He let himself out of the house and found himself face to face with Special Agent Mullins.

"How's she doing?" The agent slid his phone into his trouser pocket.

"Sleeping." He handed the letter over. "I pieced the words together. It says, 'I did it for you.'"

"Damn." Mullins thumped the plastic with his finger. "Your little lady might still be connected, then?"

Jacob shrugged. He'd never doubted Emma's potential as a target in all of this. What he wouldn't give to have been wrong this once.

"Brooks is going to insist on some sort of protective custody, or at least a detail. Stevenson said you didn't think she'd go for it—"

"Which is why I requested leave to stick close to her."

"You're both targets, then. You realize that?" Mullins' gaze narrowed.

"Maybe. Nothing he's said to me has indicated I'm a target."

"And her?"

"If he killed for her, it doesn't make a lot of sense that he'd kill her, unless there's something about him none of us are seeing."

"I study these fuckers all the time, and they always find a new, twisted view of the world." Mullins shrugged.

Jacob couldn't deny that. He'd seen enough working as a detective to have some idea of what the BAU must see.

"Can I offer you a word of advice? Job aside, I mean." Mullins' lips compressed into a tight line.

"Sure." Jacob didn't think he'd like what Mullins had to say.

"Be careful with her. Back home, I was involved with a woman who was connected to a case I was working for Interpol. Let's say it didn't go so well for either of us. Men in our position, we want to protect people, but we can't. Not always. Some are determined to stare death in the face." Mullins shook his head.

"Is she alive? The woman you were with?"

"Yeah." Mullins smile was forced. "She's got ten more years in an iron box."

"Sorry to hear that."

"I'm not." He shrugged. "I put her there. Watch your back, man."

Mullins took two steps backward before pivoting to stroll down the drive toward a waiting car.

Jacob watched them drive away, rolling Mullins' words around in his head. Whatever the agent had gone through was different than what was between Jacob and Emma. She wasn't a killer. She was a victim.

He slipped his shoes on and walked around the side of the duplex. The family sharing the other half of the house had packed up for a road trip and left, according to Emma. Which meant the suspect had practically no chance of being caught when he broke into the house.

The front door hadn't shown any evidence of being tampered with, and according to Emma, the letter hadn't been there when she'd left for the station. Which meant there was a good chance their killer had dumped the fake bomb at the courtyard and then come straight here to deliver his note. There were so many pieces, but none of them fit together. What was he doing with the eyes? Why the color-coded letters? Whose finger was sent to them?

With Emma settled for a bit, Jacob slowly searched around the exterior of the house. Officers had already been over it, but he wouldn't rest until he'd looked at everything himself. He pushed at each window, trying to pry them open. Even the back door showed no scratches from a lock pick. It was as if the killer had simply spirited the letter inside, except Jacob didn't believe in supernatural powers. Their murderer was flesh and blood.

Once Jacob had exhausted his search outside, he returned indoors and found Emma awake and out of bed.

"I called Simon." Emma sat on the couch, knees up against her chest and the TV on the local news.

"How is he?"

"Upset." Her gaze rose to his face. "Where were you?"

"Outside."

"Find anything?" There was a disturbing lack of emotion in her voice.

"No." He kicked off his shoes and joined her on the couch. The station seemed to have put together a quick history of TBK. It wasn't a lesson either of them needed. "Let's watch something else."

He took the remote from her and flipped channels.

"It's on every one of them. I already looked. Either they're talking about TBK, or the copycat. They didn't even pick a good picture of Amanda." She slumped back against the cushions.

"Do you want to talk about it?"

"Who taught you that line?" She snorted.

"My mom." He shrugged and rubbed her thigh.

"Smart woman."

"She told me girls like to talk."

"Good advice."

"My mom's pretty smart."

"Have you told her about this stuff?" She flicked her fingers toward the TV.

"Nah, Mom avoids the news. Always did. She never liked knowing what dad might be doing, if he was hurt. Once when I was a kid, a cop was shot. Mom was friends with the wife. They were having coffee one afternoon, and the news came on. That's how she found out her husband died. After that, Mom stopped watching the news."

"That's fucked up."

"Yeah." He reached for her hand and squeezed. "Talk to me?"

He wanted to make things better for her. To lift some of the burden from her shoulders, but he couldn't. Not unless she let him.

"I keep thinking I should be angry at Derrick and Amanda, but I'm not. I miss her already." She sighed. "Derrick was a waste of my time. I knew that when we got together, but I was so lonely I was okay being with him. He was a useless tool bag, but I learned a lot about myself being with him. I learned that I like myself. That I have more drive and ambition than I realized. I realized I wanted more. But I was too scared of being alone to leave him sooner, even though we were over ages ago. I don't know if that makes me a bad person or not."

"No. We all crave human connection." He tamped down on his jealousy. This wasn't about him—it was about what she needed.

Emma rolled her eyes and laced their fingers together.

"Just so you know, Derrick and I hadn't slept together in the same room in... a long time. Like I said, it was way over. I knew he was cheating, and I used it as an excuse to motivate myself into moving out. I really don't care if Amanda and Derrick were together. I don't understand them as a couple. She's way too fucking smart for someone like him, but who am I to judge?" She glanced at him and then away, her lower lip caught between her teeth.

"What's wrong?"

"Nothing. Thinking."

"About?"

"Dinner."

She was lying, but he couldn't push her. Not when she was trying so hard to hold herself together.

He could guess what she was thinking. She was drawing parallels between Amanda and Derrick to them. But she was so much more than she realized. She really sold herself short.

"Okay. Dinner. What do you want?" he asked.

"Aren't you going home?"

"No. I'm staying here. With you. Until this whole thing blows over."

"You don't have to."

"No, I don't. But I will."

"What if I kick you out?"

"You won't."

"You're pretty sure of yourself."

He leaned in close, breathing in her scent and losing himself in the chocolate brown of her eyes.

"I am. Don't kick me out, okay?"

Her gaze dropped to his mouth. He was pretty sure she hadn't heard what he'd said.

Jacob brushed his mouth across hers once, twice. The stiffness in her body eased and she brought her free hand up, cupping the back of his head. She pressed him closer and he sank into the kiss.

He'd protect her with his life if he had to. It was a truth that should scare him, but it only made him all the more ready to accept his feelings toward her. She wasn't someone who shared a history with him. She wasn't just a hot chick who understood him. Emma was a woman he could spend the rest of his life getting to know. She'd always keep him on his toes.

Was this love? He didn't know. But he'd hang around to find out, because things like this only came around once in a lifetime.

EMMA SPEARED A POT-STICKER on her chopstick and nibbled on the edges. Jacob sat on the other end of the couch, pretending as if his food were the most interesting thing in the world.

He'd been so...respectful and distant since her little breakdown earlier. She wanted to shake a real reaction out of him. It seemed as if the only time she saw true emotion from him was when he was pissed off or having sex. It was frustrating to see him so tightly contained and bottled up. She wanted to shake him up a bit, to find out what would happen.

She cleared her throat and turned to face him with her legs crossed, the TV muted. He glanced at her, but his gaze quickly flitted away.

"What about the letter from earlier? What does it mean?" she asked.

He shrugged and finished chewing his food.

"Are you sure you haven't seen anyone? No one's been bothering you?" Jacob watched her, one side of his mouth screwed up.

"I haven't seen anyone, but I have felt like someone was watching me."

"Pay attention to your gut. It's not scientific, I know, but we have instincts for a reason. You feel like someone's watching, call me, okay?"

Well, that was incredibly reasonable of him.

"So..." She pushed her food around her plate. "That wasn't the first letter he sent me."

Jacob's hand hovered above his dinner, poised to stab a piece of beef. He did that thing where he stared straight through her. She couldn't read him at all, except this time her skin was crawling and her lizard brain screamed *run!* She fidgeted with her chopsticks and dropped her gaze to the plate.

Maybe that was a bad way to poke the beast.

Jacob dropped his fork onto the plate with a clatter and *thunked* it down on the coffee table. He leaned back on the couch, rubbing his jaw. The rasp of his hand over his stubble was the loudest thing in the room.

Wasn't he going to say something? Anything?

"And that's what you're going to do? Give me the silent treatment?" she asked.

"I'm trying to understand why," he snapped. He turned enough to catch her gaze, and she almost wanted to crawl under the sofa.

Ah, there was that lick of rage, the fire in his eye.

"Why don't you ask me then?"

"Because I'm not sure I'd get a truthful answer."

"You're going to pretend as if knowing me three—what? Four days? Makes you an expert on me?"

"No, but I know how liars operate." He stood and stalked across the living room to the door, pivoted and paced back again.

"Oh, low blow," she taunted. "I never lied. You never asked me if I'd received a letter."

Jacob stopped with the coffee table between them and spread his arms. "Omitting a crucial piece of evidence."

"Still not an outright lie." She pushed to her feet, unable to stay on the sofa when he was being so, so—stupid. Okay, so maybe she had been lying, but the man needed an emotional outlet about as much as she did right now. Picking a fight might not be the best way to hash things out, but here they were.

"Yeah? Then why didn't you mention it until now?" His voice rose and a vein stood out on his forehead.

"Because I knew if I told you, you'd pull back. You'd treat me with kid gloves. I wouldn't know jack shit about what was going on because I'd become a victim before anything ever happened to me. I didn't want you to look at me with pity. I didn't want to play into this fucker's games. He wants this to go a certain way, and I'm not going to do what he wants."

"You want him to kill you, is that it?"

She stalked around the table.

"No, that's not it." She planted her hands on her hips and glared at him.

"Then what did you want?"

"For you to feel something. You sit over there so tightly contained. You're a bottle about to blow, and it's not healthy. Be fucking pissed. Get angry at me—"

Jacob grasped her shoulders so tight she gasped and her pulse kicked up. For a split second she almost wanted to fight back, to get away. But all he did was hold her and stare deeply into her eyes.

"I am angry. I'm fucking pissed that you'd intentionally put your life in danger, and—I can't stay around here and watch you put yourself at risk if that's what you choose to do. I—I can't." He pried his hands off her and took a step back.

"I told you about the letter."

"Yeah, but what else haven't you told me about? Can I trust you?"

"Yes, okay?"

"But I don't know that, now." The torment was back in his gaze.

"I told you. I'm not hiding anything else."

"Yeah, and next time?"

"What did you tell me? Trust was blind faith, or something? What does your gut tell you? I was wrong to keep the letter from you, but I still barely knew you. How was I to know that as soon as you had that letter, you wouldn't—I don't know—drop me into a jail cell for my own protection? I'd die in there." She shuddered.

Jacob stared at her, but she couldn't tell anything from his gaze. The man was a freaking blank wall again. She threw up her hands. This was pointless. He'd never open up, really let her in. The few moments of vulnerability he'd shared were clearly the extent of his ability to connect.

"Whatever. Leave me alone." She headed toward her room, but he caught her by the wrist, stopping her in her tracks. "Let go."

"No."

"You don't get to tell me off and then hold onto me. It doesn't work like that." She twisted her arm, but his grip was solid.

"You frustrate me so much. I want to shake some sense into you."

"Yeah? Well you aren't the only one. You can be pretty pig-headed yourself."

"Just—stop, okay? Stop for a second?" He hung his head and slid his hand from her wrist to lace their fingers together. "You kept something important from me."

"I did. Angry about that?"

"Yeah, I'm fucking pissed," he parroted back once more.

"Well at least we know you can express your anger in a somewhat healthy manner. I don't think the stonewall thing or the whole silent treatment really do much for you, but this was better."

"Emma, what if this guy decided to kill you last night instead of Amanda? What then? Where would you be?"

"Well, either dead or in lock-up because I'd have killed his ass."

"There haven't been any defensive wounds on the victims. They don't get the chance to fight back. He gets them before they know he's there. He's either someone you know and trust, or he's that good at sneaking up on people undetected." His voice cracked as he spoke. Was that emotion she heard?

"I made the wrong choice." She shrugged. "I didn't know I could trust you then."

"And you do now?"

"Maybe. I can't tell with you sometimes. You're so closed off and distant it's hard to figure you out. Are you here because you feel obligated? Is it the sex? Do you need someone to be pissed at? Or is this a hero complex at work?"

"I'm here because yes, I want to protect you. I'm not obligated to be here. I could have sent patrol to babysit you, but I chose to come here personally. Because, maybe this is crazy, but I care about you."

"You have a fucked up way of showing it."

"Yeah, well, you're a hard woman to figure out."

"What's so hard? I like fast bikes, big trucks, barbecue, and sex. All I really know about you is that you love your family, you're a workaholic, and you've got some anger issues. That's not a lot to go on."

The muscle on his jaw twitched.

For several moments they stared at each other.

"I hate Chinese food."

Emma sputtered. That wasn't exactly what she'd been looking for.

"Well that's a start." She couldn't help cracking a smile, though he was still stone-faced.

"I like working with my hands. Brain teaser shit. Cooking. You."

Staring into his eyes, she had to wonder if she weren't in more danger from this man than the killer. She'd told herself this was a fling, but looking down the barrel of a determined detective, she wasn't so sure.

"I'm the daughter of a drunk and a thief, sister to a felon and a hero, and I've got my own record." She crossed her arms. "I'm not exactly an upstanding member of society."

He shrugged. "Who said I was looking for perfect? Perfect is hard to match."

What the hell was happening here?

Emma's heart raced and she shifted her weight from foot to foot. They'd gone from picking a fight to...whatever this was.

"Look, this is a bad time to get involved, and we did it anyway. We're going to catch TBKiller. After that, do you think we could maybe, get to know each other better?"

"Is this that date you promised me? I don't really think asking me out for work, then bringing me over to work out your anger issues really constitutes a first date."

Oh, what the hell. He'd wake up some day and realize she wasn't good enough for him, but until then she could care for him. Love him if he ever tore those walls down far enough.

"Yeah." Jacob chuckled. "What would you say to dinner and a movie? My treat."

"How generous of you, big spender." Emma's smile was back. It loosened the tightness in his chest. A look from her and he felt like things might be okay. He was a goner.

"Before we plan out our first date in too much detail, I think you have something you need to show me?"

She quirked a brow at him.

"You've already seen my boobs."

"Not that, though I won't tell you to keep them to yourself." He shook his head.

"You want the letter, don't you?"

"Yeah, I think our FBI friends would appreciate it."

"Fine. Give me a second?" She walked around him and to the laundry door.

He listened to the second door to the garage squeak. She must have left it in her truck. Sure enough, he heard the chirp of her truck lock before she returned to him, the letter in one of those plastic sleeves she liked to use.

"Here." She thrust it at him and he held it up to the light.

I see you.

I will finish what he began.

TBKiller

"When did you get this?" He frowned at the text.

"Friday night. It was in my truck. My spare key had been moved."

"Friday night? When you were at my house?" The copycat had been outside his house, while they'd been having dinner, or maybe even when they were having sex or sleeping.

"Yeah. And I know, I should have told you, but I didn't want to be shut out. It was stupid, don't say it."

TBKiller wasn't just flirting with him. Emma was involved all along. He wished he'd been wrong.

Emma not telling him was stupid. It was more than that. She was being irresponsible with her life. He inhaled deeply, the numbers one through ten racing through his mind. Someday that trick would work.

"Okay, I'm going to call Brooks and get this over to him. I'd like to go through the victimology of the original kills and the ones we've had so far, find the parallels." But most importantly, how they connected to Emma. Again. They'd already been over it once, but that was before he knew the killer had made contact.

She nodded and retrieved the box from her bedroom. He went outside and had to wait maybe a minute before a patrol car rolled by. A short phone call later, he had the letter on its way to the FBI.

He might be off the case, but that didn't mean his brain wasn't working out the problems still. By the time he entered the house once more, Emma had each victim's information sorted into different piles. Some were thicker than others.

"Okay, everything on the table is TBK. I've put out notepads for the new victims, one through four, and this," she held up a yellow legal pad, "is for future victims."

"Five. The finger. We still don't know who that is. All the ME can tell us is that it was removed postmortem. Also, you and I go on this list." He hated saying it, but they did have targets on them.

She merely nodded and jotted down their names.

"Five kills, three scenes we know about, one unknown. The unknown actually fits. There were a number of murders early on that we knew nothing about."

"Yeah, the question is where, and who is this person?"

She shrugged. "No idea. Can we match the images in the letters with the scenes?"

"Maybe." He jotted it down on a piece of paper he wanted to reserve for things they must tell Brooks.

"Okay, so the next murder will be a family of three, if he's still going by the book." Emma hugged the pad of paper to her chest. "I don't think I know any families of three."

"Derrick and Amanda weren't a couple. He improvised there. We can't rule out that he might look for a trio, people who live together kind of like a family unit, but aren't a traditional family."

"Like—three friends? Or a single mom, her kid and a friend?"

"Yes." Jacob paced up and down the kitchen, his mind racing.

"Simon lives with two of the guys." She shrugged. "A couple of my teammates have baby mommas, but they all have like, their kid plus another. I'm not close with them though. Shit."

"Hasn't anyone ever told them about condoms?"

"I know, right? God love them all."

"We need to make a list. All of them. He could kill tonight."

"Most everyone is out at the track." She shrugged. "He can't kill anyone I know tonight."

MAX SNORTED AS HE listened to the audio feed from Amanda's house. Detective Payton and Emma thought they could guess his next move? Well, they were wrong. He was miles ahead of him.

Pretty little Emma had a larger circle of friends than she even realized. By the time they were aware of their misstep, his work would be finished.

```
Black Widow: Iron?
```

"Fuck me." He scrubbed a hand over his face, willing the private chat box to go away.

```
Black Widow: Iron, you're uploading right
now. I know you're there.
Iron: Bathroom. Whats up?
Black Widow: Just wanted to check on you.
Black Widow: I've seen the news coverage out
of Oklahoma City.
Black Widow: You're creating quite the stir.
Iron: Yeah well its what he would have want-
ed.
Black Widow: Are you sticking to your plan?
Iron: For the most part.
Black Widow: Good.
Black Widow: Did you get the ID for Acid?
Iron: In the mail.
Black Widow: Good to hear that.
Black Widow: Remember I'm here to help you.
Black Widow: If you need anything, let me
know.
Iron: Will do.
```

```
Black Widow: Make sure your internet security
is up to date. Someone's looking for us.
Iron: Updated today.
Iron: Got to go.
Black Widow: Can't wait to see your next
work.
```

Max closed the window and shivered. He glanced in the mirror above his monitor to make sure there wasn't anyone behind him. Mirrors weren't just good decorating. If you hung them all over the place, you could see around corners, in blind spots. He still didn't think it would be enough to warn him before Black Widow got him.

The cops were too slow, too stupid to catch him.

Black Widow on the other hand, well, he was skirting her rules. He'd been part of the club long enough that he'd seen several members suddenly go missing. He wasn't stupid. His plan needed a certain level of flexibility, and they all evolved. He couldn't be the same TBK that he'd been thirty years ago. If he stayed a dinosaur, he'd go extinct, and his spirit was too strong for that. No, he'd survive.

He gathered the rest of his kit. With three victims, he was traveling heavy tonight. There was a lot to plan for. He needed the camera battery charged, a couple spare changes of clothes. Three bodies could bleed a lot, and he could never have enough duct tape.

With the kill kit ready to go, it was time to make the trek to his next location. One step closer to his ultimate goal.

```
FROM: BLACK WIDOW
To: Mercy
Subject: Your concerns.
```

Hello Mercy,

I've spent quite a good deal of time going over Iron's proposed plan and his portfolio of work. It's substantial, but I'm seeing several deviations from what he pitched to join the club. I no longer feel he is on board with our vision. Please continue to keep me in the loop with his communications to you. In the meantime, I will take care of the attention he's drawing and try to do some damage control. We want to complete our missions, not cause a stir. I know you understand.

If you have the time, I would appreciate a hand moving our servers and preparing the protocols. The new members haven't experienced a shift yet, and we need to make sure they understand the rules. I'd like to not have another Slade incident.

BW

EMMA MASSAGED HER TEMPLES. SCENE BREAK.

"Ugh, I'm exhausted. The words are all starting to blur together."

"Let's go to bed. It's been a long day." Jacob grasped her by the shoulders and pulled her against his chest.

"I feel like if I make one more list, I might understand it." She leaned into him, reveling in the feeling that they were working together on this.

They'd gone through every single file, listed all the details, and made profiles of possible victims. Jacob said it was an unusual way to work, but they had extraordinary circumstances. She couldn't shake the feeling they might stumble on a key that let them into the psyche of their killer. But it slipped away from her every time she almost grasped it.

"Nope. You are going to bed." He steered her away from the kitchen and toward her room.

She wanted to whine, to say no she couldn't, but exhaustion weighed her down. She allowed him to guide her into her bedroom, among all the boxes. She turned to him, studying his face. His features were softer, or maybe it was her imagination.

"Are you staying?" she asked.

"Do you want me to?"

Did she?

"I don't want to be alone." She wrapped her arms around him.

"You aren't alone. I'm here."

She stared at his chest. So far they'd burned up the sheets together. It was passion and immediate need. He wrapped his arms around her shoulders, tugging her close. She sighed and enjoyed the simple pleasure of his arms around her.

"How about you get ready for bed and I do a circuit around the house real quick?"

"Sounds good."

He padded out of the room and she went through the motions of her nightly routine, brushing her teeth, washing her face, and changing clothes. After everything today, she should feel more. Sadness. Remorse, maybe. Something except the numbness in her breast.

Jacob returned while she was still mulling her emotional state over in her head. She wasn't sure what she wanted right now, but whenever her gaze fell on the man stripping down to his boxers, well, she had a one-track mind. She might be uncertain about where things were going with him, but she knew what she wanted from him right now.

"Everything is quiet." He climbed into the bed next to her.

She didn't expect TBKiller to come for her, not tonight. Everything Jacob had said, it all pointed to finishing off the ritual with her death, maybe Jacob's involvement. Her knee-jerk fear was that this creep might get hold of her father. At least her brother was locked up tight in jail. It was about the only time she would ever be glad that he wasn't around.

"Come here." Jacob pulled her down to lay next to him, wrapping her in the comfort of his arms. But comfort wasn't what she wanted. He'd given her that all evening and look where that had gotten her—frustrated with herself.

"Jacob?" She bit her lip and peered up at him. He'd left the bathroom light on as well as the kitchen so they weren't really swathed in darkness.

"Hm?"

"Make me feel."

9.

EMMA STARED UP AT Jacob's face, cloaked in shadows. She wanted the numbness to go away. Was it wrong?

"What do you feel?" he asked.

She placed her hand against her chest.

"Dead inside. Nothing."

He muttered what might have been, "Oh, Ems," before rolling her to her back and settling over her.

"Whatever you need, I'm here for you," he whispered. He kissed her temple, her cheek, her jaw, everywhere except her mouth.

She dug her fingers into his hair and pulled him where she wanted him. His mouth on hers. She kissed him deeply, thrusting her tongue into his mouth, pressing as close as she could get and still be in her own body, but it wasn't close enough.

He cupped her face, swiping his thumbs over her cheeks with such tenderness. This big, tough man was capable of more than she knew. She relaxed, and he took over, easing back a bit. At least their noses weren't practically breaking on each other's cheekbones anymore. She felt more from that tender touch than she had all night. It was the way he lavished attention on her mouth. She shifted, restless, but he held her in place.

Why was it this man stirred such intense desire in her? It was too soon. They didn't know each other. And yet, this was where she wanted to be. Alive. Making love to a man who quietly made her want to be better. Worthy of him.

Jacob kissed his way down her neck, pausing to suck lightly at the sensitive juncture to her shoulder. She lifted her hips, grinding against him. He pushed her shirt up and lowered his weight onto her, restricting her movements.

She pulled her shirt up the rest of the way, wiggling it off until all she wore were her panties. He made an approving sound and palmed her breast. She arched her back and surrendered to the sensations assaulting her body. The sheets were cool, soft, and smelled faintly of lavender. The coarse hair on Jacob's chest and legs rubbed against her as he moved, and his stubble scraped the sensitive flesh of her breasts. Desire coiled tightly inside of her, driving out the last bit of her ability to form coherent thoughts.

She felt a hell of a lot now. There was nothing numb about what he did to her, how he made her feel.

Her focus was on his hands, the way he made it hard for her to breathe, and the pounding of her heart.

He pushed her breasts together and licked from one nipple to the next. She shivered and grasped the sheets. He rolled one stiff peak between his fingers while teasing the other with his tongue.

She almost wanted to push him over, shove a condom on that hard cock she could feel against her thigh, and ride him to climax. Almost, because he was showing her what else he had. They might not be afraid of playing it a little rough, but he was touching her in places unavailable to human hands. It felt as though he reached inside of her and hugged her heart.

"Jacob," she moaned.

"Hm?"

"I want you."

"You have me," he muttered against her skin. He switched breasts, content to go no faster.

She shifted her feet against the bed, trying and failing to lift him, move him, make him do something.

He took pity on her and slid his hand between their bodies, cupping her mound and giving her the desired pressure. She moved her hips, grinding against his palm. He shoved her panties aside, and as she shifted against him he thrust two fingers into her pussy.

She gasped and wrapped her arms around his neck.

He pumped his hand in and out while his mouth worked on her breast. She groaned and scraped her nails over his back. His shoulders tensed as she dug deep tracks, but he didn't relent in his slow, sensual assault on her body.

Jacob sat up suddenly, his erection tenting the front of his boxers. She could feel his gaze raking over her. The cool air tightened her damp breasts.

He grasped her panties and pulled them off.

Finally! Down to business.

She reached for his boxers, but he intercepted her hands, pushing them up over her head. He wedged his body between her legs, scooting farther down the bed until his face hovered above her mound. The light glinted off his eyes, and it felt as though he saw beyond her exterior. As if he recognized her fear and apprehension and met her, toe-to-toe. Or, face to pussy as the case were.

He lowered, and she shivered as his breath skated over her skin. Last time, she hadn't had the opportunity to feel nervous. But tonight, it was as if they were each stripped bare.

He wrapped his lips around her clit and sucked. The sensation of it shot straight to her toes. She reached above her and grasped the headboard, needing something to hold onto. He rubbed his tongue over the nub, sparking off a fresh wave of arousal.

Damn him, she didn't know if she wanted closer, or to get away.

She rubbed her feet back and forth on the mattress. He had her pinned way too well for her to move against him. Her channel clenched as he continued to torment her.

Her toes curled, her body tightened, and she groaned. Her abdomen tightened as pleasure danced over her extremities. The orgasm was sharp, short, and intense, rushing through her at full tilt. She gasped and blinked at the ceiling.

Jacob crawled up her body, dropping kisses on her hip, her stomach, ribs, between her breasts, and along her collar bone. She sucked in deep breaths, her head spinning from how fast that had happened. Despite the release, she wasn't sated. Not yet. She wanted more of him, as much as she could take.

Emma pointed toward a cardboard box. There were condoms there, but he ignored her and fished his jeans back onto the bed.

"I got my own this time." He chuckled.

She laughed and stretched, feeling the soreness in her body and loving it. Loving how he drove her crazy. Every brush against the sheets heightened her sensitivity.

Jacob returned to her, sliding between her thighs and hooking her knee over his arm. Their gazes locked and her lungs stopped working. It was as if she could see straight to his soul. He wasn't keeping her out, at least not now.

He positioned his cock at her entrance and thrust. He sank slowly into her, and it was more intense because she could see the way his features changed, how his nostrils flared and his cheeks sunk in the deeper he delved. Her insides quivered, and she swallowed a whimper.

Was she supposed to feel so emotionally raw?

He invaded her body, her heart, and filled her mind. He was all around her.

Jacob let his forehead drop until their noses bumped. He flexed his hips and sank the last little bit into her. She squeezed her internal muscles around him, and she felt him smile a little against her mouth. How she wanted to see that smile, soak it in.

She kissed him, needing more connection, more of whatever it was he was doing to her. She'd asked him to make her feel.

He shifted, hoisting her leg higher and opening her up to a deeper penetration, robbing her of thought, leaving her adrift in a sea of sensation. He rocked against her, stroking deep inside her channel, rubbing all those nerve endings and coiling her desire tighter.

Jacob levered up and began a slow, purposeful thrusting. She shifted against him, but he had all the power. Her orgasm, her body, and even her heart were at his mercy.

She felt his gaze on her, and she couldn't help but meet it. Her chest ached and her heart swelled, beating hard against her ribs as he continued pushing her onward.

He didn't speak, but he didn't have to. He saw her. All her flaws and her sordid history, and yet, he still wanted her. She'd have to trust that. Trust that this man would be there for her where all others had failed her.

She dug her nails into his shoulders and gasped. Her body rippled with orgasm— sharp, sweet and sudden. He continued thrusting, drawing the pleasure out. She raked her nails down his back, and he groaned. His thrusts were rough and short. He thrust once more and froze, features tense, mouth open. He blew out a breath and covered her, crushing her mouth to his.

He rolled them to their sides, pulling her close, and cuddled her without being asked to. He knew she needed the comfort. Neither of them spoke, and that was okay. She'd wanted to feel, but now, maybe she felt too deep. He did things to her, crazy, wonderful things that made no sense.

RHONDA PRESSED DIAL AGAIN ON HER CELL.

"Come on, already. Pick up the damn phone," she muttered.

Once more, the phone line went to the answering machine, and she rolled her eyes.

"Hey, it's me. I guess you left your cell phone at home when you picked Rachel up from work. They didn't have chocolate chip cookie dough, so since you weren't answering, I picked something else."

She ended the call and tossed the phone into the seat next to her. Going a half-hour without contact from her family shouldn't be a big deal. After all, she'd gone nearly a year without speaking to any of them, thanks to a real gem of an asshole boyfriend who had a degree in manipulation. She'd vowed to never let anyone come between her and her family again.

They'd planned to go out to a movie and have a real girl's night, but her little sister had been called into work at the local barbecue hangout. Rhonda and her mother had swung by for dinner, but it wasn't the same without Rachel at the table with them.

She pulled into the drive of their little brick house. Both cars were there, including Rachel's with the dead-as-a-doornail battery. It was all where it should be, and yet, something seemed off.

If Rachel and Mom were home, why were the lights off? And why weren't they answering?

She peered at the house.

No, she could see some light from inside. Was that the kitchen?

Her gut clenched and she twisted to survey the street. Had Frank followed her home? Was he here?

Frank said the moment the cops pulled him off her that he'd make her pay. She'd been so scared. One of the officers, a woman with kind eyes and a quick smile, had checked up on her a few times and told her to take martial arts classes. Rhonda had gone mostly to get out of her own head—and found she'd liked the discipline. Maybe it was her imagination, but she felt more confident and capable for working her way through the programs. She'd become something of a dojo junkie.

She wasn't going to ignore her instincts.

Rhonda left the ice cream in her car and crept to the side of the garage. The door was busted so she couldn't get in through the laundry room, but that was okay. There was always the glass sliding door to the kitchen. Besides, with her luck Mom and Rachel were in the kitchen pigging out on whatever was leftover from the restaurant and this wasn't an emergency at all, just her overactive imagination.

She reached the door and peered into the bright country kitchen.

Nothing.

In fact, if she peered through the kitchen over the bar, she could make out their heads resting against the back of the couch as they watched TV.

Well now, didn't she feel stupid?

Rhonda shook her head and mentally kicked herself. Her paranoia bit hard sometimes. She went back to the car and snagged the ice cream, vowing to keep her delusions to herself.

Frank was not out to get her.

They were safe and sound.

She opened the front door, suppressing her annoyance that it wasn't locked. Between Frank and the serial killer the news was going on about, you'd think they would exercise a little caution.

"Hey, what's up with not answering the phone?" she called out as she flicked the locks into place.

Shit, the TV was loud. No wonder they hadn't heard. They could probably barely hear themselves think.

Rhonda headed toward the kitchen, still unable to shake the sense that something was amiss.

A shadow moved in Rachel's room on her left. Rhonda stopped as the shadow seemed to peel off the wall and become a person. Fear immobilized her for a second, but then her self-defense training took over.

"Mom, Rachel, call 9-1-1," she yelled, but they didn't move.

The man rushed her, something in his hand.

Rhonda didn't think. She reacted. She threw the gallon of ice cream at her attacker. It hit him square in the face, knocking him off his stride for a second.

A second was all she needed.

She didn't care if this was Frank, her father come back from whatever hellhole he'd crawled into, or anyone else. No one threatened her or her family. No one.

She rushed the attacker, grabbing the wrist of the hand with the weapon, and kicked his legs out from under him. He went down like a sack of potatoes, and she came down on top of him. She punched with everything she had, aiming for the face, the throat. Her knuckles and hands hurt, but she pushed that aside. Frank had taught her that, at least.

Her attacker thrashed, his arms flailing.

Plastic rattled, and the cold, heavy weight of the ice cream smacked her in the kidney, paralyzing her for a split second.

He pushed her off, kicking and throwing random objects at her. She grabbed the weapon he had—a sledgehammer, by the weight of it—and screamed. For a brief second she glimpsed his face, illuminated by the kitchen light.

Fuck, he was practically a kid.

She hefted the weapon and ran after him, but he was already scrambling to get the locks open. He sprinted down the driveway before she could get her hands on him again. She shoved the door shut and locked it, pulse racing and her body shaking.

Oh, shit. Oh, shit. Oh, shit.

Had that really happened?

The pounding in her hand, the jarred feeling in her elbow and shoulder, they all said yes.

"Mom? Rachel?" She ran into the living room, her heart in her throat.

Both women sat bound and gagged on the sofa, their eyes wide and murmurs drowned out by the TV.

"Oh my God. Oh my God."

The shaking was bad now. She looked around for something to cut them free. She needed to call 9-1-1. She needed to untie them.

"I'm going to get help. I'll get you out of that." Rhonda grabbed her cell phone from her pocket and punched in those three digits. She rushed to the kitchen, yanking open drawers she knew didn't have knives or scissors in them. She couldn't think. Couldn't process. Couldn't remember which damn drawer they were in.

"9-1-1, what is your emergency?"

"Hi, my name is Rhonda. Someone was in our house when I got home. He had my mom and sister tied up and he attacked me."

"Is he there now?"

"No, no, I scared him off. I think it was the guy who was on the news. Please, we need help." She rattled off her address to the woman and answered her questions as best she could.

Ah-ha!

She found the scissors exactly where they should be, in the junk drawer.

Rhonda flipped on all the lights, taking some comfort in chasing away the shadows.

"I'm going to get you out of this," she said to her mother and sister. The operator was still talking to her in such a frustratingly calm and composed manner. Didn't the woman understand what was going on here?

She put the phone on speaker and tossed it on the empty cushion next to her mother. The first thing she cut off was the tape over her mouth.

"Oh my God, is he gone?" Her mother gasped, tears running down her cheeks.

"Yeah, he's gone. Cops are on their way."

"Rhonda, Rhonda, is your mother okay?" the operator asked.

"I think so," Rhonda replied.

She cut her sister's gag off next. If anything, Rachel seemed pissed as hell rather than scared.

"I need to call Emma," Rachel said, wiggling in her bonds.

"Call her later," Rhonda said as she started in on the bonds holding her sister's arms to her sides. Couldn't she let her little high school friends *be* for a few minutes? Did she have to update the whole world?

"No, he said he was going after her next. I need to call Emma!"

EMMA GROANED AND SNUGGLED farther into the warmth wrapped around her. She'd just gone to sleep. Couldn't her alarm wait a little while longer?

"Ems," Jacob muttered, pushing at her shoulder.

"What?" She buried her face against his shoulder.

"It's your phone." From the sound of it, he wasn't actually awake.

She sighed and rolled over, peering at the clock with one eye.

Midnight.

Whoever was on the other end of this call was dead meat.

The phone flashed Rachel Land's name.

The teenage hostess at the barbecue place? Emma had given her a ride to work a few times. She hadn't realized the girl's number was still in her phone.

"Hello?"

"Emma! Thank God." The girl on the other end sobbed into the phone.

"Rachel? What's wrong?" Emma sat up, tossing the covers back.

Jacob's phone blared like a siren from the pile of clothes still on the floor. She glanced over her shoulder, a sense of dread settling in her stomach.

"He said he was going to come after you. Get out! Get someplace safe." Rachel continued to sob. There were other voices. Female?

"Rachel? Rachel, where are you? Are you okay? Are you hurt? I'll come and get you." Emma got up and started grabbing for her clothes. Jacob retreated to the living room to answer his call. What were the chances this was a coincidence?

"I'm at home. Mom and I got here and there was a man. He hit Mom and knocked her out, and then he tied me up. He kept saying it was for you. It was crazy!" Rachel continued to babble, but she wasn't making a lot of sense.

Jacob came around the bed, his face half in shadow, but what she could see didn't make her feel any better.

"Rachel, hold on a second, okay?" She put her hand over the phone. "What?"

"Rachel Land?" he asked.

Emma nodded.

"Looks like Rachel's sister chased away the TBKiller. They want us to stay put." He didn't seem too happy with the decision.

"Hey Rachel?"

"Yeah?" Rachel sniffled.

"Are the cops there?"

"They just got here. Emma, are you okay?"

"I'm fine. I've got cops here with me, too. I'm going to be okay. Will you call me later? Let me know you're all right?" Emma wanted to go there now, but that wasn't going to fly. She hung up with Rachel and wrapped her arms around herself.

Was this really all connected to her?

"How's she doing?" Jacob asked.

"Scared, but I don't think she's hurt. What about the rest of them?"

"No idea, patrol was just getting on the scene."

"What—what are we supposed to do?"

Somehow, this whole thing was her fault. Guilt wrapped around her, nearly suffocating her. What could she have done differently? Anything at all?

"Hey." Jacob grasped her by the shoulders and gave her a little shake. "Don't do that. I'm here. You're safe."

"But it's all my fault."

"No." He shook his head. "This is on him, whoever he is. You didn't ask him to commit these murders."

"But if it wasn't for me, Harold, Laura, Derrick, Amanda, they'd all be alive." She balled her hands into fists. She wanted to punch something. Or more like someone.

"Let's go back to sleep—"

"No." She pushed Jacob's hands away. "No, I can't go back to sleep. Not now."

She jerked on a pair of pants and stalked into the living room. He followed her, a silent presence.

"Okay, so let me pitch an idea to you."

She turned to face him. "Okay. What?"

"I think the unsub is someone you've met. Someone you know, but not like a friend. I don't think you'd even know his name."

"Really?"

"Yeah." He nodded. "I want to bounce some ideas off you, make some lists. Do you think you're up to that?"

"Hell yeah." She glanced at the kitchen table and counters covered in papers. "I'll get the card table from the garage. We can start with that."

BLACK WIDOW CLOSED HER laptop and set it on the passenger's seat. She was relying on Mercy too much. The woman had never stepped out of line, but Black Widow had run Killer Club long enough to know the patterns. People joined, they were over-zealous in their planning, but once the execution stage started... Most of them lost their way. But not Mercy. She was almost a founding member. Her list of kills stretched as long as Black Widow's.

Mercy was a better actor than others.

Like Iron.

Max Fischer had potential, but he saw himself as too much of an artist to follow rules, and rules kept the club safe. The attention from the press and the notoriety he was getting played into his delusions of rebirth, feeding his obsession. But not her plan. If this was what the boy wanted, then he shouldn't have come to her. Because her rules were law, and you only got one chance to break the law before it broke you. She'd expelled members for even thinking about deviating from their plans.

It could be that she was simply sentimental. Max was about the age of her brother, had he survived their childhood. Her brother had been her first. He'd screamed about night terrors, which had really been her experimenting. Figuring out her MO. Her ritual. In hindsight, killing her much younger brother hadn't been a good idea. But that was in the past. She'd escaped unscathed.

Max Fischer, however, would not.

She slipped on a backpack she had prepared for this little outing and got out of the rental car. There was no more Iron now. She had to start thinking of him as Max. A member on his way out.

If Max stuck to his schedule, he would have a triple homicide to carry through tonight. That would give her time to explore his hidey-hole and lay in wait for him. She liked to take time to acclimate herself to herself to her victim's homes, learn a little about them, but she already knew all there was about Max Fischer.

The people in her club thought it was all anonymous, that their identities were hidden behind handles and bounced IP addresses. There were a few smart cookies in the lot, like Mercy and Joker, but most didn't think through their choices. All they saw were others who wanted to kill, like they did. So she spoon-fed them the lines, gave them a virtual home, and reeled them in.

Eventually she'd kill them all, but it was fun to see their work and know that without her none of it would have happened. They'd all be petty little children masturbating to their murder fantasies. Only a few would have ever risen to the level at which they were now.

The foreclosed home Max had appropriated sat on a street of empty lots. She'd parked a couple blocks away and walked under the cover of night to the little, unassuming house at the end of the street.

She went in through the back door. Locks had never kept her out. She stood in the living room, listening to the utter silence.

Garbage bags were taped over the windows, and several full-length mirrors leaned against the panes. More mirrors hung on the walls, stood propped up on the floor. They were everywhere. She caught her movements out of the corner of her eye, reflected again and again.

It was enough to drive a person more than a little crazy.

There was a pallet set up on one side of the room, while an electric cord ran from the garage to a table that was no doubt Max's work station. The laptop and other equipment was nowhere to be seen. There was, however, a small mini fridge.

She opened it, and seven sets of eyes stared back at her.

Seven?

He'd only reported four victims. Who were five, six, and seven?

Later, when she cleaned house, she'd have to dispose of them. For now, it was time to dig deeper into Max Fischer's life, because in a few hours, he was going to die.

JACOB SCRUBBED A HAND over his face. Emma had her head on the coffee table, looking at another set of lists through the glass surface. They were a sorry pair.

He wanted to whisk her away from here. Maybe down to Florida or California. Someplace warm, with a beach and waves. She'd wear an itty bitty bikini, and they'd drink beer, or maybe one of those fruity drinks with an umbrella in it. Somewhere she wouldn't feel so much responsibility. If he could take the weight off her shoulders for a few minutes, he'd do anything.

"Come on." He dropped the legal pad on the table.

Emma lifted her head, blinking at him.

"Let's grab something to eat. We aren't going to see anything standing here and staring at this stuff anymore.

She didn't respond, but she did get to her feet and shuffle off to the bedroom. While she freshened up, he checked his phone for the hundredth time. He hadn't heard anything since a second call from Brooks to touch base. Being off the case was trying his nerves, but he wouldn't change a thing.

Instead, he sent the cop stationed outside a warning they were about to leave.

In a matter of minutes Emma emerged, fresh-faced, her hair brushed, clothes changed, and even a little make-up hiding the dark circles under her eyes. He guided her out to his Jeep, glancing at the unmarked police car across the street. The officer waved at him, and he nodded back.

As he pulled out onto the street, Emma reached for his hand. He brought her knuckles to his lips and squeezed her fingers.

He'd refused to think about what he would have done had it been Emma tonight in Rachel's place. He could only hope that there was something at the scene of the crime that would help them figure out who the hell TBKiller was.

They chose an IHOP near the highway. Barely past sunrise, it wasn't yet busy, and they got a table in the corner, where he could watch the comings and goings of people.

Now that TBKiller's ritual was disrupted, there was a chance the stress of not being able to complete his so-called mission might push him to do something extreme. Jacob didn't think the guy would escalate to approaching Emma in a public place, but his kills could become a thing of convenience instead of the well-planned imitations. All thoughts he kept to himself.

"Know what you want?" He flipped through the menu, though he didn't need to.

"Not really."

"Want me to pick for you?"

"Yes." She shoved her menu at him and crossed her arms on the table top.

He chuckled and flagged down the waitress. He doubled his order and asked for an extra pot of coffee. They were going to burn through that in no time.

"If you could go anywhere at all, right now, where would it be?" He reached across and took her hand in his once more.

"Somewhere remote. Far away. Like, a mountain cabin in Colorado or something." She smiled and rubbed her thumb over his knuckles.

"The mountains? Not the beach?"

"You said right now." She chuckled. "Right now I don't want to see anyone."

"Even me?"

"Okay, anyone except you. I could even settle for a decent hotel, room service, and a box of condoms."

"Hey, I got my own this time."

She smiled for the first time in hours.

"Is that a blush I see?" He ducked his head to glimpse her face when she tried to look away.

"Shut up." She twisted in her seat, but he held fast to her hands.

"No way. Miss this? Never."

"I'm going to the beach without you then."

"That's not fair."

She peeked at him through her lashes.

At some point, she'd dropped the tough girl routine with him. The Emma he saw now was someone she hid from the world.

He took her other hand and held them between his own.

"Let's go to Colorado this weekend."

"What?" That got her attention. She searched his face, disbelief etched between her brows in the little lines on her forehead. "Seriously?"

"Yeah." It was crazy and totally out of character for him, but it wasn't like he'd been all that happy. Maybe what he needed was her. To shake up his life. To show him what he was missing.

"Can we do that?"

"Why not?"

"Well if they catch," she glanced over her shoulder, "you-know-who, won't we have to answer questions or some-thing?"

He grimaced.

"Okay, so maybe in two weeks."

"Okay. All right. I'm in."

"Fantastic." He pulled her hands across the table once more and kissed the first knuckle on each.

He'd never gone on trips with women before. He'd never wanted to. They were only ever distractions from his work. A way to fill his off hours. Emma was different. He wanted to spend time with her, peeling back the layers, and be with her. There would be bumps in the road. Inevitably they'd butt heads or want different things, but she was worth working through that.

"And you should bring your bikes. Maybe you could teach me how to ride?"

"That would be awesome." Her smile nearly split her face. She was beautiful when she smiled. Radiant.

He smiled back and they laced their fingers together, staring at each other. That he'd found her during an investigation was crazy. There was nothing about how they'd begun that was normal. Which meant there weren't any rules. Hell, he didn't think Emma was suffering from hero syndrome for a second. She wasn't exactly the damsel in distress to need a hero anyways, and that was actually fine by him. They could lean on each other, instead of him carrying them both.

"Excuse me, Emma Ration?" A woman in a royal blue suit approached their table, one of those news microphones in hand and a camera man following her. "I'm from KOCO and we wanted to ask you a few questions about the TBKiller. Do you have a moment?"

Emma's eyes widened, and she glanced at him.

Shit.

Jacob slid out of the booth and put himself between Emma and the camera.

"I'm sorry, Ms. Ration will not be answering any questions at this time," he said.

"How do you feel about a copycat murderer, Ms. Ration?" The persistent reporter tried to lean around him.

"Emma, go to the Jeep." He shoved his keys at her, hating that for a few brief moments she'd be alone.

"We want to ask a few questions." The reporter tried to follow Emma when she darted around the crew, bolting for the door, but a pair of patrol officers were there to cut them off.

Jacob blew out a relieved breath and circled around the tables of staring patrons. Bet they didn't expect a side of drama with their morning coffee.

"Emma," he called out. She hadn't yet made it to the doors. A pair of men in sports coats had stopped her, and one had a recorder in her face. "Fuck me," he grumbled and dug out his badge.

"I'm not answering any of your fucking questions," Emma snapped at the men.

Jacob flashed his badge and grabbed Emma by the elbow. "Excuse us, gentlemen."

The badge distracted them for the half-second they needed to side-step them and get out the door. He was incredibly glad he'd managed a close parking spot.

"This isn't fair." Emma flopped into the passenger seat as he buckled his seat belt.

"I'm sorry, I didn't expect that."

"No, I wanted coffee. And food."

He chuckled as he reversed out of the spot.

"That I can fix."

Jacob pulled out his phone and did a quick search for the IHOP while he drove around behind the building. The hostess picked up after two rings, and once he'd given her a short explanation, was assured their meals could be boxed up and brought out the back.

"What now?" Emma asked. "Is it too late to drive to Colorado now?"

"Nope, but I think it's time we pitched our theories to the FBI."

"Do you think they'll listen to us?"

He shrugged. "Maybe."

He hoped they could figure the puzzle out before TBKiller struck for what might be the last time.

10.

MAX'S FINGERS DRIPPED WITH BLOOD. If he had his choice, he'd savor this moment. There was nothing like the warm, sticky sensation of it between his palms, but the time for savoring his kills was gone. He needed to move, now. Time was of the essence. But first, he had to get the others. Those souls he'd saved from living the pattern over again. He couldn't split without them.

The sun rose slowly on the horizon, bathing it in a pale, gray light. His time was growing short. He couldn't hide this body, so he'd have to leave it and get out before anyone noticed.

The man shouldn't have come out to check the noise. Then Max wouldn't have had to kill him. He'd at least gouged the man's eyes out. Now there would be nothing to carry forward into the next life, and no way the spirit would recognize him.

It was a necessity. He didn't like to destroy the previous lives the eyes would carry with them, but it couldn't be helped. When he was reborn, he couldn't have someone coming after him for a crime he'd committed in this life.

He wiped his fingers on the man's shirt. Time to get home.

Usually Max parked several blocks away from the house, but since he needed to move so much stuff he'd made do with one street over. It wasn't ideal, but it would be okay. No one suspected him yet.

He stuck to the shadows, going from yard to yard until he reached the end of the street. His lonely little house sat all by itself. An oasis. But not for long.

For several moments he watched the brick facade. No change. No disturbance. His haven was still there.

He peered up and down the road, but there was no one out yet. It was safe for the moment, so he struck out across the street, hands in his pockets, trying for casual.

The skin between his shoulder blades began to crawl, and a heavy sense of foreboding settled in his stomach. He stood on the sidewalk and stared at the house. The front windows were covered with plastic, but he could see in through the kitchen at this angle. The mirrors caught the morning light and reflected through the house.

A shadow passed through the light. The movement was slow, or his light-dazzled eyes might have missed it.

Someone was in his haven.

He turned and walked away from the house, his pulse pounding.

There was only one person who could have found him so fast.

Black Widow.

His body went cold and then hot, goosebumps breaking out all over his arms. The only reason she'd be in Oklahoma

City was to kill him. He'd known she'd come for him, but he hoped to have more time. To be able to finish what he'd started. There was a way to make up for last night. He could do it. But not with her here.

There'd been whispers, when he'd joined the club, that she'd killed one of their members. He'd watched several others disappear since. He had no doubt she'd kill him for breaking her precious rules.

He had to finish his mission before she killed him. Or before he killed her. He could skip the next few targets. There was really only one that mattered. Two that he wanted. And wasn't it his luck those two had taken up together?

JACOB HELD THE DOOR FOR EMMA.

"Are you sure we should be here?" she asked for the third time. She'd squirmed in her seat the second he'd said they were taking their theories to the FBI.

"Yes. It'll be fine."

"But you're off the case."

"I am. But that doesn't mean I've stopped thinking about it." He carried the box that now contained the precious folders of lists they'd compiled.

After signing her in, he escorted her back to his department, which appeared more like a busy call center than the orderly detective unit he was used to.

"Payton, what are you doing here?" Mullins sipped from a cup of coffee, looking worse for having probably not slept in at least a day.

"We've got some ideas. Where is everyone?" He glanced around for the other agents.

"Aren't you supposed to be guarding her?" Mullins thumbed at Emma.

"'Her' is standing right here. Do you want to hear the ideas or not?"

"Lady's got some fire in her. Go in the war room. I'll grab Brooks." Mullins chuckled.

Jacob led Emma into the conference room. Days ago, he'd had a table and two boards. Now, there were pages taped to walls and several rolling boards arranged in a time line with the TBK details below and the TBKiller copies above.

"Wow, this makes me look like the minor league." Emma went to the first board and examined the TBK notes.

He couldn't help but notice she completely ignored the TBKilling line.

"Payton. Ms. Ration." Brooks led Mullins and his partner into the room. "Didn't expect to see either of you here today."

"Thanks for giving us a few minutes, Agent." Jacob shook the man's hand.

"Forgive me if I ask you to get to the point." Brooks crossed his arms over his chest while the other two agents took seats.

"No, not at all." Jacob cleared his throat. "I had a theory from the very beginning that was a gut feeling. I couldn't prove it, so I didn't come out and say it, but I was certain these murders were somehow connected to Emma and perhaps myself. To our knowledge, I was the first person to receive letters. We don't know when Harold or Laura got theirs, but we do know when Emma received her first letter. I think a copycat would find value in including Emma in their plans."

"Really? You're just now springing this on me?" Brooks shook his head, his face going a little red.

"I wasn't certain, and you didn't have time to listen to me. I didn't put it together until you laid out the victim's connections to Emma, which you withheld from me." That still burned. The agents hadn't told anyone they were bringing Emma in to interrogate her. "I'm guessing everyone except your agents knew until you accused Emma to her face. How was I supposed to know that was the direction you were going if you aren't sharing information? I couldn't. After last night's botched murder, I think my theory is solid. Emma factors into the killer's plans, and if he's disrupted now, he might accelerate and come after her next instead of waiting."

Brooks' glare was enough to make Jacob rethink his word choice, though he still would have said exactly what he thought. Brooks shook his head a little and leaned forward, gaze still pinned on Jacob.

"You should have come to me before this and made me listen. You do good work, Detective. But you're a one-man team. You don't play well with others, and that's a problem for any department or team like mine."

Wasn't the agent listening?

Emma's hand wrapped around his fist, her fingers feathering over his knuckles.

"Okay guys, why don't we take a deep breath." She did as she asked them. "We all want the same thing, so why don't we calm down?"

Jacob glanced at Emma. "I thought it was strange when you had met the first victim, but when Brooks pointed out the connection with Laura, and then Amanda and Derrick were killed, that's what got me thinking. Last night Emma and I compiled lists of traits, common knowledge things about every TBK victim. Show them."

"Tell them about the other list." Emma set the box on the table and began unpacking their proof.

"Other list?" Brooks prompted.

"If my theory about the copycat is valid, that means he's someone Emma has come into contact with. A real fanatic about killers. Now, she meets with people on occasion to talk about the history of TBK. She's about the most proficient expert on the subject, apart from a few scholars. Last night we went back through her emails and made a list of everyone who has contacted her about TBK."

"I don't meet with creepadoodles." Emma shook her head.

"Creepadoodles?" Mullins laughed.

"Hush," Brooks said to his agent. "Go on."

"Most of the people I've met with are teachers, psychologists, or family members. Good people. But some struck me as creepy. We made lists and broke them down. People I met with divided into their relationship to the killer, either victim's family, professional, or curious lookie-lou. Then there's another list of people who creeped me out. We also compiled a list of everyone I rejected."

"We spent some time looking these people up," Jacob interjected. Social media was pretty damn helpful for telling you about someone's habits. "I think we have a small pool of suspects for you."

"Show me." Brooks held out his hand.

Emma handed it over then wiped her hands on her jeans. "There's four. Three are people I turned down, but when we looked them up there is substantial activity on their social media sites to indicate a serial killer fascination."

"And the fourth?"

"The fourth is a teenage kid I met with. I thought he was doing a homework assignment, but he was a total creeper. Followed me around, made threats. Eventually I had to slap a restraining order on him."

"Which is he?" Brooks flashed the list at her.

"This one." She tapped the last name on the list. "Max Fischer."

BLACK WIDOW PACED THROUGH THE HOUSE.

Patience was a virtue she exercised more often than most people, but after hours of waiting, it was wearing thin. Where was Max?

Something was wrong. By all accounts, Max killed near midnight. His whole ritual took maybe an hour to three, depending on the bodies. Granted, he'd only done a few trial runs before committing to his plan. There were always variances, but not this many.

She went to the front windows and pulled aside enough plastic to peer out.

The sun was up. Cars came and went. Blue and red lights flashed a street over.

Fuck.

She headed for the back door, but the mini-fridge caught her eye.

Max would want his trophies. But if she was found carrying them, there wouldn't be a good enough excuse to get her off the hook. She'd have to leave them and track Max some other way. God, he was a royal fuck up.

She left the door open. It didn't matter now, someone would go door to door soon and they would discover his hidey-hole. She peered up and down the street. Since the house was all by itself, it stuck out like a sore thumb. If she went for the sidewalk, anyone driving by would take notice of her.

It was now or never. Her time was running out.

Black Widow walked calmly to the sidewalk, then began jogging as if she did this every day. The small pack bounced on her shoulders, but she couldn't leave her kit behind. Her prints were all over it.

She jogged down the street, crossing when she ran out of sidewalk and continued toward the lights.

Several cop cars and an ambulance sat outside of one of the cookie-cutter homes while neighbors clustered outside in their robes and slippers. She jogged right up to a group of neighbors and stopped, breathing harder than was necessary.

"Hey, what's going on?" she asked.

The woman closest to her appeared to be near tears. "It was Mike Robinson. His wife found him dead in the backyard. They said his eyes were gone." She covered her face and muttered through her fingers, "Do you think it's that killer?"

Black Widow gasped, feigning horror. "No."

The woman nodded.

"Oh my God. I need to go check in on my grandmother. I'm so sorry."

"No, go, go!" The woman shooed her away.

Black Widow jogged off with haste. Not too fast, she didn't want to draw any undue attention, but the inbound black SUVs didn't speak well for Max. She had to find him before the FBI did.

EMMA PACED THE LENGTH of the entry to the police station. The FBI had rushed out in a hurry, save for the red-headed agent that gave Emma the creeps. The woman was like a robot.

It was all too much to take in. She couldn't think too hard about the very real possibility she'd set this all in motion years ago. Max had been nineteen when she filed the restraining order. That was nearly five years ago. Someone at the FBI had gathered up a lot of information about Max in a few minutes, and it made the kid out to be even creepier. Emma hadn't even heard it all. The agents had shut her out almost as soon as the details started rolling in.

She had a feeling they'd kick Jacob out soon too, but at the very least she wanted to hang around and see Rachel and her family. They were caught up in all of this because of her.

"There you are."

Emma turned toward Jacob's voice. Her heart fluttered at the sight of him. It was stupid. She'd been apart from him for all of five minutes. It wasn't enough time to miss someone, and yet, she had.

"Hey. Just waiting on Rachel." She shoved her hands in her pockets. Rachel and her family were supposed to help create a drawing since Max's picture wasn't online anywhere. The most recent one was at least five years old.

"Patrol is bringing them around back, through the bay, to keep them out of the eye of the press."

"Oh." Well now didn't she feel dumb?

"Want to grab a snack with me in the break room?" He thumbed over his shoulder.

"Sure." She wasn't hungry, but being near him made her feel better.

They meandered back toward his department, but detoured into a break room with a vending machine. Like the rest of the building, it was a monotone beige room.

"Don't you people believe in color?" she asked.

"I try to spend as little time as possible here. Mostly, I'm out working cases."

She shook her head. "I don't think I could do what you do."

"What? Be a cop?"

"Kind of, but more the office environment. I couldn't cut it. I need to be outside, doing stuff."

"And that's why I try to spend as much time in the field. Know what you want?" He gestured toward the vending machine. "My treat."

"Aren't you Mr. Generous? First breakfast and now a treat?"

One side of his mouth hitched up, and she had to stop herself from sighing. He'd smiled this morning at breakfast. A real, honest to God smile, with teeth and little dimples and everything. Who would have known the man had fucking hot dimples? Not her.

"Anything for you." He tucked her hair behind her ear, fingertips whispering over her cheek.

Anything? Did he mean that?

"What do you want?" he asked again.

"Chocolate."

He shrugged and punched in digits, selecting a chocolate and caramel bar for her, and chips for himself.

"When should Rachel be here?" she asked.

"She's probably already here, but they aren't going to let us back there for now." He pulled out a chair and gestured for her to sit.

"Really?"

"Let them do their job. We'll stick around until they have a sketch and decide what to do then."

"What about the guy they found dead?"

"They probably won't share that, either."

"That's frustrating." She tore the wrapper open and popped one of the sectioned squares off and into her mouth.

"Let's talk about something else."

"Colorado?" She'd thrown that out as a joke this morning, but he'd seemed serious about it. Suddenly, she wanted that trip.

"Yeah, let's talk about Colorado." There was that smile again. It was probably a good thing he didn't use it often. It was a deadly weapon.

"Would this be a friends-and-us trip?" She focused on the candy and keeping her expression neutral.

"Hell no. Unless that's what you want?"

She shrugged, not inclined to share her time with him with others.

"Are you trying to tell me you're second guessing the trip?" Now the smile was gone.

"No. Not at all, I just...well..." She shrugged and squirmed a little. "What are we? Are we friends? Are we fuck buddies? Or something else?"

Jacob put the bag down and stared at her hard.

"What do you want to call it?" he asked.

"I don't know. Should we call it anything?" If they decided to be fuck buddies, she had to stop caring for him now. But if he wanted to date her, would she have to start dressing the part of a cop's girlfriend? Was there a uniform?

"I think that decision falls to you."

"Me?" Panic gripped her by the throat and squeezed.

Jacob leaned across the table toward her, his gaze serious as always.

"I know you don't know me very well, but I promise you this isn't normal for me. It's different. And I'm not going to walk away from something that feels...right."

She swallowed hard.

"Right?" she echoed.

That sounded an awful lot like a commitment speech.

Emma had always been the relationship type, despite her independence. But he was right, with him it was different. Not just that they were plagued by the same shadows, but it was as if he knew how to lift them away. He knew everything horrible about her life, and he didn't bat an eyelash at it.

Holy shit. She loved him.

Only love could chase away the kinds of shadows in their lives. Love was the only logical reason for this crazy urge to be near him, always.

"Hey," a voice barked. It was that agent, Jade Perez. "You two need to see this."'

Fuck her and her timing!

Emma's heart pounded in her throat, and her stomach was floating in her chest. She felt dizzy and a little off balance, but then again, she'd just realized she loved a guy.

Jacob turned toward the door.

"What is it?" he asked.

"Come on." Jade disappeared down the hall.

Jacob stood and offered her a hand. She needed it. The room was spinning and now her stomach threatened to expel the chocolate.

Did people fall in love like this? All at once? Was this normal?

It wasn't as if her life had ever been normal.

Jade led them into the war room.

"We found an old picture of our suspect. Patrol went by Harold Espinoza's neighbor's house with it. Both the neighbors and the family from last night say it's our guy. He's blond now, pale and has what looks like scars on his forearms."

"Fuck me." Emma sat down hard in a chair. "He had black, long hair when I met him. He was just a scrawny kid."

Jade had been busy. There was already a board set up with Max's picture, name, and the details they'd uncovered about him.

"What about the body from this morning?" Jacob asked.

"Brooks called. They found his hiding spot, his trophies—everything except him, it seems. A street over from where they found the body. They think he was trying to get supplies, maybe money to run. There was no reason to kill the man that we can see, but they're working on it."

"Stress. His plan was destroyed, and he can't kill his intended victims. He's spiraling, so now he'll kill anyone who either gets in his way or that he comes into contact with. Our body count is probably going to double." Jacob's voice was grim, his shoulders slumped.

They knew who TBKiller was, and he was still going to murder more people. It was a terrifying thought.

Jacob turned toward her, no dimples in sight.

"I think our best bet is for Emma and me to go back to her place. He's clearly familiar with the house and her being there. If we're someplace he can find us, he might come straight for us."

"You want to be bait?" Emma asked.

"Yeah. You okay with that?"

"Yeah." She shrugged.

They were different than his other victims. They knew he was coming. And they would be prepared.

"I will communicate that to Brooks. I need to get an APB out for Max. We're going to catch him." If Jade meant her words to be comforting, they weren't. Emma doubted the woman had a warm, fuzzy bone in her body.

"Great." Jacob glanced at her, and the room faded from her awareness. "We're going to head out, get some sleep maybe, or make some more coffee. Keep us updated?"

"Will do," Jade replied and strode out of the room.

"Ready to get out of here?" he asked.

"You sure this is the best plan?" She stood and took the hand he extended toward her.

"No, but you don't run and my gut tells me he's not going to give up his end game. If I thought for a second you'd go into protective custody, I'd haul your ass off."

"Yeah, I'm not doing that, so let's go be bait." She nodded toward her collection. "We leaving that?"

"You okay leaving your scrapbooks? They might find something useful in there."

"Scrapbooks? I don't scrapbook." He glanced at the books.

"Okay, so they are scrapbooks, but I can't do all that neat, frilly stuff people do with the pages." She rolled her eyes.

He chuckled and grabbed her hands. "You scrapbook. It's cute. Come on."

She'd be adding another chapter to her collection, one that told their story. Eventually. For now, a little sleep sounded good, even if she didn't think she'd sleep for a second until they caught Max.

JACOB WAS BURNING THE last of his oil. As much as he wanted to stay at the station, he was about to fall flat on his face. Hell, he was pretty sure he'd hallucinated that moment in the break room when Emma stared at him like someone had hit her with a two-by-four.

What they needed was some sleep, another meal, and for the cops to catch Max Fischer. Once that was wrapped up, they could decide what exactly they were calling this. At some point in the last few days, he'd accepted he was hooked on Emma, and for him, there was no turning back. He didn't know if it was infatuation, lust, or love, but he wasn't going to let go. No matter what she thought or did, he was hanging on.

They walked hand-in-hand out of the precinct through a side door. He'd parked away from the building to avoid drawing attention. They'd also opted to not listen to the news, but a few of the officers had told him the media was running with the story of the Ration family and the copycat TBK murderer.

"God, it's hotter than the devil's crotch," Emma said as they stepped out onto the stairs.

Jacob laughed.

"Devil's crotch, huh?"

"Yeah." She grinned.

"You think it's this hot in Colorado right now?"

"I seriously doubt it."

He was getting into the idea of going away with Emma. Someplace they could forget what pulled them together and get down to who they really were. He was in awe of the person with him now, her strength and tenacity to face down this situation without fear. Of course, he could have done without the secrets.

"I'm thinking a second breakfast and a nap. What do you think?" He pulled his keys out of his pocket.

"I think that sounds perfect." Emma squeezed his hand and let it go.

He glimpsed something on the seat of his Jeep. Something that hadn't been there before. Something red.

"Emma, wait." Jacob grabbed her around the waist and backed up into the street.

"What's wrong?"

"There's something in the Jeep."

He glanced around them, keeping her close to his side, as he pulled out his phone and dialed 9-1-1. He rattled off his badge number and the details. Within minutes a swarm of officers had the street blocked off, and Jade Perez was there.

"He was here," Jade announced after a glance at the present left on the passenger's seat of his Jeep.

"What is it?" Emma asked.

"You don't want to know," Jacob said over Jade's answer.

"Human eyes," Jade replied. "Sorry."

"Eyeballs?" She twisted away from him and peered into the Jeep.

"You don't want to see that." Jacob pulled her back again.

"I grew up in the country. I've seen eyes before." Emma seemed much less shaken by the trophy than he did. "Did he really sneak up here and do that?"

"Yes. I want to preserve the scene until Brooks tells me otherwise. I'll get patrol to take you back to Emma's. Sorry about this, Detective." Jade shielded her eyes from the sun.

"Are you sure that's still the best plan?" Jacob asked. He hated the idea of letting Emma walk into danger.

Jade lifted her shoulders. "He's taunting you. He placed the eyes on the passenger side, where Emma would have sat. There's blood on her side, not the driver's. I think this is more about her than you."

"Or, he could be using her to get to me." Jacob shrugged.

"I want to get patrol to clear out your neighbor's homes. We can station plain clothes officers there as camouflage. I think it's the best plan. He's focused specifically on the two of you. We need to use that to distract him from the fact he'll be walking into a trap."

Jacob didn't like it, but neither could he deny that it was a solid plan.

"Sounds good. Can we get a ride home? I'm starting to get the creeps with all these cameras around." Emma nodded behind her to the reporters gathering like a pack of hyenas.

"I got it." Jacob placed his hand in the small of her back. "Come on, let's get inside."

"When will this be over?" she asked when they were out of earshot.

"Soon. They're going to catch him."

He had to believe they would. He couldn't live in a world without her in it. Not when he'd found her.

MAX PAID THE CASHIER for his bag of food and supplies. As he handed over the cash, he caught sight of his nails.

Shit.

There was still blood under them.

"Wow, looks like they know who that killer is." The man working the register took the money while he stared at a TV mounted behind the counter.

A picture of Max at nineteen floated above the news anchor's shoulder. A chill swept through his body, but he forced himself to appear casual.

"Damn. Just a kid. Hope they catch him."

"I know, right?"

The cashier turned to count the cash, only glancing at Max.

It was amazing what a change of style could do for a person.

When Max was nineteen, he'd had long, scraggly black hair and he was so pale even strangers had remarked on it. A little tan, a haircut, and bleaching his hair had been enough to fool Emma. He'd seen her a number of times over the last few months, and she'd never recognized him.

"Take care," Max said to the cashier and took his things out to a car he'd borrowed from the neighbor behind Amanda's house.

It was a stroke of luck that Max and the man were similar in build and height. A little bleach and a buzz cut, and he could pass for the blond lawyer, especially when he borrowed the man's suit. Thankfully, the lawyer kept to himself and happened to be out of town this week.

Black Widow might be on the search for him, but he'd never mentioned the lawyer, and by the time she figured out where he was he'd have completed his mission. His soul could finally rest, free to live another life unburdened by this duty he carried.

Just a little while longer. That's all he needed.

11.

EMMA STARED OUT THE passenger side window of the sedan Jacob had borrowed from the motor pool. It smelled of stale donuts, coffee, and cigarettes. She could almost see two cops doing a stakeout in a car like this. It would explain the odor. What would Jacob's Jeep smell like now?

She shuddered and turned toward him. His lips were still pressed into that tight line she hated. How could she lift his burdens enough that he could just be happy? She reached across and ran her fingers over his forearm, taking comfort in the contact.

He glanced her way.

"I thought you were asleep," he said.

"I doubt I'll be able to sleep."

"You could sleep, and I could stay up, watch over you."

Her heart pulsed. He'd do it, she didn't doubt him one bit.

"What if we get an officer to hang out in the living room, and we both sleep? It would probably be a hell of a lot more comfortable than sitting in a car. I heard the heat index is going to be up around a hundred and nine."

"Makes Colorado sound even better, doesn't it?" The corners of his mouth lifted when he glanced at her.

"Oh, hell yes." She grinned back. God, she hoped he was serious about this whole get-away plan. At first she'd thought he was talking crazy, now it sounded like the perfect escape. A cabin out somewhere on the river, lazy mornings followed by hiking, riding the bikes, or laying out on a rock, watching the clouds go by. It all sounded so heavenly.

"Do you like to camp?"

"It's okay for a night or two, maybe three, if the conditions are perfect."

"Would you be interested in hiking up someplace and doing a one-night camping trip? There's this spot I read about that has the most amazing sunsets, but you can only get there on a foot path."

"Have you been researching this trip already?"

"I might have distracted myself for a little bit searching up things to do."

"Okay, tell me more."

"Well you hike up there, camp, and then take a raft back down the mountain."

"Like white-water rafting?"

"Yeah." He glanced at her again, and she might be tempted to call the twist of his lips and flash of his teeth a real smile. A small one, but a smile nonetheless.

If this camping adventure made him that excited, she'd sign on.

"Sounds like fun. Sign me up."

"Cool."

"Would you want to stay in a hotel, or rent a cabin, or something else?" She rested her hand on his thigh and relaxed a little more, reveling in this mental vacation.

"Cabin or condo. I can't cook in a hotel room."

"Oh, so you're going to cook for me, too? We need to leave right now. Let me go pack a bag real quick."

Jacob's chuckle died fast. One glance at his unsmiling face and she groaned inwardly. Well crap. There went that moment. Until TBKiller was caught and this case was squared away, they were at a stand-still. Their lives revolved around a killer who very well might be focused on her. She couldn't think about it too much or it would drive her crazy.

She wasn't the one who'd told Max to kill people.

Max did this all on his own.

Jacob pulled into the little housing development where Amanda had lived. Had. As in used to. The past tense.

Emma sucked down a shuddering breath. Was she really gone?

"Ems? You okay?" Jacob stopped at a four-way stop sign and turned toward her.

"Fuck. I'm fine." She dashed away the tears she hadn't realized she was crying. "Can we get back to the house?"

She slid farther down in her seat as they turned onto her street. It was eerily quiet, though by appearances, nothing was different.

"They've evacuated the houses on either side of yours and a few across the street agreed to let an officer be stationed inside as lookouts. The community is really helping out."

"That's good. Amanda babysat a lot for the parents here."

"Yeah. A few of the parents mentioned that."

"Does her family know?"

"Yes."

"Shit, they're going to hate me." She scrubbed the side of her face with her hand.

"No, they were actually very concerned for you."

"Yeah, but do they know everything?"

"Not that I know of." He pulled into the driveway and the garage, squeezing in next to her truck. "Come on, let's get some rest."

They entered the house through the laundry room door. A black man in slacks and a polo shirt sat at the kitchen table, reading the newspaper.

"Morning, Payton. Ma'am."

"Hey, man. Everything quiet?" Jacob asked.

She went to the fridge and pulled out a bottle of water.

"Yup. Want me to clear out?" She could only assume he was one of the officers looking out for them.

"Nah. Would you stick around while we get some sleep?"

"No problem."

She didn't miss the slightly raised brows and quick glance her way. At this rate all the cops were going to draw the conclusion they were dating and they hadn't yet decided what this was. It was a little annoying, but in the scheme of things, it didn't rate high on her care list.

"I'm going to crawl into bed. Help yourself to anything in the fridge." Emma ducked into her bedroom and the welcoming embrace of shadows.

The air conditioner kicked on, drowning out the conversation in the next room. Since they weren't guaranteed to be alone, she changed into yoga pants and a sports bra with a tank top to sleep in. It might not be the most comfortable thing to wear to bed, but if they were right and TBKiller was coming for her, she didn't want to face him in a thong and nightie. This wasn't a horror flick and she liked living.

She crawled into bed, exhaustion weighing her down. A couple of nights together and they'd already divided the bed in half. She chuckled and splayed her hand over what was now Jacob's side of the bed.

As if her thoughts had summoned him, Jacob stepped into the room, closing the door behind him.

"He's going to stay on watch for us, so you can sleep and not worry." He padded across the room and lay down next to her. She noticed he didn't shed any clothing.

She didn't point out that if TBKiller was as bad as they thought he was, he might kill them all. No, Jacob wanted to comfort and soothe her, and she'd let him. She scooted closer, and he wrapped an arm around her waist.

"How are you doing?" she asked.

"I'm fine."

She didn't believe him, but he was the strong silent type. Or something like that.

He cupped the back of her head and kissed her brow. Such a tender, sweet gesture from a man who was so rough and tumble. She cuddled in close, letting him tuck her under his chin and twine their limbs together.

They'd get through this. They had to. Colorado was in their future.

BLACK WIDOW WATCHED THE unfolding news coverage from the safety of her hotel room. Time was running out. She'd expected this to be a quick in-and-out job, like all the rest, but Max was a real fuck up. Not only had he gone off script, the whole world knew who Max Fischer was now. At this point, she hoped the kid committed suicide and solved this whole mess for her.

Her laptop beeped. She hated how that sound spurred her to action, but it was worth it.

The message was short, a string of digits.

She blew out a breath, picked up the disposable cell phone, and dialed the number.

After this situation was resolved, she was going to have to put some more safeguards in place. Because of Max's stupidity, the whole club might be exposed. Not their handles, but their existence. They'd operated for years without detection, and now, thanks to a stupid kid, the FBI might very well start hunting them.

"Hello?" The voice on the other end was hesitant.

"Iron, nice to finally chat." She threw an accent into the mix.

"Who is this?"

"Oh come now, who else would it be?"

"Black Widow."

"You aren't as stupid as I thought you might be."

"What do you want? I'm kind of busy."

"Yeah, about that." She turned back toward the TV. "This breaks every rule in the book, Max."

"Accidents happen. I'm going to fix it."

"This can't be fixed, Max. You need to end this, and I need the assurance that you've destroyed all your electronics."

"What? Don't want this to leak back to you?"

"Something like that. Think of the club, Max. They're your family. Do you really want to put them in danger?"

"Family?" He laughed, a grating, rusty sound. "I hate to break it to you, but we aren't exactly that close."

"Fine. But should you choose to leave us vulnerable, I'll have to take it out on your friends in their little jars, and I don't think you'd like that." He didn't know she wasn't in possession of his eyeball trophies. The news hadn't mentioned them at all.

"You give them back," he roared.

"That's a terrible tone, Max. I'll tell you what, you promise me you destroy the evidence, end this man hunt, and I'll make sure they have a happy, safe rest of their lives, how's that?" They were just eyeballs, not souls or windows to the past, but Max saw something in them.

"I'm working on it. Don't hurt them."

"Then end this, Max. I don't have time to clean up your messes. I've got work to do."

Max made a few sounds, as if he were going to reply and thought better of it. Then silence stretched out for a moment before she realized he'd hung up on her. It wasn't going to be his last mistake, but it certainly put the nails in his coffin.

Max Fischer was a dead man.

"SHIT. SHIT. SHIT."

Max paced the kitchen of his newly borrowed house. All the blinds were drawn and he hadn't bothered with the lights. If he only had the cops *or* Black Widow after him, he might be able to get out of this, but with both of them out there, he was finished.

To escape the police, he'd need the Killer Club resources, but now that he'd pissed off their leader he doubted anyone would lift a finger to help him. As much as he hated Black Widow for pulling his strings, he had to think of the others. Without her, without the club, he'd never have met Mercy.

He pulled out his laptop and set the upload to fire off the raw footage of the morning's kill. Let that be a parting shot. While that was going, he opened his email and a new draft. A clean, white space, ready for him. He blew out a breath and cleared his mind.

This might be his most important letter yet.

```
To: Mercy
From: Iron
Subject: Parting Words


Dear Mercy,
   I don't know if these really will be my part-
ing words, but should these be the last thing I
ever write, I want them to be to you. I know we
haven't spoken or met in person, but the con-
nection we have is real. I believe in our next
lives, if I accomplish this mission, we might
meet again. I'd like the chance to tell you I
love you without the barrier of the internet
and email. You're a special lady, and my life
is better because of you.


   Iron
```

Max attached a zip folder titled LoveLetterstoMercy.zip. They were killers. Murderers. And they spoke the same love language. Hopefully she got his message and saw the same beauty in the words and imagery as he did. And maybe she'd carry that into her next life, a life where they'd recognize each other across a room and know they would spend a lifetime together. One that was better than any before it.

He hit send and turned away from the laptop. His neck burned, and he had to fight the urge to turn around and cut off the Wi-Fi connection before the message went through. They were honest words from his heart, and he wanted her to know.

It would be hours before the coast was clear enough for him to go visit Emma and Jacob. Thankfully he could log into the feed from the house remotely or else he'd have been screwed.

In the meantime, he had a few things he needed to take care of.

He went to his bag and pulled out a small, wooden box he carried with him whenever he killed. Inside was a quarter-sized disk of human bone. The letters K and C had been carved onto it. It was one of the rare things he'd gotten from another member of the group, and he couldn't risk anyone catching him with it. He took a deep breath, and without a second thought, swallowed the medallion.

Human stomach acid could dissolve bone. He hoped it worked fast enough.

That task accomplished, he stripped and laid out his knives and the bag of things he'd purchased at the drug store. He opened the box of topical anesthesia and squirted it in his left forearm.

This was going to hurt like a bitch, but writing "Killer Club" on his arm with a knife until he developed scar tissue hadn't been his brightest idea. He needed to protect Mercy. He was fairly certain after the area was deadened to pain he could take off enough skin the cops wouldn't be able to read the letters.

He squirted the liquid onto his skin, rubbed it in and waited for the sensation to deaden. Again and again, he treated the area until it was as numb as he could make it. He couldn't say reality TV had never taught him anything. This was a trick he'd learned watching tattoo reality shows.

When the area around the scarred letters was sufficiently numb, he selected a nice paring knife from his kit and placed the tip at the end of the word "Killer." He took a deep breath and pushed, waiting for that moment when the skin would stop resisting, that precious moment of give.

The knife slipped under his skin and white-hot fire seared his nerves. He gripped the sink with his left arm and pushed onward with his right, peeling the skin up with the blade. Blood gushed down his forearm and his vision hazed.

Fucking anesthesia wasn't strong enough.

God, it hurt like a bitch. So, so bad.

He pushed on, driving the knife under his skin, but the blood made his fingers slip and the knife went skittering and spinning across the floor.

"Shit," he spat and leaned on the counter.

This wasn't as easy to do on himself as it was to other people.

JACOB OPENED THE FRONT door and waved the officer out carrying a casserole dish, as if he were a neighbor come to visit. Up and down the street, lights were on in the homes, the occasional car passed by, but nothing out of the ordinary. Unless you watched the houses closely and noticed the TVs were off, and the occupants were watching one particular house.

It was a creepy-ass feeling—or would have been, had it been any other time. For now, those watchful eyes were comforting.

"Anything?" Emma asked from behind him.

"They found Freeman." He closed and locked the door, putting his back against the hard surface.

"Your new partner? And? Is he okay?"

Jacob shook his head, unable to form the words. Emma peered up at him, her face creased and lined with worry.

"H-he's dead. They found him chopped up in garbage bags and buried around Max's hiding place." He cleared his throat. "Development said they were going to pour new foundations over where they found the body parts. His eyes were in a fridge. Along with his other victims. There's two we don't have identities for."

"Oh, Jacob. I'm sorry. I'm so sorry."

"I barely knew him."

She hugged him tight, but the worst part was he didn't feel anything. Nothing. He'd barely known Freeman. They'd worked together for a few weeks. He'd transferred in for the chance to work Homicide.

Jacob patted Emma's shoulder. He should have spent more time with him. Gotten to know his new partner better. But the first letter had arrived after they'd been teamed up, and Jacob had been so focused.

"Let's sit down." Emma guided him to the couch.

They'd slept most of the day, only waking up for food and updates from the officers up and down the street. After they'd found Max's second victim that morning a few blocks from the station, the trail had gone cold. He'd vanished. There wasn't even a glimpse of him on security cameras in the area.

Was it too much to hope Max was dead?

He put his back against the door and admired Emma as she stretched, still groggy from sleep thanks to the lack of coffee.

"What are you staring at?" she asked, dropping her arms to her sides.

"You."

"There are better things to look at. I'm a mess." She pulled the ponytail holder out of her hair and ran her fingers through the locks.

He crossed the floor to her and pushed her hands aside, taking over the privilege of stroking her hair. She let her eyes close and tipped her chin up a bit as he massaged her scalp.

"I like you this way," he said.

She snorted. It was an indelicate sound he'd grown fond of.

"I'm serious. There's no pretense, no window dressing, I don't have to act a certain way around you. I can be me. Do you know how rare that is?"

Emma peered up at him through narrow slits.

"People have some fucked up expectations sometimes. Screw them," she said.

He chuckled. So eloquent, his Emma. He'd have to warn his mom eventually, but he'd worry about that later.

"I'd rather screw you, to be honest," he said.

Her eyes fluttered wide, and her jaw dropped. She sucked in a breath and pressed her hand to her chest.

"Did you just make a joke?"

She startled a laugh out of him.

"Maybe so?" He grinned and his cheeks hurt.

"I don't believe it. You laugh, too." She tried to step around him, but he had his fingers dug so deep in her hair she couldn't get away from him. "Hey, any cops listening? This isn't Jacob. He smiles and laughs and makes jokes. I think we have an impostor."

He laughed harder, which seemed to only make her laugh as well. He'd get himself almost under control and she'd giggle, which sounded so damn cute he'd snicker and then she'd laugh again. It was contagious, and probably a result of too much stress, but he didn't care.

She looped her arms around his waist. Her body shook with mirth, giving her a mischievous, pixie-like air. She was trouble to the bone, and he wanted to drink up every drop of it. Hold her inside of him, protect her, laugh with her.

He curled his fingers in her hair, tightening his grip, and bent his head. Her gaze slid to his mouth and one corner of her lips hitched higher.

"What?" he asked.

She sputtered, laughing for no reason.

"What did I do?"

"I'm sorry, I can't seem to help myself. Come here. Give me a kiss." She lifted up on her tip-toes. "Has anyone ever told you your dimples are adorable? I didn't notice them before today."

He rolled his eyes and groaned. "I try to forget about them."

"Why?" She cupped his cheek. "They're so cute."

"Yeah, I'd be okay if they went away."

"No," she wailed. She pressed her finger in the spot where the damned dimple always showed up. "It's cute."

"Cute. Great. What every guys wants to hear." He rolled his eyes.

"Hey, it makes you more relatable. Otherwise you're too hot to be real, so embrace the dimples." She snickered again. "You don't choose the dimple life, the dimple life chooses you."

"All right, enough of that."

"What?"

He picked her up and she squawked, laughing and clutching his shoulders as he carried her to the couch. Maybe he'd let her tease him about the dimples, but there were limits, and she was stomping all over that line. He tossed her onto the sofa, still laughing. If poking at his dimples made her forget what else was going on, he'd let it go. This time.

Jacob lowered himself on top of her. She stretched her arms toward him, pulling him down, still with that smile tugging on her lips.

"So, what's next? Want to play paddy cake?" she asked.

"Not really."

"Hm, how about Monopoly?"

"You're asking for trouble, you know that?" His cheeks and stomach hurt from laughing and smiling.

"Yes."

"Well, I have a better idea." He lowered his face to hers.

"And what would that be?" Her lips whispered against his as she spoke.

"Stop talking."

Her reply was muted by the press of his mouth over hers. Not that she protested too much. She opened her mouth, kissing him back as if she hungered for more. He wanted all of her. Everything she had. Everything she was. If he could press their bodies together, it might not be enough.

"I like this plan," she muttered when he lifted his head.

"Good. There's more."

"Oh really?"

"Yup."

"Stop talking and kiss me."

He chuckled and did as she said. She twined her fingers into his hair, pulling the short strands as he thrust his tongue into her mouth. She sucked on it, flicking the tip of her tongue out to flirt with him, tease him more. He shuddered in her arms, wanting this to go farther.

But it didn't mean he couldn't worship her body. There were a lot of things to appreciate, after all.

Jacob pushed her tank top up and sports bra up under her armpits, freeing her breasts. Angry red lines marked where the elastic had cut into her. He kissed the lines, soothing away the hurt in his own way.

She tugged on his hair, but he ignored her. He had a feeling teasing Emma might become his new favorite pastime.

IT WAS TIME.

Max pulled on his shirt and tucked the sleeves into his gloves. He added some tape to the cuffs to keep them sealed. The rest of his outfit was simple, jeans and canvas shoes he could dispose of quickly. He was traveling light for this one.

No spare change of clothes.

He couldn't stay in the duplex for longer than it took to knock the two of them out. He'd have to drag them across the backyard and into the lawyer's house so he could take his time with them.

No video equipment.

This kill was for him. For his soul. And the mission he was born with. He might not be able to complete the ritual as he wanted, but he could put Emma and Jacob to rest, which would have to be enough.

The club wouldn't get this one.

He gathered his considerably lighter pack and slipped the straps over his shoulders.

He was ready.

Max exited through the back door. He'd spent so much time in this house, it was familiar to him, all its quirks, the way it shifted. It wouldn't have been possible, had the lawyer not been having an affair. There were plenty of day trips and spending the night elsewhere.

It had allowed Max to prepare this location, unlike the others.

He pulled the decorative bush up out of the ground. It had taken an entire evening to unearth the roots, put it in a plastic bucket and disguise the hole, but it was necessary. He'd needed to get to the privacy fence. A piece of plywood slid between the shrubbery and fence went over the hole so he didn't trip in it. That had happened once and he'd learned his lesson.

Getting over the fence was out of the question with all the cops around. He'd watched them come and go all day. Thankfully his need to be able to get those close to Emma had pushed him to this. While going in, out, and under Derrick's trailer house was an easy thing to accomplish, Amanda's was the other place where she spent her time.

Since he couldn't go over the fence, he'd made a gate. He'd unscrewed several of the boards, nailed them together, and created holds to drop the new bar into so the fence appeared untouched. The bush disguised his creative entrance.

He lifted his gate out of the secure spots on either side and propped it up so he could crawl through the space between the boards.

He peered into the backyard, but the privacy fence was too tall for anyone to see into the yard. And the couple inside was too preoccupied to notice his approach. The cameras were one of his better ideas. It made keeping tabs on Emma so much easier.

Max crawled through into the yard and dusted himself off.

This was really happening.

He was almost too giddy to focus. The other victims hadn't expected him. There was an added element of danger that had his blood pumping extra hard. But he needed to focus. His head had to be clear for this one. He sucked in a deep breath, counted to ten and pushed it out.

The key in his pocket felt as if it weighed five pounds. He fished it out and crept toward the back door.

Emma and Jacob lay on the couch, limbs entwined and bodies grinding together. He eyed the distance from the door to the couch. There was no way he could unlock the door without them hearing. He'd oiled and worked the lock many times, but it still scraped and clicked. Jacob would be up and on him by the time Max was through the door.

Plan B it was then.

He sighed, not liking this one as much. Ducking under the window in the door, he skirted the house until he came to the second window in Emma's room. He'd jammed the locks so they appeared to be secure, but when he grasped the bottom and lifted—it went without a complaint. He pulled the lamp through the window, unplugging it and set it on the ground before hoisting the lightweight table out as well. Using it as a step-stool, he easily entered the bedroom.

Max stood in silence, listening to the moans from the other room. Would he have to listen to them fuck? Or could he hope they were so distracted by each other he might be able to surprise them before they got too naked?

He tip-toed around the room to the box Jacob had commandeered as a night stand. A wallet, a phone, his badge, and cuffs, as well as a few other odds and ends, lay in plain sight. Max pocketed the badge and cuffs. They might come in handy.

Max retreated to the deepest shadows of the room and slid his pack off. He pulled out the spade he'd stolen some time ago on a whim. Earlier he'd cut the handle down until it made a nice, portable weapon.

His skin broke out in goose bumps. Years of work, research, and honing his craft had led to this moment. This one special act.

It was time.

12.

EMMA ARCHED HER BACK AND MOANED.

Fuck, he had a beautiful mouth and he used it so well. She sat up as much as she could, which wasn't very far, and started to tug her clothes off.

Jacob grabbed her wrists and lifted his face from her breast.

"Don't do that," he said.

"What? Why not?" Yes, she was whining. The man was sexy, she needed a distraction, and he was it.

Jacob scooted up until he could plant a quick kiss on her mouth.

"Because, haven't you seen horror movies?" he asked.

"This is not a movie."

"No, but it's a bad idea to go there now." He kissed her cheek and jaw.

"Why?" If she had to pout, she sure as hell would.

He sighed and sat up.

"Because, what if—and I'm just throwing this out there— we're having sex and—"

"I get it. I get it." She tugged her shirt and bra down. Horny she may be, but stupid she wasn't.

"But..." One side of his mouth kicked up and a little glimmer of mischievousness lit his gaze. He kissed the center of her collarbone and tugged her neckline town. "One of us could at least get off."

He pulled her shirt back up and kissed lower on her stomach, but one leg slid off and he rolled off the couch to sit down hard. They blinked at each other for a second before bursting out laughing.

"Are you okay?" She sat up and propped her elbows on her knees.

"Yeah." He pushed to his feet and grabbed her wrist. "I think it's time this moved to the bedroom before I brain myself on the coffee table."

"Now that would be fun to explain."

"I'd prefer not to." He twirled her around until she was walking backwards toward the bedroom.

"Are we two-stepping now?"

"Maybe. Let's see if I can remember how." He took her right hand in his, placed his other at her waist. As he began to sing, "Blame it all on my roots," he shuffled her backward.

His voice wasn't quite twangy enough for the song, but that he could sing it and knew the words made her laugh all over again. Granted, it was pretty damn sexy when you took in the whole package—he cooked, he sang, he'd even keep you from dying in a horror movie. It was about as perfect as she could hope for.

They danced through the doorway into the bedroom. Was it her, or was it getting hot in here?

Hands gripped Emma from behind and jerked her out of Jacob's embrace. She yelped, stumbling over something.

Jacob stood in the doorway, his gaze not on her, but behind her.

Oh, God.

TBKiller.

Max.

"Easy now, man. Careful with that knife." Jacob had his hands at his side, fingers spread in a non-threatening manner.

How had he gotten inside? Where were the cops?

She gripped the arm banded across her chest with both hands.

Emma's heart hammered against her ribs and she couldn't get a breath into her lungs. She didn't want to die. There was a lot left to live for.

Colorado, for one. She wanted to go away with Jacob. Her motocross team had a big championship and she was supposed to lead the training. Thoughts slipped through her fingers like sand. The only thing she could hold onto was the regret that she hadn't had time to know Jacob better. To tell him she was falling in love with him.

"Let go of my arm," Max growled.

He'd said he'd come for her, and he had.

Fear and anger mixed. She wanted to punch his lights out, to give him as much pain as he'd given her friends. He pressed the blade against her throat. It was a hunting knife. One of the medium sized ones Simon used during deer season. Max meant business.

She released her grip, balling her hands into fists. Were they wet? No, they were damp and sticky. But not with sweat. Something else. What the hell?

"There are zip ties next to the door. Put those on your wrists, or I'll start with her throat." Max's voice had changed from the gangly teen she remembered. It was deeper and more mature now, but he would have aged.

"Max, you don't have to do this," Jacob kept speaking, his voice low, calm. It was crazy how composed he was. One second he'd been her lover, and the next he was the cop.

"Of course I have to do this. The cuffs, or she gets it." Max pressed the blade to her throat, just a bit.

Think.

She had to use her head.

Emma sucked down a deep breath.

She wasn't going to go down without a fight.

If Max got his way, she wasn't going to walk out of this situation. He was only there to complete his ritual. If he were trying to get away, he shouldn't have come after her. At this point, his end game was their death, probably followed by his own. She'd studied men like him. She knew this. Which meant there was no point in cooperating with him. She was dead one way or the other, which meant going along with what he wanted got her nothing but dead his way.

Those thoughts made her stomach knot up. The adrenaline pounding in her veins made her palms sweat and for a blessed second the clamor of thoughts quietened.

She didn't run from anything, and she wasn't about to let this creepadoodle kill her without putting up one hell of a fight. If he killed her, she'd make sure he had to work for it.

But she wasn't alone, either. She had her cop.

Against Jacob and her, she didn't think Max had a chance. Not if she could get out of his hold. Until she was free, Jacob would do whatever he asked. It was that damn, rule-following cop part of him. He had to be willing to take a risk, even with her life.

Jacob's gaze flicked to her. He shook his head slightly, as if he knew she was thinking of doing something. Well, he knew her pretty damn well if he realized that. She nodded, slightly. Max wouldn't get what he wanted. He wouldn't get to kill them both.

She sucked in a deep breath, calming herself as much as she could. It was hard to think past the knife slowly sawing at her neck as he shifted behind her.

"I'm going to bend down and get the zip ties, okay buddy?" Jacob said.

"Do it already," Max snapped. He jabbed the knife toward the ground, where the thick ties lay on the floor, ready for this moment. How long had he been there if he already had this set up?

This was her opening.

Emma slammed her elbow into his ribs and kicked backward. He grunted and stumbled.

She ducked and twisted away from him, striking out again, but he dug a hand into her hair, yanking her back. She shrieked and clawed at him, but his hold was too tight. He brought his knee up and drove her face down into the blow. Pain jolted through her body and she gasped. Her vision swam and hazed to black.

Fuck, that was going to leave a mark.

"No! No, Emma," Jacob yelled.

The hell she was going down without a fight. She twisted again and felt hair rip from her scalp. She punched Max straight in the junk with everything she had. His grip on her hair loosened and she was free.

Jacob roared as he shouldered past her, slamming into Max. The two men crashed into the boxes, knocking them over as they grappled and struggled with each other. All she could see were legs kicking.

Max came out on top of Jacob. She saw the flash of the knife, heard Jacob cry out, and she screamed. She grabbed the closest thing to her—a broken shovel? What the hell? She swung, hitting Max with everything she had in the back of the head. He slumped forward. Jacob rolled with him. He punched Max a few times. Max's body was completely limp.

"Get my cuffs," he yelled at her.

She looked around at the mess. "They're not here."

"Zip ties."

She grabbed them and pushed the boxes away from Max, who was groaning. Any second now he'd come around, and she didn't want a repeat of what they'd gone through.

"Oh my God." She shuddered. Max looked completely different. Blond. Clean shaven. There wasn't anything of the kid she'd met before. In fact. "I know him."

Max's hair had been darker a few days ago. He'd made some joke when she was paying for gas that she'd laughed at. He'd been in her life for months.

"Emma. Christ. I can't let go of him. Put the zip ties around his wrists."

"Like this?" She bent and did as he asked.

"Yeah, that's good. Fucking hell. Where's my phone? Call 9-1-1." Jacob groaned and sat back on his heels. Blood stained the front of his shirt.

"You're bleeding." She stared at the growing stain. She'd seen people bleed plenty. Motocross wasn't a tame sport, but those people weren't Jacob.

"Emma, my phone?"

She searched in the area where Jacob had last placed his things, but everything was gone or tossed on the floor except for his keys, which were now by the bed.

"It's not here, either. There's nothing. Just your keys. My phone's gone, too."

"Oh fucking hell." Jacob got to his feet and quick stepped out of the way as Max came to and began thrashing around. "Get out of here, Emma."

"I'm not leaving you."

"You aren't leaving me, you're letting me do my job." He grabbed her by the arm and dragged her out of the bedroom.

"But..."

Someone pounded on the front door.

"FBI."

The boxes tumbled around in the room as Max struggled even more.

"Jacob," she yelled as Max stood up, his hands free.

Jacob whirled to face the threat. The front door burst open, and officers spilled into the house. Lights from the backyard indicated more coming that way.

Max stepped into the doorway, a smaller knife in his hand.

Blood dripped down his left arm.

He stared straight at Emma and said, "I'll see you again."

"Fuck never," she said before she could think better of it.

Her words turned into a scream as Max plunged the little knife through his ear. He gurgled something and fell forward, landing on the knife.

"Oh my God," she said over and over again as shudders took her.

A pool of red formed around him in a matter of seconds.

"Emma, Emma, come on." Jacob wrapped his good arm around her and ushered her out of the house.

The quiet street was alive with people, lights and cars. She blinked around as officers and people rushed past them.

"Don't you ever do that again." Jacob pulled her in, hugging her to his side.

She wrapped her arms around his waist. Who cared about a little blood when they were still breathing? She buried her face against his shoulder. He squeezed harder and shifted.

"Fuck," she bellowed, backing away and cupping her hands over her nose. "That hurts."

"That's probably because your nose is broken. Come here." He took her by the hand. This time, she hugged him and kept her aching face up. "We're alive."

Emma sucked in another deep breath and blinked back tears. She was not a girl who cried, but damn if that wasn't a lot to process.

"We're alive," he whispered again and kissed her brow.

She clutched him tighter and rested her forehead on his shoulder. Yup, blood was dripping from her face. Just great. But—she was alive to bleed, and laugh, and love.

JACOB CLOSED THE DOOR to his house, flipping the locks into place. He shuddered and twisted the locks once more. Max had to have come in by way of a window at Amanda's. He'd have to check those as well so he could rest knowing Emma was safe.

Emma had already kicked off her shoes and padded into the kitchen.

The sun was creeping up over the horizon, bathing the room in a warm glow. He still flipped on all the lights. It would be a while before he would be okay walking into a dark room. Those images of Max with a knife, Emma against his chest, would stick with him. He'd almost lost her back there.

How had someone he'd just met come to mean so much to him? The idea of his future without Emma in it made his chest constrict and his stomach tie into knots.

She was alive.

He shook the dark thoughts from his mind and followed her.

"Can I get you anything?" He carried her bag into the den and set it down on the couch.

"Something to make my face stop pounding would be awesome." She sounded completely congested. Her face had swollen, and dark bruises were forming on her cheek bones.

But she was alive.

"I could give you some of my drugs." He pulled the pharmacy bag out of the pocket he'd stuffed it in and rattled it at her.

"You need that more than I do."

He'd popped one pill on the doctor's orders after getting the stab wounds looked at and hadn't been able to walk a straight line. Between them, they needed a ride from the hospital to his house. It was a pretty pathetic situation, but *they were alive.*

"Want something to eat?" he asked.

She shook her head and glanced away, through the back doors into the yard. The officers had shown him the set-up at the house behind Amanda's. It had appeared as though Max's plan was to force them from the duplex to the house and go through the ritual there. They'd even found Max's laptop with the surveillance running. He'd left out all except the most necessary details when filling Emma in on things. She didn't need to know. Because while she was tough, she wasn't unbreakable.

He went to her, pulling her into another hug. She might not need it, but he did. For the span of a few minutes, he'd been certain she was going to die. A hundred outcomes had flashed through his head, all of which resulted in her death.

She clenched him tight, proof he wasn't the only one who needed support.

Losing her would be losing part of himself. At some point she'd stolen his heart, and he didn't have a hope or a prayer at getting it back, not that he wanted it. His heart was better left in her hands. So long as she stayed among the land of the living.

The words, those three little words, stuck in his throat.

They'd faced death and lived; yet admitting how he felt still scared him.

Emma stared up at him with a very serious, somber expression. There was no light, no laughter. She'd pulled her hair into a knot on top of her head, tendrils hanging around her face. His heart clenched at the thought of the pain she had to be feeling and the torment she'd been through tonight.

If only he'd been a better protector...

"I love you," she said.

He stared at her. Had he passed out? Was this a dream?

"I know it's stupid, and fast, and you're probably going to read me some psycho-analyzing bullshit, but I love you. And I could have died tonight without telling you that." Her voice trembled and her gaze dropped to his chest. A fat tear rolled down her cheek, the first he'd seen.

"Hey, hey, don't cry." He could handle anything—except her tears. And her death. So two things.

"Look, don't make this awkward, okay?" She sniffled but allowed him to lift her chin. He hadn't really thought a tough, independent woman like Emma, who had to have a line of guys waiting for their chance, would tell him she loved him.

"It's only awkward if you don't mean it."

She glared at him.

"Don't make fun of me," she said.

"I'm not. I'm just saying...I was standing here thinking how much...how much I love you too, and that it scared the shit out of me to think about saying it."

Her glare lost its heat, her eyes widening and jaw dropping.

"I thought it would be too much to put that on you, but—"

"Say it again."

He took a deep breath and the last bit of tension left his body.

"I love you."

She blinked at him, as if she wasn't sure he was serious.

"I went to meet you expecting you to be something you weren't. You've surprised me, pissed me off, made me laugh, and more than anything, you make me want you. So yeah, I was too scared to tell you I loved you first."

Her smile was the most beautiful thing he'd ever seen. She relaxed, leaning into him. "It's not weird?"

"I'm sure there will be plenty of people who will call us crazy." He shrugged and tried to keep his gaze away from her mouth.

"Kiss me—gently, okay?"

He chuckled at her insistence and, very carefully, pressed his mouth to hers. The things he wanted to do to her would have to wait. She lifted up on tip-toes.

"Ouch." She twisted away, cupping her hands over her face. "Not fair!

She laughed despite the pain.

"I'm sorry."

"It wasn't your fault," she grumbled.

"Come here." He gathered her to his chest and squeezed her as tight as he could without aggravating his shoulder or her broken nose.

There would be a Colorado in their future, and much, much more.

BLACK WIDOW THREW THE remote across the room. "No! God damn it."

The top story was about the TBK copycat's suicide.

Max hadn't run, he hadn't done the honorable thing and taken his own life *before* there was a scene. Hell, she hadn't even been able to clean this mess up.

She paced the length of her living room, seething. She'd planned for an instance like this, but this was too early. There were still plans in the works. Max's shortcomings could seriously fuck up the chances for the rest of them to succeed.

Which was all the more reason for the club to go to ground, to hide, retreat.

There would come another day, another time to kill.

Epilogue

ONE MONTH LATER...

Jade Perez shuffled the latest case file back into its folder. A little paperwork and she could call it done.

"Hold the phones, don't go anywhere." Lali Smith, their tech-kitten—as she called herself—strode between the desks, a stack of papers in her hand.

"What's happened?" Brooks had his coat over his arm and briefcase in hand. It had been another long week and they were all ready to go home.

"OKC forensics finally sent over the autopsy report and tox screen, and I think you're all going to want a look at this." Lali handed the papers to Brooks, her lips tightly compressed. She was a petite, slender woman who often made Jade think of a butterfly, though Lali was rather sedate. Like her, she was a woman edging into the men's club, and she had to play by their rules.

Brooks flipped through the report. "Conference room. Now."

Mullins and Abraham groaned. The two were no doubt lining up their ladies for the evening. Not only did the guys work together, they'd gone in on a sizable house last year. If Jade didn't know they were into women, she might wonder.

She gathered her notebook and tablet, heading to the room. Truth was, she'd been waiting for this report after the initial autopsy had been performed. In short order, the whole team was seated at the half-circle table facing the projection wall.

Lali lost no time in pulling the report up on the screen. "According to the ME, Max Fischer didn't have any drugs in his system."

"What about his arm?" Mullins had his own notepad out and flipped through the pages.

"Right—they were able to examine the scar tissue and it appears as though he'd performed some scarification on himself." Lali flipped through a few of the digital pages until a picture landed on the display. "It says Killer Club. How creepy is that? But that's not the really weird thing. Remember the coroner said he found something strange in Max's stomach? Well it turns out it was a piece of bone. A circular disk, probably a femur, that matches the DNA of a missing girl from Calgary who went to Chicago for the weekend and never came home. Make it even weirder, Killer Club was carved into that as well."

The room was silent for a few moments while they all took it in.

"Max attempted to remove the scar, correct?" Jade asked.

"Correct." Lali replied. "It looks like he started with a knife, and when that didn't work out, he used a clothing iron to disguise the words."

"Someone doesn't want the idea of this Killer Club to get out," Mullins remarked. He clicked a pen and shook his head.

"Lali, were you able to recover anything from Max's laptop?" Brooks asked.

"Not a lot. He'd wiped it of almost everything. I got a few recent emails, some browser history, and the surveillance footage from that night, but everything else is gone."

"We don't have proof he used that laptop to make the letters?" Mullins sat forward.

Jade rolled her eyes. "You seriously won't give up the idea that Detective Payton and Emma Ration are involved somehow, will you?"

"I'm just saying they fit." Mullins shrugged.

"Mm, except their alibis check out, both in the real world and digitally. I have credit card activity and security footage of both of them during the time of death on at least two of the victims." Lali shook her head and didn't look at Jade. They were in agreement that the couple couldn't possibly be involved, but Mullins could be pig-headed. "Also, Detective Payton just applied for a credit card at a major jewelry store. Wonder what that's for?" Lali glanced at her, flashing a smile.

"Any purchases?" Jade asked. She couldn't help herself. She might not understand love, or even know how to feel it, but it fascinated her.

"None yet, but I might watch out so we know when to send congratulations."

"Okay, focus." Brooks pulled out his seat and sat down. "What are the chances we're looking at a club of killers?"

Want to know when the Killer Club will strike again?

Sign up for the New Release Newsletter at
www.SidneyBristol.com
to get inside scoops and a free book.

Dangerous Attraction

Part One

November 2015

Part of the Seven Naughty SEALs boxed set.

A new romantic suspense serial featuring Travis Ration, a former SEAL who has been to the ends of the earth and back. This time he's not only battling his inner demons, he has to save *her* from the terror that stalks the night.

Warning: It won't end happily ever after—this time.

Part Two & Three due out November/December 2015

TRAVIS RATION HUNCHED OVER the hotel desk and flipped to the first page of the autopsy report. The lights from the Vegas strip cast globes of colored light onto the paper, but the glitz and glamour held no sway for him. Only the poor woman.

She was blonde. Like the rest. Pretty. A Vegas native named Linda. She'd been social, so her disappearance had been noted within hours by friends and family, but by then it was too late. Whoever was in the business of abducting blonde, attractive young women was good. And if the list of missing blonde women were a hint, the perpetrator had operated in the Las Vegas area for years—without anyone connecting the dots.

There was a serial killer in Las Vegas, and no one wanted to admit it.

"Hey man, ready to go?" Mason Clark, a new hire to the Aegis Group security firm, stepped into Travis' room, one hand braced on the door.

"No, man. Hit the strip without me." Travis didn't glance away from the report.

It read almost exactly like the last one had. Judging by the time of death, the girls lasted for anywhere from seven to twelve months before being murdered and dumped. Linda was an exception. She'd been missing for almost two months. What was really telling was that from the time of death to the next abduction was somewhere in the twenty-four hour mark, which meant these crimes were well thought out. The perpetrator organized and focused on the details. Travis hadn't even touched on the disturbing facts yet.

"No? What are...No, you are not on that again." Ethan Turner, Travis' best friend, groaned and shouldered past Mason. "I thought you were going to take a break from this."

"I said I was taking a break from work." Travis picked up the hotel pen and jotted down the injuries and observations that were different from the previous victims. That was where he'd fine the clues. The guy doing this was too methodical to deviate from his plan, so when and where he did was important.

"What are you doing?" Mason crossed the room and peered over Travis' shoulder.

"He's playing hound dog for the FBI." Ethan popped the top on a long neck from their freshly stocked mini fridge.

"What is this?" Mason snagged the first page of the report with the autopsy pictures clipped to it and dropped it almost immediately onto the ground. "What the hell?"

Travis punched Mason in the thigh, not hard, but enough the other man bent over and rubbed the spot.

"Don't fuck with my stuff." Travis grabbed the piece of paper and the photographs. He straightened the documents out, ensuring all of the pieces were securely in place before putting it back in the folder.

"What the hell is that? Why do you have pictures of a dead woman?" Mason's eyes were wide, his lip curled. They'd all seen death. Everyone who worked for the Aegis Group had served over seas. They'd all killed. But they weren't all good at it. Travis had reservations about Mason's hire, but he wasn't the boss.

"None of your damn business," Travis replied.

"Is this a job or something?" Mason glanced between Travis and Ethan, who shook his head and took another swig of his beer. The Aegis Group was a private security company on paper, in reality, they performed a wide range of services that often skirted the law.

"Don't worry about it," Travis said.

"The fuck we won't." Ethan gave Travis the thousand yard stare. Travis was pretty sure Ethan was about to try to deck him for the hell of it.

"I thought we were here for a protective detail," Mason said.

"You are. I'm not." Travis flipped the folder closed. FBI and CONFIDENTIAL were stamped across the front of the brown surface.

"What did you get us into this time?" Ethan took two steps toward Travis, and stopped, the beer clenched in his right hand.

"You aren't involved," Travis replied.

"The hell I'm not. What is this?" Ethan pointed at the folder.

"Just something I'm looking into."

"Is this why you wouldn't go home for Christmas?" Ethan's gaze narrowed.

Travis studied Ethan, the blood shot eyes, the clenched hand. This wasn't about Travis or his side gig researching potential cases for the Behavioral Analysis Unit, a specialized FBI team that tracked down the worst kinds of killers, something he'd gotten involved with after a copycat murderer recreated the horrors from his family's past.

"Molly refused to split Christmas with you, didn't she?" Travis shifted his weight onto the balls of his feet, ready to move if Ethan rushed him. The worst fight they'd had happened the day Molly told Ethan she wanted a divorce. Some emotions could only be worked out with fists.

For a second, no one moved or spoke. Travis was not looking forward to a hotel bill for trashing the place.

Ethan blew out a breath and sat down onto Travis' bed as if a one-ton weight were on his back. The spring squeaked and the pillows bounced under the man's bulk.

"Yeah, she did," Ethan mumbled.

Mason's brows rose, but he didn't comment. The kid had some brains.

Travis stood and stretched. No fight then, which was a good thing. He'd hate to have to break Ethan's nose, then take his place on the protective detail because he was too scary looking.

"When will you get to see Nate?" Travis crossed to the mini fridge and grabbed his own beer. The case weighed heavily on him, but he'd gone through SEAL training with Ethan. Travis had been the best man at Ethan and Molly's wedding, and the first one there to load out boxes of Ethan's things when he moved out. They were brothers in every sense of the word, save blood.

"Before he goes back to school. The second through the fourth. Three days. Three fucking days." Ethan took another long pull on his bottle.

"Make the most of those days, don't dwell on what you don't get." Travis clinked his bottle to Ethan's.

Travis knew what it was like to have an absent father. At least Ethan wanted to be in his son's life. Travis was pretty certain his father hadn't wanted to live, but he hadn't wanted to die bad enough to do something about it. That was the kind of mark a serial killer left on a person, and it was the same darkness passed down to Travis.

"What's the deal with the FBI?" Mason picked up the folder from the desk and looked at the cover. "This is the real deal, isn't it?"

"Yeah. Leave it alone." Travis watched Mason, not because he didn't trust the kid. Anyone who worked at Aegis underwent a thorough background check and multiple people had to vouch for the new hire. In the field, Travis would trust Mason with his life, but he didn't know the guy.

The younger man seemed to consider his options for a moment, then did the smart thing and laid the folder on the desk.

"What's the case this time?" Ethan asked.

"Some sick fuck is kidnapping young, blonde women. He keeps them for months, maybe a year, then kills them." He left out the horrific parts about the abuse and the pregnancies. Some things the others didn't need to know.

What did he do with the babies?

"Why is this your problem?" Mason asked.

"Ever heard of TBK?" Ethan glanced at Travis.

If Mason hadn't already known, he would find out. It was only a matter of time until someone told him.

"Wasn't that on the news a while back? Last year?" Mason screwed up one eye and pressed his lips together. "I was getting out about that time. It's all kind of a blur."

"Nah, man, TBKiller and that dude are two different people. TBKiller was a copycat," Ethan said.

"My old man's family was murdered by a serial killer. Called himself TBK. Torture. Blind. Kill." Travis peeled part of the label off his beer. Murdered was putting it lightly. They'd been tortured in the most sadistic fashion, then before their deaths, their eyes were removed.

TBK had terrorized Oklahoma City before Travis had been born, but TBK had shaped Travis' life. TBK's last victims were Travis' grandparents, and his father had been forced to watch it all. His old man had never fully recovered. Travis and his half-sister Emma often bore the brunt of the dysfunction.

"Fuck. I didn't know," Mason said.

"It happened before you or I were born." Travis shrugged. "Last year this guy goes ape shit. Starts copying the TBK murders and leaving these sick notes for my half-sister, Emma. They killed him trying to finish Emma off. Turns out this guy who'd worked at the corner gas station she went to all the time, is part of this...serial killer club. The BAU is—"

"BAU? What?" Mason blinked.

"Behavioral Analysis Unit. They're the FBI unit that specializes in serial killers. They're trying to track down the club members, but no one wants to have a serial murderer on their hands."

"And that's where Travis likes to help out." Ethan thumbed at Travis.

"How?" Mason asked.

Travis could see the skepticism in Mason's eyes. The kid had been around Aegis long enough to hear rumors, stories about the Z-Team. He was probably wondering what a felon like Travis could do that the FBI couldn't.

Well fuck him.

"I let their team know where I'm working. If they have any leads, I'll look into it." Travis sipped his beer and stared at the mirror.

"Why?"

"Why the fuck do you want to know?" He scowled at Mason, but couldn't blame him. The whole gig was strange. "The FBI has to be invited into an investigation unless it crosses state lines. Like I said, no one wants to have a serial killer on their hands."

"So you, what? Find a reason for them to come here?" Mason asked. "Why you? You're just a body guard."

Travis gripped the edge of the dresser.

Just a bodyguard.

"What the fuck do you know?" Ethan flipped Mason off.

He was right. All Travis was good for these days was an under the table gig, and to catch the bullets meant for someone else. But that was his own fault. Reputable people didn't hire a felon, even an ex-Navy SEAL felon, no matter what his credentials were. But some jobs were made for him. He'd tracked some of the worst kinds of people across deserts, oceans and mountains. This serial killer wouldn't know what hit him.

Want to know when you can get your hands on Travis?

Sign up for the New Release Newsletter at
www.SidneyBristol.com
to get inside scoops and a free book.

Dear Readers,

I hope you have enjoyed the story of Emma and Jacob, two beautifully broken people. I'm not nervous about releasing books as much as I used to be. I guess that's what comes with putting out 20+ books, huh? **Blind**, however, it's been giving me the jitters since I finished it in 2014.

Every so often authors write a book that's purely what they want to read. For me, **Blind** is that book. I wanted to read characters who didn't ride off into the sunset with their lives perfectly figured out. I wanted to see messy, broken people who were strong and capable. And so Emma and Jacob became clear voices on the page.

I hope you like this book. I hope the rest of the BAU cast is as near and dear to your heart now as mine. Oh, the stories they have to tell...

Let's do this again.

Acknowledgements

Books take a village. Readers, you are why I do this. Thank you!

Thank you to my editing team, Dayna and Jessica, for sticking with me and believing in this project. Your enthusiasm and encouragement kept me going.

To the earliest of beta readers, I lost the list of your names, but your feedback in the very beginning told me I was on to something.

All of the officers and agents who have patiently answered my questions, thank you. I hope you never, ever read my books, but you have made them a little more real with your feedback.

Charity, you stuck with me when I was being difficult, when I wasn't positive about the cover direction. You, lady, are a champ and a master at what you do.

My very own Team Awesome, Reb, Lea and Soph, you ladies know how to keep a girl's spirits up.

Jayne and Carrie Ann, your guidance and support during the drafing process was huge. Thank you for telling me to stick to my guns.

My Crazy Crew, Bambi, Rachel, Joe and Matt, thank you. Movie nights are an anchor in an otherwise turbulent and busy ocean.

Lastly, Shawn, you put up with hours of Criminal Minds and The Following during editing. Thank you for believing me when I said I wasn't going to kill you in your sleep. I meant it.

Book List

Aegis Group
Dangerous Attraction, parts 1, 2 and 3
Bayou Bound
Picture Her Bound
Duty Bound
Bound Memories
Bound & Tamed
Other BDSM Titles
Committed
Bound with Pearls
Collar Me in Paris
Festive Seduction
Electric Engagement
So Inked
Under His Skin
The Harder He Falls
His Marriage Bargain
Good Guys Wear Black
Hot Tango
Line of Duty
Standalone Titles
Falling for His Best Friend
Dream Vacation (free read)
How Zombies Stole Christmas
Anthologies
Hot Ink
High Octane Heroes

ABOUT THE AUTHOR

It can never be said that NYT & USA Today Bestselling author Sidney Bristol has had a 'normal' life. She is a recovering roller derby queen, former missionary, and tattoo addict. She grew up in a motor-home on the US highways (with an occasional jaunt into Canada and Mexico), traveling the rodeo circuit with her parents. Sidney has lived abroad in both Russia and Thailand, working with children and teenagers. She now lives in Texas where she splits her time between a job she loves, writing, reading and fostering cats.

Sidney is represented by Nicole Resciniti of the Seymour Agency.

You can find Sidney here:

Website: www.SidneyBristol.com

Twitter: @Sidney_Bristol

New Release Newsletter:
http://sidneybristol.com/newsletter/

Facebook Page:
www.facebook.com/Sidney.Bristol.Romance.Author

Facebook Profile:
www.facebook.com/Sidney.Bristol.Author

Cheesecake Reader Lounge:
www.facebook.com/groups/CheesecakeReaderLounge

www.ingramcontent.com/pod-product-compliance
Lightning Source LLC
Chambersburg PA
CBHW021217250626
47155CB00008B/2840